Books by R. C. House

Requiem for a Rustler*
Trackdown at Immigrant Lake*
Drumm's War
The Sudden Gun
Vengeance Mountain
So the Loud Torrent

*Published by POCKET BOOKS

REQUIEM FOR A RUSTLER

R.C. HOUSE

POCKET BOOKS

New York   London   Toronto   Sydney   Tokyo   Singapore

This book is a work of fiction. Names, characters, places, and
incidents are either products of the author's imagination or are used
fictitiously. Any resemblance to actual events or locales or persons,
living or dead, is entirely coincidental.

An *Original* Publication of POCKET BOOKS

POCKET BOOKS, a division of Simon & Schuster Inc.
1230 Avenue of the Americas, New York, NY 10020

ISBN: 0-671-76043-2

First Pocket Books printing August 1993

10 9 8 7 6 5 4 3 2 1

POCKET and colophon are registered trademarks of
Simon & Schuster Inc.

Cover art by Bill Maughan

Printed in the U.S.A.

With deep affection for
Jonathan D. House
"Pals Forever"

REQUIEM FOR A RUSTLER

· 1 ·

The wind always blew up here, big and wide and frisky, sweeping things clean and sending the stench of cow manure and the warm milky odors of calf slobber down to the next county.

Luther Moseley sighed with a rare contentment as he paused on the pine-shaded shelf to rest in his sweaty saddle, taking time just to think about wind. Below him, milling placidly about the broad valley, thirty head of quality beef grazed, symbol of a new start in life for Moseley and his family. The war and the futile attempts to start over had taken their toll and left their scars.

But now was a time of renewal and the start of that new life for Luther Moseley with a future that at last held hope.

On the far side of the herd, a bull turned playful with a cow. Go ahead, old feller, Moseley thought happily, making a little poem; all that means, is fun for you, and money in my jeans. His mind turned back to the wind.

Wind was almost always at work soughing in the pines on the high ridges such as this or combing the grass into golden wavelets or keening up the valleys and draws. Wind, Luther thought, as he watched a party of riders coming toward him on a trail bordering the vast prairie basin, could be wistful if a man was feeling wistful or merry if that was his frame of mind. Just now Luther Moseley's frame of mind was happy.

Cedars were scattered here among the shading pines, their tangy fragrance reminiscent of pleasant night fires in numberless camps along long-forgotten trails, further spreading a serenity over Luther Moseley's soul. He was doing the right thing at the right time at the right place.

Nearby, a range of low mountains stood blue and jagged against the sky, a calming sight for a man. He might just be, he thought, getting over the summit of the troubled post-war years and now the downslope would be easier; time to enjoy home and family.

Hope was what men lived for and Luther Moseley, a big, dark-haired man pushing forty, had the eagerness and bright outlook of one much younger. It hadn't always been that way for him. Now, starting with a small herd of cattle, he expected to build it to the point he'd have enough to somehow make up to his wife and children for his absences during the war and over the lean years that followed; those years when it seemed that fate dealt from the bottom of the deck.

About ten men rode to meet him as he sat his horse, waiting.

"Howdy, boys," Luther called; Moseley regarded himself as a man of peace and of ease with a naturally generous and open nature. He figured others were of the same disposition until their actions proved otherwise.

"Huh!" The long-legged, powerful man riding ahead of the rest only grunted crossly as he pulled his powerful stallion to a stop and regarded the rancher with eyes impassive as a snake's. Those eyes seemed to fairly smoke.

Obviously the leader, he wore a black broadcloth suit, white shirt and string tie and a low-crowned, wide and flat-brimmed ebony-colored hat. At his waist the long skirt of his coat on the right was pulled back and hooked over a black-gripped six-shooter. The man's manner was so hostile that Moseley began to feel ill at ease. Deep inside, Moseley also felt a twinge of resentment and he drew his brows together at the callous intrusion into the enjoyment of his reverie.

Under the wide-brimmed hat, the foremost rider showed matted hair the color of new bricks. His blunt nose perched over a crisp, reddish mustache. His great paw of a left hand, on which large knuckles stood out against the bronzed skin, gripped the stallion's reins. The red-haired man's right hand rested at his jutting hip, close to the sinister Colt. His wide, bony shoulders poked against the material of his coat. The man was rawboned as a starved steer. A glinting flame played deep in the man's hard and bright eyes.

Those with him were of kindred stamp, though not so pronounced. Four wore Mexican outfits—steeple sombreros, tight-fitting flared pants, and short jackets—and were dark of skin, glinting of eye. The rest were men from north of the line, tight-mouthed and wearing sun-faded range clothing and thick leather batwing chaps capable of resisting the thorns and snags of chaparral. Their grim faces also registered hard-edged dispositions.

All were heavily armed, Moseley perceived at a quick glance, not only with Colt revolvers, but with shotguns or carbines in saddle boots. Their habits, the uneasy rancher decided, were far from the peaceful kind. His thoughts conjured another rhyming word: unrefined.

"The name's Moseley, gents," the cowman said, fighting to control a growing tremor in his voice and speaking only to break the tension he was under at the leader's cold stare of hatred. "Luther Moseley. I'm runnin' a herd through here. And who might you be, sir?"

The snake-like eyes flicked lazily to the cows that Moseley had run into the grassy hollow to graze.

"Huh!" The leader of the strange-acting group of riders repeated his ugly grunt. Every line of the man's form seemed sharp with hostility. When he finally spoke, his voice rasped like a dull saw in tough wood. "You're a stranger in these parts, Moseley. At least to me. The name I go by is Doan, Jubal Doan." As Moseley showed no nervousness at the name, he added, "I said I was Jubal Doan. That doesn't mean anything to you?" A sardonic grin flitted at the corners of his mouth, not pleasant to behold.

Moseley felt the fury in the man's words rattle along his spine. "Reckon not. Should I know you, Mr. Doan?" Moseley forced a grin. He was aware there were plenty of tough characters in this end of the territory. And he wasn't looking for trouble.

"Maybe not," Doan's harsh, rumbling voice broke in. "Been back east two years."

"Leavenworth vacation," one of the riders chimed in, grinning.

"Shut your face, Sandy!" Doan snapped. He turned back to Moseley. "How long you figure on stayin' in these parts, mister?"

"Why permanent, of course," Moseley answered easily. "Got a house and corral I'm building over the hill yonder."

Moseley unclenched a nervous, sweaty, claw-like grip on his reins and moved his lips to ease the tension in his jaw.

"Huh! That all the cattle you run?"

"Huh-uh. I got about two hundred head to start. Of course, the others got more—like Sam Carson and the rest."

Doan's eyes squinted to thin lines. "Carson? And the rest? What are you telling me?"

"They're my friends that came into this country with me. We're settlin' here, Mr. Doan, proving up our land claims legal and proper. Got a start on a little town, too. Berdan, she's called, in north of here. Not much yet, but we've got high hopes."

Doan's eyes narrowed and snapped in fury. "Well, we'll have to see about that," he roared. "This is my range, savvy? Squatters and nesters got no place here! Damned nuisances, bringin' in folks and the law and putting down roots, staking corner markers and runnin' fence around everything. Me

4

and my boys will just have to have us a look-see into all that business, and that's for certain. Who's behind all this?"

"Why, Mr. Rathburn, the banker in town. He's fixed it all up legal," Moseley protested, sensing his outrage rising. "You got it all wrong, Mr. Doan. This land wasn't proved up—open range—before we came. You'll have to take it up with Mr. Rathburn and Sam Carson."

"But I'm taking it up with you here and now, mister," Doan snarled. "Joe, you and Sandy and the boys drive them beeves out of here. We need meat back at our place." A quick shadow of cruelty came to Doan's eyes.

"Wait a minute," Moseley snapped. "Those are my cattle!"

His hand moved upward in a gesture of objection. Jubal Doan hardly needed an excuse. The black-gripped Colt by his right hand flew out and up, exploding, and Luther Moseley's dreams ended with a bullet to the heart.

Three days later, the alert, keen eyes of the young rider coming into Berdan from the south crinkled with satisfaction at the new buildings of the settlement he now regarded as home.

Though raw-boarded and rough at the edges, the buildings along Berdan's Broad Street projected substance and integrity. The tent town that had sprung up in the first months of settlement had given way to timber and stone.

Broad Street, as the youthful rider's horse clopped along it, was unnecessarily wide at this point in Berdan's life. The town founders insisted on the width with the future in mind. There would be abundant wagon-and-team parking in the years ahead for others to pass without hazard or inconvenience.

These days, though, Broad Street became a morass of mud in rainy times and a golden haze of powdery, nostril-clogging dust after a dry spell. Rome, Jim Carson mused happily, hadn't been built in a day, and Berdan would be no exception—but progress was clearly on the way.

Midway along the street, Carson halted his chestnut mustang and swung out of the saddle with a youthful, limber bounce. He dropped the reins over a convenient hitch rack near a square board-and-batten building marked by a sign in large, red letters against a black background: BERDAN LAND COMPANY. The building's rough-sawn siding still carried the distinctive aroma of green lumber.

Jim Carson's blue eyes narrowed again at the building and the sign. His father's name was up there as well in letters only slightly smaller than the company title. SAM CARSON, PRESIDENT. To Jim it spoke of family pride and of progress and of good times ahead.

At the right of his father's office building was that of Martin Rathburn, the investment banker who had under-written the new settlement and most of its citizens. The two buildings, sharing a common wall, were at the heart of the burgeoning community and the sprawl of ranches it sup-ported.

Jim Carson was as wiry as the plains mustangs he caught and broke to saddle, an outdoorsman to whom this land marked both home and adventure. Hunting, dangerous work with wild horses and cattle, scouting out good grazing pastures and choice locales for ranching spreads for his father's ventures all appealed to his free, unbridled, and daring spirit. The beauty of the Ramirez Plateau and Black River country had become part of him.

With clean but sun-faded range clothes and quality boots fitting as though he'd been born to them, Jim Carson kept a sand-hued Stetson cocked on his brown hair. His pleasant and open sun-bronzed face was clean shaven; he shaved every morning on the trail or at home. Beards bred vermin and besides, he liked the fresh feeling that came with a good shave.

Jim's smile came easily to his good-natured expression, his eyes were level and direct as he surveyed his new town and considered his family's role in it. Optimism, Jim had long since decided, nurtured itself in a man's spirit, and negative feelings did the same. He fought hard to sustain a positive attitude in his life.

Thinking as positively as possible, he viewed Berdan and saw but a few structures, set back from the Black River canyon on the western side of the stream. In the pine-fringed elevations nearby, giant springs had been discovered and dug out. Their increased flow was diverted via ditches, the way the Mexicans far to the south and west constructed their irrigation ditch-like *acequias,* providing enough water to supply the settlement as well as the numerous small ranches whose owners had been encouraged by the company to prove up new ranch sections.

It was an unusual spot, Jim thought, still studying the new town, this oasis in the generally parched surroundings. For untold centuries, the land had lain fallow, crossed only by animals and now and then by the red men who had paused to camp and rest by the river and its feeder springs.

Now permanent settlement had come, the new inhabitants eager to raise cattle and to establish homes. Already, Jim was aware, the land had grown in value as it improved with habitation and human support.

Young Carson's eyes swung farther down the single, reddish dirt street to a small saloon, the Berdan Bar, the meeting place for men who came to town—to slake a thirst, to talk, to argue and complain about politics, cattle, and taxes. Berdan also supported a general store, as yet carrying only a few basic supplies—flour, hardtack, canned and dried beans, canned pears, peaches and tomatoes, shovels, bolts of cloth, and sunbonnets. The store also had ammunition for the ranchers' hunting rifles and Colts, both front-loading and the single-action variety.

Frills and fancies, Jim figured, as he stepped down slowly from his horse, could come later; these days folks worked toward a time when such things would be accessible and appreciated. Jim stamped his feet a few times to relieve the stiffness in his legs. From behind him came the pleasant clank and rhythmic ringing anvil tap of the blacksmith shop.

7

Jim pushed back his hat and, with a little breeze cooling his forehead, lifted his gunbelt and let it settle more comfortably.

Young Carson's reverie was interrupted as he became aware of movement out of the corner of his eyes. Every small town had to come equipped with a town character or two and Berdan was no exception. Dad Burns was considered a town loafer, an imbiber who settled into a life of mooching drinks, drifting in sometime soon after the saloon opened its doors.

Jim grinned inwardly with the thought of the mothers and wives, widows and spinsters of Berdan who frequently clucked among themselves that old Burns was a "foolish eyesore" in the decent, Christian environment they tried so hard to encourage.

Old Burns, however, was tolerated by the townsmen and ranchers, most of whom understood the old geezer's failings and through unspoken common consent, anted up for his bar bill; after all, none knew when he might find himself old and dependent like Dad. Dad wasn't taken seriously, Jim mused as Dad approached him; neither was he openly ridiculed. Berdan people, he thought—the menfolk at least —and the people of the West in general, were more accepting of strangeness than people elsewhere.

The good-natured old-timer, maybe a has-been prospector or cowboy, had never given his name. The most evil phrase he'd uttered was "dad-burn it!" and the saloon's hangers-on humorously had pinned the name Dad Burns on him.

Now Dad hobbled into Jim's vision, a familiar foolish, eager grin splitting his face. "Howdy, Jim," he greeted, licking his loose lips. "You dry as me this dry mornin'?"

Dad wore the same tattered, cast-off clothing and the battered felt hat with holes in the crown he'd worn the day he hit town. He claimed the holes were made by bullets. For a glass of whiskey, he regularly told the story of how it happened, though since the details differed and were more dramatic each time, Dad was looked upon simply as a source of amusement. The vague old fellow's black whiskers and long hair were salted with gray and the ingratiating grin seemed fixed in his face.

"No, not today, Dad," Jim countered with an understanding grin. "But here, have one on me." He tossed Dad a two-bit piece, and the old-timer disappeared into the bar with amazing speed for a man his age.

Jim leaned back against the hitch rack and watched the saloon door shut with a familiar wheeze and whine of hinges and clacking of double batwing doors.

A small, familiar buckboard wagon among the cluster of conveyances across the street at the general store attracted Jim's attention, and he ambled to it. At the store's large front window, Jim shoved his face close and shielded his eyes, squinted against the glare of the glass, to peer inside.

He was caught red-handed as the first thing he saw was the smile of chestnut-haired, dark-eyed Melissa Douglas, eighteen-year-old daughter of George Douglas, another Berdan settler. Embarrassed, Jim grinned sheepishly, remembering that seeing Melissa was on his mind throughout the slow days of his week-long hunting trip.

Before Carson could recover from his surprise, Melissa popped out the door, her face brightening in recognition and pleasure, and he heard the familiar warmth of her easy laughter. "Jim Carson," she enthused, "How pleasant. Where have you been? You've been missed." She caught his arm and pulled him into Estevan's Mercantile.

Jim was still shrunk a little inside for having been caught peering at her through the storefront. He would acknowledge only to himself that he was drawn to the young woman, with neither the courage nor the forwardness to come right out and express his feelings.

The girl beside him held a man's eyes with her compelling olive complexion, a strong neck and body and substantial and capable wrists and hands. Her face was young, a soft oval framed by the bonnet that hid most of her hair. To Jim,

Melissa Douglas represented the fiber and grit of old pioneer stock. She was abundantly suited to the life she would no doubt lead one day as a rancher's wife and mother of a large and happy brood.

"Oh," he apologized, by way of explanation. "Been hunting on the other side of the range. Left a few haunches of elk, antelope, and bighorn out there with Molly Redfeather at the Indian camp to cure up for us into jerky and pemmican and make up boudins. Enough for your folks and mine. Paid her in fresh meat. We'll have that to look forward to M'liss. Are things all right out your way?"

Jim found himself becoming lost in the depths of Melissa's dark eyes as they made small talk near the front of Estevan's store. "Oh, all fine. Dad and Vic have the barn and stable well along and the herd's healthy. Aside from that, we're all well as well." Melissa chuckled over the little word-joke, a delicate and merry tinkle of laughter. Jim realized her eyes were probing as deeply into his, and he was certain his cheeks had reddened.

"I just happened by," he said, nearly stammering. "Saw your rig outside. Figured you were in the store."

"Some dress material I ordered is in. I've got to see Mrs. Estevan at the back. Can you stay a minute till I'm through?" A smile, tender and happy, settled on her lips and in her eyes.

"Oh. Yeah. Fine." Melissa flashed him a grateful look and skittered along the counters to the back of the establishment. Jim hung around the front self-consciously, studying the activity in the street and looking over Mr. Estevan's latest merchandise.

José Estevan, whose family had been in this country for generations before Berdan was founded and settlement began, was busy with a customer.

Jim wandered over to lean down for a look at the guns in the glass-topped pistol case. A couple of the new Colt Bisley models rested on the green flannel cloth under the glass, along with a new long-barreled Smith and Wesson revolver.

Jim carefully lifted the glass lid and alternately hefted the latest model Colt and the Smith to get a hang of their feel.

The Bisley was for all the world a dead ringer for Colonel Colt's world-famous Single Action Army, save for more of a hump-backed grip and a flat, low-curving hammer spur.

The Smith and Wesson's grip was slighter with less heft and didn't fill the hand or have the substantial feel of a Peacemaker like the dark-blue steel weapon in the holster on Jim Carson's hip.

He put the new guns back and drew out his own Colt sixgun to heft it for comparison. Now there, Jim mused, thoughtfully allowing the comfortable feel to invade his system, there's balance. The grip had an uncanny, almost eerie natural nestling the way its backstrap conformed to the center crease of his right palm. The back-curving lower grip settled comfortably and familiarly into the flesh of the heel of his hand. He could hold the gun muzzle up with the hammer area resting in the crotch of his thumb, fingers relaxed, and balance the weapon perfectly. Neither the Smith nor the Bisley could claim such precise balance.

And, Jim thought, the single-action's aiming balance was the same whether the gun was long- or short-barreled. To Jim Carson, the gun hadn't been made to equal the Old Six Shooter; the Bisley and the Smith and Wesson would never have the popularity of the 1873 Colt's design. A man locking his palm and fingers around the grip of Colonel Colt's Peacemaker had a vague sensation he'd held the gun in another life, even though he knew that was altogether impossible.

Jim was roused out of his reverie by Melissa's voice ringing with crystal clarity as she returned to him near the front door, eyes agleam, gaily hugging a brown-paper-wrapped bolt of dress material.

She had other purchases, necessities for the Douglas ranch; Jim helped her take them out to the family buckboard.

That finished, Jim stood self-consciously wondering what

he'd do next. Somehow he was always tongue-tied around Melissa, and never knew the proper thing to do. The morning air around them was balmy, promising heat by midday. Just now it was near perfect.

"Don't suppose you've the time for a short stroll around town?" Jim asked.

"I was thinking to myself before I caught you peeking into the store what a nice idea that would be, if I had someone to stroll with," she responded, her smile coming slowly, crinkling the corners of her mouth.

Jim knew he was reddening again, and he could sense the hot blood stinging his cheeks. Melissa took his arm and the two started along the shady side of Broad Street, with Carson carefully shortening his pace to stay in step with the young woman at his side. As Jim looked at her, a cloud seemed to come into her eyes.

"Oh, dear, Jim," Melissa exclaimed before they'd gone but a few steps. "I was so surprised and pleased to see you that it slipped my mind. Such a tragedy!"

Carson was alerted. "Tragedy?"

"I'm sure you haven't heard. Mr. Luther Moseley's been killed. Murdered. Some of his stock taken."

Shock sent a tremor along Jim's back; Luther Moseley had been a good friend of his father. "No! What happened?"

A silence came between them as though Melissa didn't know how to soften the dreaded truth.

"They found him shot through the heart, not far from the river flats. My dad and yours probably know more. I got the impression there was a trail showing that quite a few men met him, shot him, and drove off his cattle. Dad thinks rustlers did it, but the men who searched lost the sign a few miles northwest, up in the thicket country."

"Huh!" Jim grunted. "Luther Moseley's been doing so well. What'll happen to his wife and children now? Anybody still out there checking? I'd sure like to be in on bringing in the killers."

"Some of the ladies have been with Mrs. Moseley, and

folks have sent food and offered help. They're well looked after. Some of the men looked around the better part of two days, but they didn't find a trace. After a while, all of them had to get back to their chores at home. Mrs. Moseley will have to take the children back home to Ohio now."

"Well. That's too bad. No, it's awful. A terrible tragedy. Maybe I'll drift that way where he was shot for a look-see myself. Things are quiet at home and Rick's out there to look after things when Dad and I are away anyway."

Melissa's dark eyes were on him. Her hand was warm and firm as it gripped his. "I'd rather you wouldn't, Jim." Anxiety and apprehension rang in her voice. She knew Jim Carson and what lengths he might go to to right a wrong. "They must be dangerous men."

Jim's mind was on Luther Moseley; he'd come to Berdan to settle because of Jim's father.

Near the new land office, Jim and Melissa saw a buggy poking ahead of a dust cloud from the south along the river trail. "Here comes Mr. Rathburn," Jim said. "Wonder if he has any ideas about Mr. Moseley and the rustlers?"

Melissa shrugged. "I don't know. He's been away on business. Jim, you ought to let Mr. Rathburn and your dad and the others decide what to do about the killing."

Jim's shyness around Melissa had become secondary to the urgency of the tragedy. "Melissa, it's not going to hurt for me to do a little checking. I'm not going to do anything rash."

Melissa's silence acknowledged her acceptance, though her eyes continued to register disagreement.

As Rathburn's buggy neared, Sam Carson stepped out of the land office. Nearing fifty, the elder Carson was a solid, steady man with earnest eyes and brown hair graying at the temples. He was heavier than his son, but they bore a close resemblance. It was plain that Sam Carson had looked much like his oldest son when he had been Jim's age. Both were stamped out of the same tough leather. Sam's face had only gained in sternness with the passing of years.

But now, Jim noted, an unfamiliar sadness lingered in his father's eyes, something that went deeper even than grief over Luther Moseley's killing. It was an expression of bitter disappointment, the shattering of a dream. Now something had come along to tarnish, taint, and forever cloud the dream.

Though Sam Carson was in no way responsible for the murder and rustling, his eyes seemed to say that he had somehow betrayed a trust, had proven unfaithful to those who had trusted him.

This was something that the character of Sam Carson could not tolerate.

Jim sensed, as well, a deep melancholy in his father's subdued tone. "Jim!" he said. "Glad you're back."

Studying his father's crestfallen attitude, Jim Carson swore to take whatever steps were necessary to avenge the awful wrong done to this man who had taught him the very moral code that both of them now found challenged.

Rathburn's buggy rattled to a halt near his office. The sweaty horse dropped his head almost gratefully after the long uphill pull from the river ford. The light carriage leaned with the compression of its springs as Rathburn—a large and heavy man—heaved himself out; it popped fully upright again as the banker's weight was released to the hard-packed dirt of Broad Street.

Jim observed that his father's business associate had a large head, as befit a man with his physical frame, perched on a thick neck as strong as the rest of him. Rathburn's nose was broad, and his teeth gleamed when he smiled, which was often. He was a tall, robust man of commanding appearance.

Frothy sideburns and hair worn full at the sides and back nearly covered his large ears. He cloaked most of his hair under a wide-brimmed tall black Stetson.

Rathburn's black frock coat hugged his corpulent form strangely, in some places appearing tight enough to burst, and in others loose and baggy. His black broadcloth trousers were tucked into knee-length black stovepipe boots. Rathburn's face was perpetually flushed and his blue, bug-like eyes carried a constant glitter.

Dangling across his vest was a thick gold watch chain with a large wolf fang fitted into a gold cap, worn as a fob. Rathburn's younger days, Jim knew, had been spent as a wolfer, trapping, poisoning, and shooting the wily pedator that created so many problems for Western cattle ranchers.

Now, Martin Rathburn's bearing showed nothing of the coarse, crude life of a wolfer. Everything about him bespoke respectability and benevolence. Those qualities were even there in his deep, friendly voice that now greeted the three standing on the raised sidewalk, there by chance, but looking like a welcoming committee.

"How was the trip, Mart?" Sam Carson inquired, step-ping out to shake Rathburn's hand in a welcome-home gesture.

"Good enough, very good indeed, thank you, Sam. Missed you yesterday when I got in, I'm afraid," Rathburn boomed. "Jim, my boy! How are you this fine morning? And the pretty Melissa. Always a pleasure to see you, my dear." Rathburn bowed graciously, lightly gripped and lifted the young woman's hand, and kissed it.

Jim grinned awkwardly as the color came and went in Melissa's cheeks. She tried to smile prettily at the compli-ment as Rathburn pinched one of those cheeks in a fatherly manner. To Jim, such gallantry belonged to a bygone past; though he never would have expressed it openly, he some-how suspected Rathburn of devious motives in such demon-strative displays. But he couldn't put anything definite together, and thus tended to dismiss it. After all, to everyone in Berdan, Rathburn was respected, the one person who had made it all possible, and given the settlers the chance to own their land and homes.

By all appearances, Jim mused, his mind full of the catastrophe that had visited Berdan with the murder of the kindly Mr. Moseley, Rathburn was also uncommonly kind.

Almost too kind, Jim thought, again disturbed with himself for what he considered spiteful thoughts.

Martin Rathburn had lent large sums of money with which the settlers bought the tools, lumber, hardware, and other necessities for settlement. To the newcomers helping build Berdan, Rathburn was a benefactor who had magically appeared to help them. And it seemed his only interest was altruistic, though by all indications, he could afford it. For all they knew, and from hints Rathburn had dropped, he had big investments in the East and throughout the West.

Rathburn's smile faded, but did not disappear completely. "Sam," he asked, "could I see you inside? A matter that came up during my trip . . . we need to talk."

"Sure, Mart."

"Besides," Rathburn added, "these young people probably haven't seen each other in a while and have their things they need to talk about."

Jim reddened, and shot an embarrassed look at his father.

"It's all right, Jim," the elder Carson said softly with an understanding nod. "Please excuse us, Melissa, business calls. Jim, I'll see you at home."

"I've needed to tell you, Dad. Don't expect me. There's something more I need to do out on the range. Tell mother I'll be home tomorrow night."

Suspicion glinted in his father's eyes. "I know you, Jim." His voice trailed off for an instant and then went on. "It's the Moseley thing, isn't it?"

Jim's thin, excited face was also grim. "Dad, I just need to know that everything possible's been done to track the killers. One stone may have been left unturned."

"Son, let Mr. Rathburn and me and the other men handle it. We're staying on top of the situation."

Jim looked at Melissa, weighing his words, then turned decisively toward his father like a man whose mind was made up. "Dad, I'm not a little boy. I've spent a lot of time out there on the prairie. I know the land. I'm good at

16

tracking. Maybe I'll find something the others missed. It's just a day to do some looking, some checking."

Sam Carson's face furrowed with thought. "All right. But be careful, son."

"Depend on it, Dad."

His father's face broke into a melancholy grin; he knew his son.

After the older men disappeared into the banker's office, Melissa and Jim finished their stroll at the girl's wagon. "I've got to be home in time to help with supper," Melissa said.

"Maybe I'll just ride along. With evil men around, I'll feel better seeing you home safely."

Melissa was pleased with Jim's concern, secretly hoping it involved a bit more than her welfare in light of recent events; Jim hadn't needed an excuse to ride with her to her home before. But he'd always had a reasonable alibi for the mission. Jim, she knew, was a decent, caring young man who, she was well aware, was awkward about expressing his feelings. Maybe, she thought, some day he might find his true voice.

Increasing heat waves danced out of the dust as Jim rode his chestnut mustang alongside her vehicle. Jim found subjects of small talk to fill the near hour it took to get to her home. As they rode in, the Douglas spread was as beckoning as an oasis in the desert—which in many respects it was. Grass lay a rich yellow in the sunlight. Like a green gem against the sun-baked open land, the clot of trees clustered along a spring-fed stream provided ample shade for the good-size cabin and corral. A barn and stable under construction nearby rounded out the headquarters of George Douglas's Square D ranch.

In the air was the dry, tickling pungence of cured grass and sage and of a day building up to an oppressive heat.

Melissa's father was at work in the yard as they approached. The front and back of George Douglas's shirt were dark with sweat as he shod a work horse with the help of Melissa's seventeen-year-old brother, Victor. Douglas was the picture of a man working hard for his family in his faded blue Levis and work shirt. His ample pants cuffs were turned up, providing a handy receptacle for his horseshoe nails.

Douglas had the look of a man accustomed to hard work, but one who enjoyed it, and seldom shirked. His thick, stocky body also spoke of the feisty and dogged disposition of a terrier. His kinky black hair was cropped close for comfort and cleanliness, going salt-and-pepper on top with gray showing in a band at the temples and circling around the back of his neck. The character of his hair and his naturally tan skin that deepened with the sun hinted at a strain of African ancestry some generations back.

The West, Jim knew, was full of men—and women— from broadly diversified ancestries. Melissa's father had many of the telltale marks of having been a cowboy; his nose, once almost noble, drifted off center, broken at some time, possibly in a saloon brawl or some mishap on the cattle trail. He had hard, rope-burned hands. The first joints of his right third and fourth fingers were missing, accidentally severed, Jim surmised, during George's cowboying days, when he wasn't fast enough in taking his dallies around the saddlehorn with a singing lariat to control a steer, moving at express-train speed, that popped the rope taut. More than a few cowboys carried similar telltale signs of their occupation.

Douglas didn't stop work as his daughter drove up with young Carson in the saddle beside her. He merely nodded; he liked young Carson well enough, but hardly had the idea of regarding him as Melissa's suitor. Douglas believed that his daughter was still much too young to marry and leave his home for one of her own.

Melissa's younger brother Victor, however, had a more cheery greeting. "Hello Jim, you old scalawag! Where've you been?"

"Hunting for a week. Next time, maybe you can come along," Jim called, helping Melissa take her town purchases to the house. Vic's father looked at Vic and then at Jim, the hint of a glower on his face. A lot of work needed to be done at his ranch, and he considered hunting trips—unless out of necessity—altogether without purpose.

In the Douglas kitchen, Jim Carson got another kind of warm reception—a warm, motherly hug from Melissa's mother, Hanna Douglas, and an invitation to stay for supper.

That night, with the excuse that the Douglas place was closer to where he intended to go in the morning than his parents' ranch, he slept in the unfinished barn, his plans made before his eyes closed.

· 2 ·

By dawn, Jim was in the saddle with the excitement of the chase stirring his blood. This time he wouldn't be tracking animals but men, far more dangerous quarries than the bears and other game he was accustomed to stalking. The night before he had learned from George Douglas most of all he needed to know of Luther Moseley's murder—where the body was found and other details of the townsmen's hunt for the killers. A determination grew in him to track them where the others had failed.

The morning sun reddened the streamers of night clouds in the eastern sky as Jim hunted over the ground near the Black River trail where Moseley had died. The sun touched the peaks of surrounding hills but lower down the darkness yet lay. The sign was cold and trampled over by less skillful searchers. Still Jim found enough to assure him he moved in the proper direction, reading sign as he went. Trampled grass and stirred-up dirt created by a small herd being moved through the land charted his course. His horse traveled well, alternating trot with lope as Jim watched for sign.

What track he saw could only have been the rustled Moseley herd, and led northwest. After a few miles, the

20

country grew thick with thorned brush and scarred with numerous branching arroyos.

Through the afternoon, Jim rode back and forth across the brushy flats. The country was open, flats and low ridges, coulees and benchlands. At last he came to timber, a dense, thickly twisted and nearly impenetrable barrier. Abruptly the land lifted and the gully he followed terminated in an impassable thicket. Jim swung his horse to the right, toward an opening he had noted from a distance. The going was rough, and evening shadows blued the narrow entrance.

There, the cattle spoor he followed played out to the point he felt it hopeless to continue. But, he thought, studying the waning sun as it slowly slid down the heavens to the west, the rustlers might return any time and perhaps a bit more patience was called for. He climbed to a high spot, a concealed vantage point that gave him a clear view of the thicket where he had lost the trail of the rustled cattle. He made himself comfortable, vowing to wait as long as he could for whatever clues might turn up.

The long evening dusk was almost at an end, and the thicket was shadowed, the brush along its perimeter nothing but dim clumps. The hills and timber held the darkness to the bottom of the thicketed gulch.

He estimated that his wait had consumed an hour when —near deep dark—a horseman emerged along one of the cattle or game trails leading into the thicket.

Jim's breath caught as the rider was joined by others; he tried to make himself smaller in his hillside point of concealment.

He recognized none of them, so could only assume he was looking at some of the men involved with Luther Moseley's death. The first man who had ridden out, obviously the leader, was a rawboned, red-haired man in a black suit and hat who rode with a hard-edged posture in the saddle, as did his heavily armed followers.

Light from a crimson sun bulging on the western rim of the world glinted off rifle barrels and cold Colt steel, and Jim had a hunch his wait had not been in vain. He counted fifteen riders filing out of the thick tangled area of trees and brush. Rather than riding casually, they appeared to be on a determined mission that took them in the direction of Berdan. Jim slid back to where his horse was hidden, mounted up and followed, careful to stay out of sight.

With full darkness, he had trouble following them, but with the silvery lights and shadows of an emerging full moon, he drew closer and was not far behind when they entered the settlement and walked their horses down Broad Street toward the Rathburn and Carson offices.

Jim swung down from the saddle and hid his horse behind the Estevans' store, carefully crossing the street to come up along the alley behind the buildings; the riders he had tracked were already behind closed doors in Rathburn's office. As he crossed Broad Street, Jim also noted that Rathburn's buggy was still in town.

Sliding along the building in the dark, Jim found Rathburn's rear window partly open. He crouched there, ready to spring to Rathburn's aid if necessary. He was confident the men were the rustlers who had killed Luther Moseley. What business they had with Rathburn he felt he'd soon find out as he crouched in the dark below the office window and peered in cautiously.

Even at his remote vantage point, Jim could sense the tension in Rathburn's office.

Inside, the big brick-haired leader was already standing belligerently in the center of the office, facing Martin Rathburn. The financier sat rigid behind his flat-topped desk. It was a well-furnished office, with a carpet, comfortable chairs, and a conference table. A map of the old Ramirez Grant, which constituted the land around Berdan, nearly filled one wall.

Close behind Rathburn stood a cabinet containing decanters of liquor and boxes of cigars. A small stack of papers was on the desk near his hand and a large oak file cabinet stood against the wall.

The black-suited leader, obviously angry, paced up and down before Rathburn's desk. His voice rasped as he reviled Berdan's benefactor. His every word was clear to Jim. Through the several-inch opening of the lower sash, Jim could see the other riders ringing Rathburn's desk in imposing attitudes. The atmosphere inside the office seemed charged with menace.

Jim's heart throbbed and he felt he couldn't pull enough wind into his lungs.

"Get one thing straight, old man," charged the leader, shaking his fist, his voice growling deep in his throat. "You and these fool squatters are not wanted around here. This country's my stamping ground and you know me. If you don't, you'd better! I go by Jubal Doan. When I left here two years ago this was open range and I ran my herds in and out of here freely. Now you've got these nesters comin' in here with their herds, stringin' wire and crampin' my style. It ain't going to be tolerated."

Doan's voice was low and clear, every biting word crisp and tart. Fury touched his lips and again and again Doan's long, harsh-knuckled fingers wrapped around the black butt of his holstered Colt.

Jim Carson crouched in the dark beside the building listening, ready to draw his own Colt. Eight of the chief rustler's cronies were inside. He wondered where the rest were, but assumed some had drifted down to the saloon. He yearned to find out, but dared not leave his vantage point under the window for fear harm might come to Rathburn.

Much to the eavesdropping Jim's amazement, Rathburn —rather than appearing intimidated—laughed. Rathburn studied Doan's lean form with shrewd eyes and an amused glance. "Sit down, Mr. Doan," Rathburn's voice boomed cheerily. "Sit down, for heaven's sake. Your men can sit around the table there. Don't be bashful. Have a drink. I'm not armed, so you can relax your gun hand. Here, try some of my fine Napoleon brandy. I reserve it for special occasions."

Jim admired Rathburn's nerve, faced by such fierce outlaws and killers as Jubal Doan's band. Jim hugged the rear wall, silent in the dark, puzzled by the portly financier's casual, friendly attitude.

Rathburn turned in his chair toward the liquor cabinet and carefully and slowly selected a decanter with a large red diamond on its label. He poured a stiff drink of the rich, golden brandy for Doan, smiling benevolently at the red-haired rustler. Doan blinked in guarded astonishment at Rathburn's unexpected civility and accepted the glass.

He raised it to his lips to swallow the contents in a gulp, but Rathburn stopped him with a sinister chuckle and a wave.

"Don't do it, my friend," the banker said softly and ominously. "It's heavily laced with enough strychnine to kill a he-wolf and all of you in this room as well." Jim raised his eyes over the sill to see Rathburn watching Doan with a sinister smirk.

Doan reared back, rage welling up in him, his flinty stare on Rathburn as he still held the evil brandy snifter. Doan's eyes were icy, his lips compressed in new outrage. Their glances met with angry impact. "Poison me? Why you damned old sidewinder," he rasped, starting for his sixgun again.

Rathburn now smiled broadly, disarming Doan's scowling glare and holding up his hand to let him speak before Doan unleashed his pistol. "That was only to show you that I'm not as helpless as I seem, Mr. Doan."

Doan's hand dropped from his pistol butt, and Rathburn studied him with another self-satisfied smirk. "Not as helpless, nor as easy to buffalo, Mr. Doan. Don't think that all fat men are soft. I could have killed you, but I didn't. Could have done in you and your men at once and I'd be a hero in this town for doing away with the killers of Luther Moseley. Just now you need me, and I need you. We can work together."

Rathburn—to Jim Carson's total surprise—chose another flask. This time he poured a drink for himself and downed it before he pushed it toward Doan and brought out glasses for all in the room.

"Drink up, boys," he said. "Never fear. This is the good stuff."

If Jubal Doan was astonished by Martin Rathburn's reception, Jim Carson was struck dumb, his energy drained. His mind could scarcely believe what his eyes and ears had recorded.

Rathburn coolly regarded Doan and his henchmen now sipping gratefully of the heady, expensive brandy. Jim struggled now through the confusion in his brain to hear what was said.

"As I said, Doan, don't sell me short. And don't judge me by appearances. Do you know what a wolfer is?"

"A wolfer? What the hell are you getting at?" Doan took a step forward, a savage hatred in his face. The hospitality of the brandy had not penetrated the outrage he'd brought with him into Rathburn's office.

Rathburn brought his hard-clenched fist down on the desk, its rattle resounding in the room, taking the outlaw group by surprise. "I asked you a question, sir! Do you know what a wolfer is?"

"Who doesn't?" Doan's voice had lost some of its aggressiveness, but he was hardly intimidated by the fat man.

Rathburn's eyelids flickered. "Because that's how I started in this country. Years ago. Two dollars apiece for wolf scalps. Strychnine, my friend, strychnine. That's how I got 'em. More often than shooting or trapping. Baited dead cattle, and often I had to kill my own bait and at times that bait wore a brand, but I could have cared less of a damn. Wolves are cunning, but they're also dumb. Sometimes I'd get four or five kills at a carcass. After a while, I had crews working for me and I cleaned up."

Jubal Doan studied Rathburn now with a kind of admiration. "I'm a son of a gun," Doan muttered. A silence settled between the two men before either spoke.

Rathburn continued. "I went east ten years ago with my capital. I plunged in real estate, paper securities, and such. Owned a riverboat—a floating gambling emporium and whorehouse plying between St. Louis and New Orleans—for several years. When the railroads came close to connecting east and west, I saw the handwriting on the wall and sunk nearly everything into the cattle business. That's mostly what brought me to this part of the country. Cattle need land, need growers, and I decided it was time to get back West and get in on the action."

"So I take it," Doan growled, setting his glass down on Rathburn's desk, "you've got a scheme up your sleeve, Rathburn. I got to hand it to you for sand."

"Precisely. These people you wish to drive away, Doan," Rathburn said, his eyes narrowing, "these very people make the land valuable. It's worth a fortune simply because it's being proved up. Sam Carson's company has lent the money—my money—so they may further improve their properties."

"I still don't savvy," Doan said gruffly. "You set 'em up. They start herds and increase 'em. Then they sell some, pay you off, and they're in the clear. What's in it for me, or even for you?"

Rathburn's smile was patient but condescending, his plump hand up, gesturing for the opportunity to proceed.

"Why don't you leave the details to me? I've had a great deal of experience in such affairs. It's all legal, to the last scratch of the pen. Even the powers that be in the territorial capital can't indict me as long as I play the cards close to my vest. I will tell you this much. These ranches have been started and there are always other men waiting—eager men, stupid men, coming West—with cash to buy such improved places. The main dependence of the cowmen here is on their herds. Without cattle to market, they don't meet their obligations." Rathburn affected a mocking, singsong voice. "I'd like to help but I'm just a simple businessman. I have no

26

alternative but to foreclose and evict them. Proved-up properties are more desirable to interested buyers than raw land—and worth more money. Do we see eye to eye?"

Jubal Doan was fascinated. "Why you sly old rascal!" he exclaimed as the scheme dawned on him. "Could be real money in it."

"There is," Rathburn said. "I've been watching for a connection like this for some time. When Moseley was found dead and his herd rustled, I knew I'd found my connection. I was trying to think up ways to get a message to you, or whoever was in charge. And here you are; stroke of fate."

"I got to hand it to you, Rathburn."

"No, soon I'll be handing it to you, Doan. You take the herds out of the territory. I'll arrange the foreclosures. We proceed carefully, cautiously, discreetly, so we don't tip our hand. Do I make myself clear?"

"You sure do."

Rathburn hit the desk with his chubby fist. "Not clear enough! None of this gunning down ranchers in cold blood and running off their herds, leaving a trail a mile wide and an inch deep that a blind man could follow!"

Doan's anger flared instantly. His breath wheezed with his words. "Why, you . . . !" His hand started to drop to his sixgun and he quickly thought better of it. "What do you think I am, Rathburn?"

"A clumsy ox, if you want the truth. The Moseley affair was sheer stupidity. There's no law around here but if you keep pulling stunts like that, Judge Winfield up at the territorial capital will have a man in our midst in no time."

"You want me to rustle their cattle or don't ya?"

"Of course, man, of course. But by slow and easy degrees. They say the best way to boil a frog is to put him in a pot of water and gradually increase the heat. By the time he realizes what's happening to him, he's practically cooked."

"I don't get it."

"If you toss a frog into hot water, he'll hop right out. Bring up the heat gradually and he'll stay until he's cooked and ready to eat."

Doan's eyes glinted with understanding. "Take a few cattle at a time. Don't rile them up. By the time they realize what's happening they've hardly got any cattle left."

"You're getting it, Doan. A couple of them have a bad year and are forced out. Nobody needs to bring the law in for that. That's the way life is, get it? I don't propose to have a virtual fortune wangled away from me."

"Sounds like a gold mine," Doan said. "It's a deal. But I'm the one at risk. They hang rustlers. I think the split ought to be better than fifty-fifty."

Rathburn's eyes narrowed. "It'll be slow, sad music for both of us if we're caught, Doan. If I'm implicated in a land swindle, don't think these people won't form a vigilance committee in a trice to give me a hemp necktie, forget judge and jury. Sure it's risky. Easy money always is."

"You got a point there, Rathburn. Okay. Equal shares." Doan now grinned at his new partner in crime. "By God, you're hard as nails, but you still got plenty of tricks up your sleeve."

"You'll run off each brand of cattle as I tell you," Rathburn continued. "We'll start with the Square D. That's George Douglas. He's got a heavy obligation with me and his improvements are well along. Without his stock in trade he'll be ruined and have to pull up stakes."

Jim Carson's heart was a rock of ice. He felt weak as he heard Martin Rathburn disclose his true character as a deadly opportunist who had used Sam Carson to lure in victims to be fleeced. Details were not all clear to Jim, but he'd heard enough.

He was so stunned by this turn of events that he failed to hear the soft tread of a man turning the back corner of the building. Jim stiffened as he felt a breath of movement behind him. He tried to whirl, to get out his Colt. Before he could move, a pistol barrel slashed at the side of his head and with an abrupt burst of light and pain, darkness dropped like a cloak over his awareness.

Doan's men dragged him inside limp and groggy, to hold him up before Rathburn and Doan.

"Good Lord!" Rathburn exclaimed. "That's Jim Carson." Rathburn's gleaming face had turned grim.

"Listenin' outside the back window, Jubal," one of Jim's captors growled.

Jim's awareness slid back in time to hear the man speak. "I didn't hear anything, Mr. Rathburn," he lied, his head a mass of ache. "I saw your light and came over to see if you were all right, and these men jumped me."

"I see," Rathburn said ominously, turning in his chair. He picked up the decanter with the red-diamond label, poured a measure of it into a glass and held it out to Jim across the desk. "You look shaky, my boy. Here. This drink will calm you." Rathburn smiled at Jim as he offered it.

Carson shook his head, even though it hurt to do it. The agitation in his voice robbed his words of conviction. "I . . . I don't need anything to drink." He was well aware of the drink's contents.

"He heard everything," Rathburn said, glowering at Jim.

Jubal Doan cursed and jumped at Jim, whose arms were quickly pinioned by a man behind him. Doan's lips had a cruel twist as he punched Jim in the stomach. As Jim doubled over, Doan hit him in the face, smashing his lips into his teeth.

Jim tried to fight, but men were all around him. He went down under their weight. Doan, swearing a blue streak, began kicking him with sharp-toed, spurred boots. Carson's body convulsed and trembled with the intensity of Doan's attack, his head and face a bloody mess. He passed out again.

Rathburn watched, his expression unchanging until Doan's men had finished with Jim. "You'll have to get him out of here and disposed of," the banker said, breathless over how near he had come to being exposed. "When you come here again, Doan, be more careful. Our connections must not be suspected."

· 3 ·

Against the stillness and depth of dark night when vision decreased, sounds and smells sharpened for the forty-odd head of cattle bunched in a grassy hollow several hundred yards and over two hummocky hills east of George Douglas's Square D ranch house.

The riders approaching quietly and cautiously out of the night from the opposite direction caused no great alarm among the longhorns bearing the boxed *D* brand bedded-down along with a smattering of unbranded calves that nestled in the dark close to their mothers for both security and sustenance.

The cattle had gotten wind of many of the approaching riders before, in daylight as well as dark, as several times in recent weeks the rustlers eased in cautiously to cut out and silently drive off as few as three, sometimes as many as eight, of the Douglas herd.

Their heads turned suspiciously toward the approaching sounds, the clustered longhorns, though alert, stayed calm and quiet, almost as if waiting their turn to be driven away. In the soft, diffused light afforded by a cloud covered full moon, they were dark clots of resting animals against a pewter-colored land. The riders, expert at their trade and moving with swift, assured precision, split and fanned out a respectable distance from the bunched cows.

One of the riders, last to approach them out of the dark, eased his horse into the bed ground and quietly and carefully urged a longhorn steer to his feet. With expert maneuvers, his cow pony cut the steer from the herd, guiding it away into the night in the direction from which they'd come.

Nearby riders eased into the flanks of the herd and skillfully urged others to their feet to follow the lead longhorn. Obediently, still without significant sound, the others rose stiffly and with guiding riders keeping them bunched, moved off singly or in groups, calves dutifully trotting near the haven of their mothers' flanks and close to the precious udder. The only sound from the invading riders was the occasional sharp slap of coiled lariat against the thickness of leather chaps to encourage cooperation; flank riders—silent, gliding silhouettes in the night—kept the drowsy cattle pointed down trail, stringing them out for better control.

From behind, two cowboys rode drag, hurrying along the stragglers and keeping their eyes peeled for bunch-quitters.

Lush grass deadened the sounds of retreating hoofs. In the soft light of moon and stars, a silvery haze of dust rose above the cattle's bed ground, settling softly as the sound of the last riders and their rustled livestock blended with the night and the distance.

In the Square D ranch house, George Douglas was mysteriously awakened by a vague, disquieting dream; he could have sworn he heard the sounds of moving cattle. He was glad to become aware of the realities of his physical body and of the darkened bedroom. Outside the window, the sprawling land was silent under a night sky. Beside him, Hanna was a warm, familiar bulk under the blankets. Her breathing was heavy, raspy, and bordering on a snore. His mind at ease again, George watched a few minutes out the window at the sky and its hidden moon and ample dusting of stars.

Still, there was in his mind the gnawing anxiety of a number of missing cattle; at least he suspected some were missing. Work on the barn had kept him from saddling up, riding the back country and making a tally. With a note coming due to Mr. Rathburn, a roundup and a drive to market couldn't be delayed much longer.

Vic, his boy, could make a quick tally, but he needed Vic's help with the barn. Besides, if there were—as he suspected —rustlers at work, such a ride into the trackless prairie could have its dangers. Vic was a good friend of the other Carson boy, Rick. The two of them would be good at tracking down errant cows. But Sam Carson's family had its hands full these days with concern over Jim.

Douglas found his ears pricking again for unheard sounds, leftovers of his dream. Lots of work in the morning, George, he told himself as he watched puffy clouds erase the field of stars and brighter planets from his low vantage point under the window. He settled into a comfortable sleeping position and tried not to think troubled thoughts. He felt himself drifting toward sleep, his mind calmer.

Deep in the plains east of a mountainous escarpment of sheer granite—a towering monarch hazy and softened by great distance, boldly rearing its head several thousand feet at the end of a sloping range—Jubal Doan crouched by the morning cook fire with his coffee as he gnawed a glowing, whip-thin cheroot. A gentle breeze fanned the smoke of the stogie along with that of the fire to his eyes. He squinted against it, lending a characteristic glower to his features.

Tawny trail dust dulled the black of his flat-brimmed, low-crowned hat; a voluminous tan duster reaching nearly to his boot-heels protected his black business suit. Behind him, a few paces from the bed of embers and feeble flames, the range cook, a portly, dark Mexican in grimy clothing with an even grimier rag around his middle, dithered and clattered among his pots and pans at the broad work shelf provided by the chuckwagon tailgate. After breakfast and their post-meal smokes, Doan's crew had mounted and drifted off toward the herd, a thousand head, all of dubious origin and with freshly doctored brands; they'd be Montana bound in the morning.

Doan regarded a growing distant dust cloud from out of the south with grim satisfaction. Curly and Duke and the boys were bringing up the last of the Square D cattle after a carefully planned night raid.

Old Rathburn might have a fit over them taking so many in one gulp but, thought Doan, what the hell; they'll be out of the territory in a day and a half and nobody will be the wiser. He needed to start trailing a herd north; for a man of his profession, warmed-over brands—too many of them— were pure poison in this neck of the woods.

"Roberto," he growled back over his shoulder at the cook. "Riders comin' in. How's the coffee and grub? They'll be needin' to eat." The portly Mexican stopped his work to shield his eyes against the sun, seeking the figures of riders and cattle against the hazy dust cloud.

"I make the beeg pot again, Joo-bawl. *Mucho* coffee. Cooked greets we got lots hot een kettle. Beeskets in dotch oven an' gravy hot. Still *mucho frijoles*. Always *mucho* beans. Roberto feed 'em right, Joo-bawl. Never you mind."

Doan roused up to walk out into the prairie to greet his approaching hands. Duke and Curly rode leisurely at point and he could see the flank riders emerging out of the dust. Duke raised a hand and pointed to his left, motioning the crew to circle the newcomers near the main herd. Duke and Curly rode on toward Doan.

The rustler chief's shrewd eyes tallied about forty head turning off toward the branding fires. It would take the rest of the day to blotch Square D brands before they'd be trail-ready. Only for a moment did he wish he had a man with better skills at doctoring brands. He strode out to greet his two top hands.

On another morning two weeks later, Federal Judge Isaac Winfield, the law in Fort Walker and in this corner of the New Mexico territory, paced his ample office, his gnarled old hands clasped behind his back as he stared at the framed wall map of his jurisdiction.

Winfield was a burly figure in his advancing years; his broad face and mane of straight, white hair had earned him the nickname, "The Lion of Fort Walker." Indeed, when it came to upholding justice in his portion of New Mexico, Isaac Winfield possessed a lion-like ferocity.

"Berdan," he murmured, studying Sam Carson's letter. "First I've heard of it." Winfield didn't need a map to visualize the several hundred square miles under his control. As a Federal judge committed to its law and order, he knew this land. In his long-gone youth, before age pinned him to a swivel chair, Winfield had ridden those danger trails himself, as a lawman in pursuit of outlaws and fugitives, while guns roared and flamed over the vast red-earth plains of the east, the chaparral sprawl and the foothills and mountains to the west, and the *malpaise*, the badlands, in the southern reaches.

Later, with his law degree in his saddlebags, Winfield rode the outlands to help interpret the law that protected decent people and inflicted punishment on the scalawags and scofflaws.

Winfield pictured, too, the sandy flats, the red mud in the wet seasons, the choking dust in the dry months along the northern boundaries where the wind blew all the way from the Arctic with nothing to stop it but barbed wire in the northern plains states.

Closer to home, Winfield knew the vast Ramirez Grant, being broken up by eastern settlers like those in this new town of Berdan. The Ramirez Grant was once a great sprawling rancho and had a history dating back generations before America's war with Mexico brought these territories into the embrace of the United States. Winfield's mind conjured the sprawling Ramirez Grant, rising to ten thousand feet in the mountains, a tremendous semi-arid plateau split by dry canyons and the great, lush Black River basin. He envisioned the bottom lands choked with cactus and other thorny growth, and the immense rocky mountains thrusting into a hot, azure sky.

"No need for a map. I remember that Black River country," he mused, as he studied the map anyway. He could close his eyes and see it. "According to this letter from that man Carson, that'll be about where Berdan now stands." With a red pencil, he made a small cross at a spot along where the Black River etched its serpentine coils through the old Ramirez Grant. The map acknowledged the area where prolific natural springs poured forth their richness to create a green oasis and add their flow to the mighty Black River.

Winfield's calm this day was an unusual thing. He had all the fierceness of disposition usually attributed to a Southern gentleman like himself, as well as the gentility. Nothing frayed his temper like reports of citizens being abused by an outlaw element.

He called out loudly and his clerk, Robertshaw, appeared in the doorway, stood a moment in hesitation, then stepped inside. He looked expectantly at Judge Winfield. "See if Cole Ryerson is about this morning, Bob. Then send him in." Robertshaw ducked with a sort of bow and disappeared.

Footsteps soon echoed in the narrow, wood-floor corridor, the stride measured and unhurried. A tall man edged into the room, his gray-green eyes registered concern as they sought Winfield's. United States Marshal Cole Clement Ryerson, already a legend described by the nickname Boot Hill Cole, stood well over six feet in his polished, spurred boots.

Because he was the man Winfield had picked as his personal representative, Ryerson was always given

Winfield's toughest assignments. Winfield studied the tall lawman. He had purposely appointed Ryerson following the latter's several spectacular years of lawkeeping in Abilene after the tragic assassination of Sheriff Mose Laramore. Ryerson had quickly tracked down and brought in Laramore's assailant, a Mexican known only as Greaser Jack.

Still, Boot Hill Cole showed few of the aspects of a quick-triggered fighting man, unless his keen eyes were studied closely. Instead, in his fresh blue shirt and red bandanna, with dark trousers tucked into boots, Ryerson seemed little more than a good-natured cowboy.

His hair was jet black, with a sheen that spoke of health and youth. His legs were long and powerful, his shoulders broad, but his hips, from which hung a belt supporting his blue-steel Colt cap-and-ball Navy, were narrow.

Not that Ryerson was stern or severe, for his wide mouth somewhat relieved any severity his other features indicated. But in him appeared to be the rippling ferocity of a leashed panther, and Winfield knew that the man could move with devastating speed.

Though Ryerson's lazy slouch might have deceived others about his swiftness in a fight, Winfield was aware that the large, clumsy-looking hands of his top marshal could clear leather and fire his Colt Navy from its supple, oiled holster like the lightning dart of a serpent's head.

Ryerson found his boss pacing up and down in his large, well-appointed office in the territorial courthouse.

"Mornin', Judge." Ryerson's voice, too, was low, lazy and drawling. Yet when necessary, it could thunder with respect-commanding authority.

"And a good day to you, Cole," Winfield greeted. "Glad you were in. I received a letter here from a man named Sam Carson. It appears he's head of a settlement and a bunch of one-horse ranchers who've moved in on the old Ramirez Grant along the Black River. Established a town—Berdan. Seems they got along fine for a while, but rustlers have hit 'em. I think I know their head man, Jubal Doan, though Carson doesn't mention him by name. One of the circuit judges put him away in Leavenworth for a couple of years for finding another man's horse to put under his saddle and other men's cattle to put under his brand. Now it appears our Mr. Doan is back at his old stomping grounds and up to his old tricks, as lean and mean as ever."

"You're suggesting here's a jasper that might stand some taming," Ryerson said softly, his mouth hinting at a grin.

Winfield grinned back. "Cole, so long as that owlhoot seems determined, it's up to my office—and, yes, you—to cool his enthusiasm a bit."

Ryerson's gray-green eyes flicked to the wall map and Winfield's recent red mark, and then back to the judge. Winfield frowned, his frosty brows knotted and ferocious, his lips set and grim. He cleared his throat and rattled Sam Carson's letter.

"The law," he said, "needs to look into things over there. Listen to this." Winfield perused the letter. "Da-dah-dah, and so-and-so. Yes, here. 'I write this discreetly, and I trust in your confidence, Judge Winfield. One of our ranchers, Luther Moseley, was shot in cold blood,' obviously by Doan's cattle thieves, for they ran off Moseley's herd. 'My oldest son, Jim, has disappeared because he rode out to trail them. I'm not prepared to admit they've killed him, but I'm gravely concerned. As you can well imagine, I have my hands full with his mother. She's beside herself with care and grief. My business partner, Martin Rathburn has been very consoling and has offered his resources to help me find Jim. He is upset, almost, as I am. Further, one of my best friends, George Douglas, who has had cattle rustled and had trouble finding enough beeves with his brand to fill a consignment shipment, has been foreclosed. He's left his family with me and has gone farther west to scout for a new homesite. George's problem is the least in a series of bad turns of late. There's no formal law here, Judge. We need help, and quickly.'"

Winfield's voice shook. Suddenly, his anger flaring, Winfield banged his fist on the desk, the sound nearly echoing in his large, high-ceilinged courthouse office. "Dammit, Cole, you and I have worked too damned hard to make this territory safe for settlement by honest, God-fearing people! When I hear of folks being used this way, I'm about ready to saddle up and take matters into my own hands," he bellowed. "Decent people being set upon by a cussed band of mongrel cattle thieves!"

Winfield folded into his office chair, his face graying, propped his elbows on the desk and shook an angry finger at Ryerson. "Hanging's too good for the likes of this Doan, Cole, but justice has to prevail. I want that man stopped! Just now, one man can do more than an army. Do I make myself clear, Mr. Ryerson?"

Boot Hill Cole retained his composure. "Totally, Judge Winfield. Totally. I'm to have me a look-see into this man Doan's carryings-on. Is that what you're suggesting, Judge?"

Ryerson's blood warmed with excitement; this was the kind of challenge he had been born to, his zest for such confrontation honed by a war and a long career at law-keeping.

Judge Winfield launched himself out of the chair and strode to look thoughtfully out the office window. "You'd better straddle leather, Cole. But be careful," he said, a new note of calm in his voice.

By midday, with a warm sun spreading a yellow glow over the grassy courthouse square, the old judge watched from the same second-floor courthouse window as Ryerson approached a stout trail horse, a roan. The horse danced in excitement and nuzzled the marshal's caressing hand.

After checking over his traveling gear loaded on the horse, Ryerson swung into the saddle. Under one leg, a well-kept carbine was snugged into its boot. His saddlebags contained only essential provisions and extra ammunition. The tall marshal could live for weeks in the open with a bit of salt, coffee, and sugar. His voluminous yellow slicker—his "fish"—was tied behind the saddle, as was his big off-white canvas ducking ground cloth and cover wrapped around clean bedding blankets and quilt-like soogans for comfortable night camps. Boot Hill Cole knew how to live well off the land.

Winfield watched him start out to the west toward the old Ramirez Grant, feeling almost as good as if he himself were riding Rusty on the way to carry Federal justice to the wilderness.

"Huh," Winfield grunted to himself, "Boot Hill Cole Ryerson. There's a man who travels his own trails."

Years later, Cole Ryerson would remember with a kind of nostalgic reverence the long, lone ride to Berdan. Days in the saddle passed like long episodes of glory; clear, open skies and clear, clean open country. World without end, amen. As he rode, the land rolled before him like some rumpled magic carpet under the blue heavens and he was its only passenger. There was almost a music in the silence of the unending, somber, solemn, and sun-spread land.

Nights were like dark but vibrant counterpoint to the days of his odyssey with their soft night fires steeped in rich aromas of crisping bacon, warmed-over beans, and coffee.

Boot Hill Cole Ryerson was a man accustomed to accepting and enjoying where he was as well as who he was.

Riding toward his thirty-eighth summer, Ryerson sat his horse with the shoulder-back posture bred into him over four adventure-filled years in General Jo Shelby's Rebel cavalry in Arkansas and Missouri. When—after four years of arduous service—Shelby registered his disgust with Lee's and Davis's disgrace at Appomattox and took his battling brigade across the Rio Grande to seek new fields of combat in Mexico, Ryerson petitioned for his discharge. With it he rode into Abilene to pin on a deputy sheriff's badge under Sheriff Mose Laramore.

In the course of maintaining law and order under Laramore, Ryerson was boxed in eight times when only his Colt Navy could get him out—with the result that he sent eight men to Boot Hill. After Laramore was backshot by Greaser Jack in '68, his protégé and deputy, Ryerson, pinned on Laramore's old badge and successfully took the trail after Greaser Jack. Already known as Boot Hill Cole, and now also as sheriff, Ryerson went on to send six more hardcases sliding down the chutes to hell.

It didn't seem to matter that a dozen more went off to the hoosegow for long stretches. Whether as a lawman he terminated life or merely confined it in prisons, Ryerson seemed to gain about five enemies for each man sent to Boot Hill or to the calaboose. He stood to be challenged any time, at any place and often by someone with no more connection than that he wanted to make a name for himself by gunning down the famous Boot Hill Cole Ryerson.

Ryerson had been hit three times, but in each case, when the smoke cleared, he was the one left standing.

After Abilene, Ryerson became infected with the itchy foot, especially after Judge Isaac Winfield offered him a U. S. marshal badge in the territory to the north and west of Abilene.

Now on the trail to Berdan, east of the famed Ramirez Plateau, Ryerson and Rusty neared the deep canyon of the seldom-dry Black River, headed for a crossing several days north and east of Berdan, when Ryerson straightened, peering into the distance.

Rusty's laid-back ears alerted him. A horse's actions, Ryerson knew, could tell a man a lot. "Somebody out there ahead, eh, Rusty?" Ryerson grinned at his absent-minded foolishness in talking to a horse.

Still, Ryerson felt his breath tightening in his throat.

Expert at tracking and always alert, Ryerson had slowed his pace for several minutes. Faint dust in the air and the disturbed sandy rut of the trail wrote a message of warning that he was not alone.

An intuition about such things fine-tuned his senses, urging caution. His badge as U.S. marshal was safely tucked in his shirt pocket; in an investigation such as this one, Ryerson gained as many pertinent facts as possible before declaring who he was.

He was still far from Berdan, and there had to be settlements to the north and south; possibly the man ahead of him would turn off to one of these soon.

Rusty moved up to a rise in the road, hooves gripping for holds in the loose gravel. Stands of clumpy mesquite and pine clothed the hills. With a growing sense of foreboding, Ryerson had trouble adjusting his feelings under a sun high in a blue sky. Around him, birds picked off insects on the wing or fluttered among the scrub chaparral growth along either side of the tawny ruts of wagon trail Ryerson followed. It was too fine a day for the gnawing anxiety that seemed to fill him.

Boot Hill Cole drew up at the top of the rise, the country for about two miles to the west spread before him like a tapestry of gold and green tones. The land was thinly grassed, broken up by woods and rocks. Sunlight, growing low in the west, threw long, reddening waves of light across the sagelands. The horizons filled with a powdery haze. A few cows grazed to the north; beyond them a thin plume of smoke indicated an isolated cattle spread. Ryerson spied a north-south trail branching off, evidently to a lonely ranch. Nearer to him, his east-west road ran like a thread to disappear over the next wave-like elevation, fringed with dark trees.

His sharp eyes next caught sight of the traveler who had delayed him. At several hundred yards, Ryerson could see that the man rode a black mustang, wore rancher's clothing and a tall and large Stetson. At the crossroads, he turned north onto the trail toward the distant ranch. In the open country, under a crystal clear sky, Ryerson had a good view of the rider and the surroundings.

As Ryerson watched from the shield of the bluff around which the trail curved, a dark figure emerged from the mesquite, coming from behind the distant rider. Sun glinted off a Colt barrel, and with a quick exclamation Ryerson snatched his Winchester from the under-stirrup boot, levering a cartridge into the breech.

The soft air around him had suddenly become electrically charged with menace and he felt his blood racing hot.

The action spread below him was too fast to be checked, and too far off. The rider, alerted to someone behind him, chose to fight, ripping at his reins, seeking to draw his pistol as the backshooter fired. The horseman sagged, fell out of the saddle, and his weight stopped the startled horse so the killer could seize the reins.

Holding the Winchester at the ready and spurring Rusty toward the action like a cavalry charger, Ryerson realized he had been witness to one of the swift and terrible tragedies of these lonely, dangerous spaces; a desperate man killing another for his horse and his possessions.

Busily searching the pockets of his victim, the killer in grimy trail clothes was stooped over and did not see or hear the approaching Ryerson until he was within twenty-five yards of him. The thundering of the earth under the roan's hooves warned him, and with a quick oath he turned and rose. His Colt, sheathed as he robbed his victim, leaped into his hand.

"Drop it!" thundered the marshal.

Ryerson's glance at the adversary rising to challenge him was of a sharp-faced, long-nosed man, red-rimmed eyes snapping viciously as he brought up the long-barreled sixgun. The man had not shaved or cleaned up in days and every inch of him said savage. In that quick glance, his mind on his own need for survival, Ryerson's only impression was that he faced a wild, predatory beast.

The fury in the man's eyes was deep seated, reflecting something profoundly evil that had lived with him too long to be controlled.

Ryerson had to shoot quickly. The heavy Colt in the killer's hand rose to drill him as he charged. Ryerson swung out the carbine with both hands, guiding Rusty with his knees, aiming through the swirl of dust that rolled ahead of him on the downwind breeze.

A spurt of dust from the man's Colt kicked up a few feet ahead of the roan. Ryerson's Winchester bucked against his shoulder, its report cracking in the warm, dry air. The dry-gulcher threw up both hands. Pitching his handgun into the air with the massive jolt of Ryerson's bullet slamming him, the assailant turned once, staggered, and fell.

· 4 ·

Wheeling to a halt beside the double-death scene, Ryerson leaped from the saddle to quickly determine that the dry-gulcher was not playing possum. Ryerson's bullet had drilled a hole between the man's now-fading eyes.

"Sorry it had to be done, pard," he said, studying the face of the corpse. "You asked for it, and you probably had it coming." Ryerson turned away from the body to check the surroundings. The story was as easy to read as if it had been printed in a book.

Around him a breeze skipped through the grass, and, as he looked up at a hint of movement, he watched the lazy, spread-wing glide of a distant hawk, light as a feather, not moving its wings, just tilting round and round on the updrafts.

Ryerson sensed a paradox; so much beauty in the sky and in the hawk's graceful flight to contrast the bitter ugliness he had witnessed and been a part of down close to earth.

Off the trail, hidden in the bush, lay a dead gray mustang. Its ribs showed savage spur gouges, its flanks scarred by welts from the man's quirt. The horse had been driven and beaten to death. The desperate rider, perhaps fleeing a noose, had gotten his dying horse hidden, and lay in wait for some victim to supply him with a fresh mount.

The nearby black horse of the dead rancher wore a brand. The man looked to have been about forty, and bore no marks of the owlhoot breed. Among some papers on the ground, dropped there by the thief, Ryerson learned the victim's identity—his name, ranch and brand, and the area in which he lived.

Ryerson glanced to the north; the smoke from the ranch house some miles off was still visible. To take the body there would mean the loss of a half a day, and Ryerson was pushing to avert more tragedy in Berdan. The living just now required his help more.

With his stub of a pencil, Ryerson scratched an explanation on a scrap of paper and tucked it in the dead rancher's shirt pocket. Securing the body over the saddle, he started the black stallion off. The animal dutifully trotted up the trail, obviously knowing the way to the home stable.

Turning his attention to the bandit, he looked down at the quiet face of the man he had killed. He lay on his back, his Colt on the ground beside him. Ryerson searched the man's pockets, finding some money and other sundry possessions. He secured them in his saddlebags to turn over to Judge Winfield along with his report when he got back to Fort Walker. In the inner pocket of the dead outlaw's black leather vest was a soiled note. The significance of what Ryerson read in it hit him with a jolt.

The outside of the paper indicated it was for the attention of Jubal Doan; Ryerson read the inside with great interest:

> "Heres Kenny Rollins best man with a running iron in these parts but its too hot for him round heer and he needs a furlo. put him to werk. Bisness good heer come on over Some time. Roy."

Ryerson's eyes crinkled in excitement. He refolded the letter and stuck it in his shirt pocket for future use. Rollins was running from the law and on his way to Doan's for a while until the heat cooled.

In the yellow sunlight of the next morning, Cole Ryerson rode the roan along Berdan's Broad Street. One glance sufficed, almost, for his bleak eyes to take in the store, a saloon, and the square wood-sided building with the sign of the Berdan Land Development Company, with Sam Carson as its president. Beside it was a similar sign: MARTIN RATHBURN—INVESTMENTS.

Ryerson grinned and rolled his first smoke of the day, his eye picking up the familiar earmarks of a saloon up the street.

The Berdan Bar struck Ryerson as a splendid place to begin his investigation on the sly. It offered refreshment for the thirst he'd built, and a chance to stand close to the man who probably knew as much as most anyone about Berdan —the bartender.

Dropping Rusty's reins over the roughly polished hitch-rail near the saloon, Ryerson was stopped by a figure that seemed to pop from nowhere to greet him.

"Well, howdy! Howdy, stranger," came the tattered old-timer's lusty greeting. "Welcome to Berdan. Mighty dry day, ain't it?" The man seemed harmless, a frontier mossyhorn with a wide, long-in-the-tooth grin lancing his whiskered cheeks. His clothing was overdue for replacement and his old felt hat had two large holes in the crown.

For Dad Burns, a new arrival in Berdan was usually good for at least a free drink. He held open the saloon's batwing doors with a patronizing air for the newcomer, and then trailed after him like a faithful pup. The saloon was empty except for the barkeep. A few rude benches were scattered about the plank floor and a bar was a wide board secured to two giant hogshead casks. A fancy bar would probably come later, Ryerson thought. Bottles and glasses were stored on shelves behind the bar. The place, Ryerson perceived, was efficient, not fancy.

"Set 'em up for two, barkeep," Ryerson barked, as he thought a man named Kenny Rollins might do, and motioned for the old scalawag standing expectantly a few steps away to join him. Dad strode up, his bright eyes eager and lips moistened by his darting tongue. Dad downed the amber fluid in the thick-glass tumbler in one expert toss of head and hand and turned eagerly toward Ryerson.

"Have another, old-timer," Ryerson invited and Dad slid out his glass to the bartender. After his second, Dad figured he'd mooched enough, had satisfied his thirst for the moment, and turned talkative—as if in some kind of thanks or payoff.

"Yes, sir, mighty nice town, mister—uh, didn't get your handle, stranger. But you're a gent, all-around gent. Gent of the first water."

"Or the first whiskey," chimed in the florid-faced bartender, mopping at the yellow pine plank bar with a damp, sour-smelling rag.

"This is your town then I take it, my friend," Ryerson remarked.

"Made it so, I reckon," Dad said. "Last place I lived, I see a feller hangin' around the saloon porch and I goes up to him and I says, 'Mighty dry day, ain't it, mister?' He up and says, 'You think so, hey?' and uncurls a big plowhandle Colt and puts one right through my brand-new Stetson. This 'un was new then."

Dad Burns hauled off his hat and thrust a finger through the holes, once .44-caliber size and now nearly an inch wide from his poking.

"Dad Burns tells the story different to every stranger that comes to town," the bartender informed Ryerson. The barkeep's almost ridiculing tone rankled Ryerson a bit.

"Sam Carson about town this mornin'?" Ryerson inquired. "The name's Rollins. Kenny Rollins. I was thinking maybe of investing in a section or two in these parts. Interested in ranchin'." He thought it best to satisfy the barkeeper's curiosity at the start. He also figured some of

Doan's riders might drift in, hear the name as part of the bartender's usual gossip and Ryerson would be that much closer to his connection with Doan.

"Carson?" the barkeep said. "He's over at his office prob'ly. Seen him a half-hour ago when he rode in from home." The man behind the bar shook his head. "Poor Sam's come down a notch or two. Since his boy came up missing—they figure he's dead—Sam just ain't been the same."

"Mighty sorry to hear that," Ryerson said, tossing down more than enough silver for the bar bill. "I'll sure keep that in mind when I'm dealing with him and try to be understandin'."

"I'll show you his office, Mr. Rollins," Dad Burns said.

Braced by his shots and puffed with self-importance as an official town guide, Dad Burns trotted ahead of the tall marshal to the door of the Berdan Land Company. There Ryerson thanked him, knocked and walked in.

The solidly built middle-aged man behind the oak desk looked up from his papers. His brown hair was white-streaked, his face drawn and thin. Dark lines under his blue eyes reflected the strain of his suffering. Ryerson considered dropping the Kenny Rollins charade to reassure Carson that help had arrived. "Mr. Carson?" he inquired.

Carson was alone in the office, its walls covered with maps of the area blocked out by sections. An oak file cabinet stood in one corner; a chair or two, an equal number of cuspidors, saucers for cigarette stubs, and a large table for discussions and spreading out papers completed the furnishings.

"Yes, sir. Sam Carson." He shoved out a hand. "What can I do for you?"

Ryerson studied Carson's careworn features. If there was any devious business in this part of the country, Sam Carson was not part of it. Ryerson saw that right off and he seldom misjudged character. Carson's feelings were too apparent in his eyes and in the grim set of his mouth.

Ryerson moved closer to the desk. He looked around to

assure himself no one else could hear. In his cupped hand lay the silver shield identifying him as a U.S. marshal. "The name's Cole Ryerson. From Judge Isaac Winfield's court up at the territorial capital." He said it in a low voice. "We got your plea for help."

Carson stood up to grip Ryerson's hand, some of the strain easing from his face. Still, he seemed to hold himself together with great will power.

"I . . . I hoped somebody would come, Marshal Ryerson. I know the name. Cole Ryerson. Hmm. Wait a minute. Boot Hill Cole!"

"Well, some call me that. Actually, I believe I've sent more men to Leavenworth than I have to Boot Hill."

"Judge Winfield sent us his best man."

"I don't know if I'd go so far as to say that, either. But I'm here to try to get at the root of your problem and see what can be done."

"Mighty glad you're here. We've been having a tough time of it. My son's gone, as you know from the judge. It's a hard blow for a man to take. Disappeared without a trace. Other tragedies haven't lightened the burden."

"Your son hasn't turned up yet?"

"Not yet. And it's the uncertainty that's killing his mother. His horse came home, its saddle gone. We know Jim was trying to track the men who laid Luther Moseley low. Best I can figure is that they caught Jim on their trail and done for him." Tears welled up in Carson's eyes.

"I'll sure keep my eye out for sign of him, Mr. Carson. We'll know something definite before this is all over."

Sam Carson gave Ryerson a grateful look.

"I know with you I can keep my true identity confidential, Mr. Carson. At least for now," Ryerson said. "I'd like to work quietly until I'm sure of things. The handle I'll go by is Kenny Rollins. There was an incident on the way here. I'm taking the identity of a dead man, apparently coming here to join the local rustlers. The law must have been after him where he came from. Supposed to be a top man with a running iron. That ought to give me a foot in the door with the bunch we're after."

Carson watched Ryerson eagerly, his eyes brighter. "Maybe you can really find out what happened to Jim. I'm sure he must have confronted them."

"And it might not take too long. I'll make my reports to you. Utmost secrecy. You mustn't even discuss it at home. If there's a leak, my hash will be settled. For all intents and purposes, all you know of me is that I'm Kenny Rollins, a cowboy looking to invest in a spread."

"If it will bring news of Jim, I'll cooperate in every way I can."

"What's the feeling of the ranchers?"

"One more's on the brink of selling out and moving on. His herd was suddenly thinned, but not to the extent Moseley's was. After Moseley's death, they hit George Douglas's spread. Or so it seems. Enough to cause him to lose his land claim. Damn! It goes totally against George's grain to owe anyone, or be in arrears in his obligations." Again Carson's eyes began to fill. "My son Jim was kind of sweet on the Douglas girl, Melissa. I have Mrs. Douglas and the kids at home with us for now till George comes back. George's claim reverted to my business associate next door, Mr. Rathburn. He'll find a buyer and I hope there'll be something left to sustain Hanna Douglas and her brood. You'll probably want to talk to Mr. Rathburn."

"That would help. Casual sort of thing. For now, I still want to keep my real reason for being here just between us. The fewer people who know who I am the better."

"I need to stop by and see Mart on business. You could just tag along and say howdy," Carson said.

"Wouldn't hurt, if you could spare the time, to ride out to your place so I could meet Mrs. Douglas and Melissa and the rest of their family. A few careful questions about what happened at their spread might add to my information about the rustlers."

Carson brightened. "Easy enough. I've a section out that

way I could show you as potential property to settle on. Ought to work."

Sam Carson now had turned eager to get into action. He led Ryerson across his quarters and through a connecting door into Rathburn's well-appointed office with its carpet, handsome walnut furnishings, and framed pictures on the walls. Ryerson immediately observed that it had much more handsome furniture than Carson's work-oriented setup next door.

The man behind the desk was large, with abundant and thick black hair and sideburns. His nose was broad, and his teeth prominent in his frequent smiles. He wore a black broadcloth frock coat.

Behind Rathburn was a well-stocked liquor cabinet, which also held boxes of cigars. The smoke from a Cuban cheroot filled the air with its fragrance, mingling with aromas of fine brandies. Rathburn had a glass of his best vintage at his elbow.

Carson laid some papers on Rathburn's desk. "This is the final filing notice on the Matson claim, Mart," he told Rathburn. "Mr. Rathburn, I'd like you to meet . . ." For a moment, Carson forgot Cole Ryerson's alias.

"Ken Rollins, Mr. Rathburn," Ryerson offered, shoving out his hand. "But I go by Kenny. From up north. Been cowboyin' and thinking it's time to start a spread of my own." He didn't trust Carson's memory; the rancher-businessman was too rattled to think straight.

Rathburn's smile was benign as he rose to shake Ryerson's hand. Ryerson studied him; he came across as almost too glib, too slick. "You're thinking of investing here?" he asked, offering the cigar box and brandy decanter to his guests. "Good. Always pleased to have more hard-working folks in our midst. Right, Sam?" Ryerson and Carson politely refused the offered drink and cigar.

Ryerson tried to affect the look of a man who knew his cattle and had a better-than-common head for business. As he sat down to chat further with Carson and Rathburn, his eyes took in the office and its details, whether ordinary, peculiar, or uncommon—anything that might prove handy later. Most of the bottles in the liquor cabinet had varying degrees of fullness. One, marked with a red diamond, appeared to have been opened, but little of the contents removed. It was the only one of several similar bottles to have a special marking. Interesting, he thought, but probably of little significance.

A glance toward the back of the room revealed a double-sash window, the lower sash raised a few inches to allow what breeze there might be to waft through the office; a passerby in the alley might be able to overhear conversations inside. Ryerson made a mental note to remember that.

He continued his charade. "Been figuring I might like to have a place of my own at last, as I was telling Mr. Carson here. From the word I hear around the area, others have found this a good place to settle and grow beeves, and maybe a family. So this might be the place for me, Mr. Rathburn. Looks like good range. And believe me, I know my grass and surroundings for breeding and cattle raising. This is some of the best land in the state."

"The grass is good. Rich." Carson put in. "We've also set things up so everybody has access to the Black River and plenty of water for the stock. Never an argument in Berdan over water rights. We saw to that. Mr. Rathburn can help with financial backing if you need it."

"On cowboy's wages, I haven't been able to put aside enough to buy land and get everything I need for a start, that's for sure."

"We'll help you," Rathburn said abruptly, almost eagerly, his eye gleaming. In that gleam, Ryerson saw something unexpected; maybe it was greed, he thought, or maybe hunger—for wealth and power. Ryerson was hard put to come up with the word in his mind. But he read something in the eyes that belied the attitude of the man. He was also curious about the fancy-fitted wolf fang dangling from Rathburn's watch chain; what, he wondered, is the significance of that?

He dismissed his main misgivings as only pessimistic hunches. Still Ryerson's spine tingled as he heard the smooth words and saw Rathburn's suave smile. He felt he had somehow played into the man's hand by suggesting they might make a business transaction.

"Sam," Rathburn put in, "this gentleman might like a look at the old Douglas spread. I've had to put it back on the market."

Ryerson saw Carson grimace. It didn't seem fair that Rathburn acted so decisively severe and almost premature about the Douglas foreclosure. But Ryerson knew that a businessman had to be hard-headed and that policy was policy and an obligation was an obligation.

Ryerson was, with only mild reservations, favorably inclined with his first impression of Rathburn. From all Carson had told him, Rathburn had helped the settlers and was their friend. So far he had observed nothing about the setup to arouse even mild suspicion. Rathburn generally appeared to have an open, good-natured manner much like that of Carson.

"I'll be back in a day or two, Mr. Rathburn, and maybe there will be some business we can discuss," Ryerson said, getting up. "I'm riding out with Mr. Carson now to look over some land on the other side of his spread."

Rathburn saw them to the door.

Now it was time, or nearly time, Ryerson mused, to start looking into Jubal Doan's connections. He'd have to start by figuring ways to find the obvious outlaw thief.

His ace in the hole was Kenny Rollins's note of introduction to Doan, and it was high time for Boot Hill Cole to play his hole card.

· 5 ·

Sam Carson tightened his horse's cinch and mounted up. The sun was warm on their shoulders as he and Ryerson rode out of the settlement. A hot breeze rustled the dry brush of the Black River country spread before them. "Doan's stamping grounds are northwest of here," Carson remarked, "but it's hard country to find your way around in."

They rode several minutes in silence. "Strange," Carson said, hauling off his hat and swiping a sleeve at his streaming forehead. "Strange how excited one can become about an aspect of his life. As I was about this country and its rich promise, Cole. And then how a tragedy such as our loss of Jim can so quickly turn it all so meaningless, so sour."

"I didn't get the impression before when we were talking that you'd abandoned all hope, Sam."

"I haven't. Not by a long chalk. But it's tough to generate enthusiasm for a pet project like this one when a loved one disappears without a trace."

"From all I can see, you and Mr. Rathburn have worked hard in this valley, Sam. Not only with your own personal plans, but in helping others with theirs. All that's got to mean something to you."

"Oh, it does. I guess what I'm saying is that until all this evil is resolved and we learn what's happened to Jim, I feel—well, I feel like half a man."

"I guess I can understand your feelings," Ryerson said. "I'm here to see if I can bring you some kind of encouraging news before long."

"Just your being here, a man with your reputation and background, does have its compensations. I feel good about it. I've a hunch things will turn more promising before long. I still can't believe Jim's dead. Maybe he's hurt or he's Doan's prisoner."

"I appreciate those thoughts. And remember, when we get to your place, you're to refer to me as Kenny Rollins."

Sam Carson's teeth showed slightly as he spoke, but there was little mirth in his smile. "I'll remember . . . Kenny."

Ultimately, the riders eased up a low mesa. The buildings of the Carson spread came in sight below them and they followed the trail down the slope. Its rectangular ranch house was of native timber with a split-shingle roof. Ryerson's keen eyes saw the long, hand-dug, wood-trough flume that snaked from the nearby elevations, bringing life-giving water to Carson's barnyard holding tank. The tank was more a pond with the dirt that had been dug out forming a mounded dam around the edges.

Cattle grazed on the grass of Carson's claim.

Roundabout, fenced acreage gleamed with a hay crop and grain plots for winter feed; nearer the house, a small truck garden seemed sufficiently abundant and varied to provide the Carsons with vegetables and greens to add to family meals. The buildings were clearly of recent construction, some of them not yet finished. Ryerson's eyes appraised a small corral, a barn, and several sheds under construction. A young man with an eager face, ruddy and sweaty, was at work in the corral, preparing to break a mustang to saddle. He stopped to greet his father and the visitor.

"My other son, Richard," Carson offered by way of introduction. "We call him Rick."

Rick shook hands with "Mr. Rollins," and took his father's horse to unsaddle and rub down. Ryerson saw to his own mount and when he strode to the open door of the house, Mrs. Carson greeted him warmly but with a reserve that Ryerson was convinced stemmed from the ache in her heart over the disappearance of their son; there was also a soft slanting of her eyelids and a faraway look in the eyes themselves that reflected the grief the kindly woman suffered.

She was short but substantial, with rosy features as sanguine as her welcome would be under more favorable conditions.

"Mr. Rollins," she said. "How nice to meet you. Mr. Carson says you're thinking of settling here. Come in and let us give you a warm Berdan welcome." Nora Carson stepped aside to let Ryerson enter first. The kitchen he passed through was warm; a coffeepot steamed on the stove.

The Carson home, though simple and modestly furnished, had a warm, homey feel. Nora Carson ushered Ryerson to the front parlor—more like a main lodge room—from the kitchen. Sam Carson stood, studying some papers, and as Ryerson entered, he indicated a comfortable chair for his guest, and took another himself.

"Well, Kenny, what do you think of the place?"

"The kind of home I'd like to have myself some day," Ryerson responded.

A slim blond beauty of sixteen, who was introduced to Ryerson as the Carsons' daughter, Penelope, affectionately called Penny, came in with a tray of cookies and cool lemonade.

As Ryerson and Carson talked, the Carson's house guests filtered into the room from other parts of the house. In turn, Sam introduced Mrs. Hanna Douglas, her son Victor, who went by Vic, and in a few moments the chestnut-haired and beautiful Melissa Douglas, her fresh loveliness like a flower in a drab room. Ryerson quickly noted that there was character as well as beauty in her face. The girl's dark eyes were sad, and Ryerson was touched with pity for these people who mourned the loss of the Douglas spread and Jim Carson's disappearance.

Mrs. Douglas excused herself to go help Nora Carson in the kitchen. Vic Douglas, who looked to Ryerson to be about seventeen, and Sam Carson quickly got into an interchange on their personal preferences in horseflesh. Ryerson, sitting near Melissa, found the setting appropriate to a few questions of the young woman about Jim Carson. He was careful that his questions not appear to be prying; he couched his inquiries instead, in a tone of concern for what had happened.

The girl drew her slender shoulders to squareness and responded in a soft voice tinged with the tragedy. Unfortunately, as Ryerson found in their conversation, Melissa was not able to add much more than Ryerson already knew.

While they talked Ryerson sensed a dull fatigue spreading over him, brought on, he surmised, by the quiet, relaxed atmosphere of the Carson home. The tension, though, was very much in evidence in the air with the unexplained disappearance of Jim Carson.

It had been a long ride to Berdan and both Ryerson and Rusty needed rest and food. After a supper with the Carsons and the Douglases that took on almost banquet proportions, he spent the night at the ranch.

In the early morning, with a warm breakfast under his belt and a rough understanding of the surrounding country, he rode toward the wilds in which Jubal Doan probably had his sanctuary.

As he urged Rusty along, the morning mist rose and the sun appeared above a ridge to the east, its yellow glow diffused and, for the moment, without heat. Ryerson sensed the day would soon begin to glow with warmth.

"They may keep a lookout. We've got to be careful how we approach," he murmured to Rusty, again grinning at his conversation with a horse.

Animal tracks, of horses shod or unshod, of stray cattle and game, crisscrossed the land with numerous trails and winding paths. The country a few miles northwest of Carson's spread rose steeply, and the valley of the Black River curved that way. It was a solemn, solitary land Ryerson faced on his ride, transmitting an awesome depth of loneliness that might depress a man if he allowed it. Cole Ryerson chose not to allow it.

When he calculated he was in the vicinity of Doan's mysterious hideout, he sought a high point to watch the surrounding territory. Doan's place, or the trail to it, might be anywhere in the dense thickets and deep draws that marked the land under Ryerson's view. He continued his ride to the high ground, looking all about him as he traveled, searching for sign.

Securing the roan below in a shaded, grassy swale, Ryerson climbed to a prominence that allowed him to see for miles in all directions as he searched with his telescoping glass. Time seemed to hang in limbo over the long, cloudless afternoon. His eyes probed the skyline for riders, but nobody showed.

The sun rode high, yellow and warm, and birds and insects flitted and hummed around him. As he watched the land spread blissfully sunny below him, Ryerson saw no trace of smoke or movement to help in his search for the rustlers' stronghold. Ryerson sensed frustration; he had never had much patience in the stalk. Still, they were in the area someplace. But where?

"Nothing to do but wait," he whispered to himself, his words escaping in a sigh. He settled himself as comfortably as possible for what might be an extended stay and rolled a smoke.

The long hours proved unproductive, the tedious, taxing day trailing off into evening twilight. Nothing human had disturbed the wilderness quiet. There was a silver lining in the cloud under which he waited, he thought: It was good that there could be such calm and apparent peace in the world when his brain was a battleground of anxiety and impatience for something to happen. Anything.

Night at length drew its cloak around him and with it the inability to see distant movement. Ryerson eased up stiffly to stroll through the deepening twilight back to Rusty's hiding place. He fixed a simple meal, looked to his horse's comfort and slept in his soogans and tarp with his head on his saddle.

At mid-morning of the next day, sweeping the sun-yellowed land with his glass, he observed with a spurt of excitement a line of distant riders, dark specks in the distance, coming along a deer trail from the dense woods to the northwest. Studying them through his telescopic glass, Ryerson perceived eight well-armed men in the faded clothing of working cowboys.

In time, the queue of riders passed within a half-mile of Ryerson's position, apparently riding for a cattle range near the Black River.

He watched them out of sight and earshot before creeping down warily, saddling Rusty and beginning a backtrack of the riders' trail. The tracks of the shod, outbound horses were as easy for the marshal's sharp, seasoned eyes to read as a newspaper page.

Their trail was nearly identical to any of the hundreds in the vicinity, but this one led to the thicket and he followed it, the hoof-worn lane narrow, with thorny branches reaching out to scratch or snag a horse's hide or a cowboy's clothing.

Ryerson grinned, his eyes puckering narrowly, in a kind of admiration of Jubal Doan; the man knew how to set up a hideout and keep his tracks covered. Ryerson missed a turn, soon finding himself on a cold trail, and retraced his course. Trails through the dense brush formed a veritable maze and only by the sheerest luck did he finally again define the one showing recent marks of the passing of shod horses.

The density of the thicket waned and the trail meandered

into a broad draw with a trickle of water; the draw, he could see, worked its way upstream to a narrow canyon cutting through a silent, sun-baked and tawny mesa.

For all Ryerson could observe, he might be the only human for hundreds of miles. A fitful afternoon breeze channeled down the canyon, sometimes buffeting him and drumming, only to soften to a pleasant zephyr a moment later.

Ryerson picked his way cautiously, aware that sentries might be posted anywhere. Doan probably had his men primed to shoot an interloper without so much as a challenge. Only moments passed before Ryerson became gratefully aware that he'd been wrong in that assumption.

A huge shoulder of gray-brown rock loomed ahead. Ryerson slowed the roan through the narrow high-walled draw where it switched back on itself, and poked cautiously around the point of rocks, aware that in his situation, he was a sitting duck for a concealed and armed sentry anywhere nearby.

A hoarse voice boomed out of the nearby dense chaparral. "Reach!" Ryerson could neither see the challenger nor determine exactly where the voice had come from. Wisely he halted Rusty, stared straight ahead, and poked out his bent arms to hold them loosely at chest level.

"Easy, mister," he called. "Take it easy."

From a rock ledge over the trail a carbine muzzle emerged, followed by a man's head. The gun was aimed for a direct, killing hit.

The sentry's voice clipped through the silence around them like a bullet. "State your business."

"Easy with that howitzer," Ryerson called up to the man. "I'm looking for a man by the name of Jubal Doan. Got a feeling I might be in his territory. A friend sent me."

"You got a name. Use it!"

Ryerson studied his antagonist. He appeared to be little more than a hard-edged, tough-looking cow waddy who found rustling under Doan's command easier than honest work. His blue eyes were hard and cold as ice and his jaw jutted stubbornly.

It would be time for a hardcase like Kenny Rollins to take charge.

"I told you to lower that cannon," he ordered. "The name's Rollins. Kenny Rollins. I've got a letter from a friend of Doan's named Roy from out east of here." Ryerson spoke with as much of a growl as he could muster.

Ryerson realized in a spurt of panic that he didn't have a last name for Roy. He'd stuck his foot in it for sure now. When he couldn't come up with Roy's last name, that menacing carbine was sure to go off.

"That'd be Roy Chalmers," the man said, to Ryerson's eternal relief.

Ryerson grinned. But it still could be a ruse, a fake last name tossed in to test the intruder. On second thought, he doubted the man confronting him possessed that level of shrewdness. Ryerson took a risk.

"Then you'll let me pass to go show Roy's letter to Doan?"

The sentry offered no further challenge about the name. "Take out the letter and put it on the ledge beside you. Then back off so's I can have a look at it."

Ryerson did as he was ordered. The lanky, crusty rifleman slid down from his perch onto the canyon floor and snatched the Kenny Rollins letter and studied it, keeping one eye on Ryerson. The sentry shifted his head to stare steadily at the intruder.

"How do I know you ain't makin' all this up?"

Ryerson affected an impatient tone. "Well, take me to Doan and let him see the letter. He ought to know Roy Chalmers's handwriting."

They eyed each other with a cold wariness and distrust.

"You ride on ahead of me, and no monkey business."

Ryerson moved on slowly, aware of the guard's horse safely behind him but still at a deadly gunshot range. He had no doubt that the man's Winchester was pointed squarely at the small of his back.

The canyon floor rose and the sheer rock face at his right dwindled away to a grassy shelf with the wall on his left becoming a bluff that gradually lost its steepness. Eventually the two riders emerged onto a great circular basin hemmed in by craggy, nearly impenetrable cliffs.

Live oaks clustered here, providing welcoming gray circles of shade. Horse herds made the most of the cool shadows, most standing stoically. Others grazed on abundant, sun-drenched grass, sneezing and whickering in complete contentment.

Commanding the entrance to the canyon—apparently the only way in—a good-size ranch house was built against a sheer rock wall, using that wall as its backside. The basin's cliff-like wall towered another twenty feet above the house.

It was an ideal spot, Ryerson mused, for Doan's carryings-on, building up his herds with a catch rope and a running iron. Water was close at hand for stock; probably the house was perched over a spring to assure its inhabitants a constant water supply in a siege.

A siege, of course, would be virtually impossible because of the long, rugged, and steep canyon trail leading into Doan's fortress-like position; an army of besiegers could be stood off, almost, by a single sharpshooter.

Doan's huge and ample log ranch house would be impervious to bullets; instead of glass, huge plank shutters with rectangular rifle ports protected the windows. Jubal Doan, Ryerson was coming to understand, was a canny, formidable adversary. He saw no cattle around except for a few kept handy for fresh meat. He surmised that Doan's rustled herds were driven directly north to railheads or on to other markets to the north.

An aging, grizzled cowpoke lounged on the ranch house porch, a large cemented fieldstone affair of veranda-like proportions, shaded by a slanting, ripple-tin overhang.

"Clute!" Ryerson's captor shouted. "Go tell Doan we got company!" The shout alerted men down by the corrals who turned and stared. Others appeared at the window openings and several emerged onto the porch, one of them obviously Jubal Doan.

The rawboned, copper-haired man wore a white shirt, open at the throat, and black broadcloth trousers tucked into black boots. Even as he might have been busy plotting new rustling schemes with some of his top hands, Ryerson noticed Doan kept a long-barreled dark-blue-steel Colt secured in a black latigo holster at his hip.

A big man of spare build, Doan had large, angular joints showing through his shirt, which clung to him like an afterthought; one hand rested on his hip, close to the Colt, its knuckles and finger joints large and prominent.

Doan's narrowed, flashing eyes locked on Ryerson's. Others of the men who had sidled close to the porch regarded the interloper with mild suspicion, alert to any gesture of threat toward their boss.

"He's carryin' a note from Roy Chalmers, Jube," called the sentry who still held his rifle at the ready from his horse. His voice was harsh and cold-toned. Ryerson cautiously fished out Roy Chalmers's note and offered it to Doan from horseback. As yet, Ryerson hadn't been bid to step down from the saddle; in this case the tense situation kept him from it more than did common range etiquette.

Doan, his slitted eyes bleak and wary, snatched the paper from Ryerson to read it laboriously, occasionally forming his lips around difficult words. Finished, Doan folded the note and handed it back. When he spoke, his voice was harsh, even though the words were meant to be cordial.

His cruel-looking lips peeled back from long teeth in what might have passed for a smile. A hard cynicism seemed to touch the corners of his mouth when he smiled.

"So you're Rollins? Roy says you're one of the best brand blotters in the territory. Get down and come on in and set a spell. We'll talk." Doan turned to Ryerson's captor. "Chris, you get on back down there where you belong. The next one nosin' in here probably won't be carryin' a letter and you'll have to put a window in his skull."

The one called Chris poked his Winchester into the under-stirrup boot and wheeled his horse back down the canyon. "Come on, Rollins," Doan invited warmly. "Come in and have a drink. You look like you could use one."

"I don't need to be asked twice," Ryerson said dryly, following Doan through the front door. He was relieved. He'd cleared a dangerous hurdle. His long trip, followed by his day of watchful waiting and a cold night camp had left him with a definite cheek stubble and grimy face, hands, and clothing, a fit disguise for his pose as a hardcase on the run. He was aware of the crew's considerable and natural suspicion of an outlander, but saw no looks or other evidence that his posing as Kenny Rollins was anything but accepted, however grudgingly.

Ryerson made a point of swiveling his head, feigning an appraising eye, taking in at a glance the small circle of Doan's men come up to have a look-see at the newcomer. His glance was calculated as nothing more than to reinforce his guise as a tough hombre expert in the field of altering cattle brands with a running iron and a man who could be dangerous if crossed.

Satisfied that Doan's men generally accepted him for who he claimed to be, Ryerson stepped to the porch with a lithe jump to follow Doan into the house's dark, cool interior. Jubal Doan led Ryerson into the square central lodge room, a comfortable-enough-looking place. A huge stone fireplace stood at one end of the big room, surmounted by a trophy elk head. Nearby was a framed English hunting scene. An outlaw's measly way of trying to appear prosperous and genteel, Ryerson thought grimly. Fancy furnishings, like clothes, he mused, don't make the man either.

From somewhere, Doan had freighted in several well-padded chairs and a large and ornate velvet brocaded chaise lounge that Ryerson surmised might have spent much of its prior life in a bordello.

Thick woven wool rugs, colorful in geometric Navajo designs, were scattered on the rough board floor. The peeled log walls supported a rifle case—more an arsenal—which Ryerson noted contained two dozen lever-action rifles of the Winchester make or style, a variety of single- and double-barreled shotguns, and several sinister-looking sharpshooter or long-range hunting rifles built on Sharps or Spencer actions and equipped with long brass tube-like telescopic sights. He surmised that two large drawers below the weaponry contained an ample supply of ammunition for each.

Elsewhere around the room the walls supported coal-oil lamps and candle sconces. A wagon wheel hung on chains from the center ceiling beam with lamps bracketed to the wheel felloes at the end of every other spoke.

Ryerson took it all in in a single, appraising, information-seeking glance; knowledge of the room's layout and contents, as well as similar information on the rest of Doan's ranch, might be important before this was all over. The general cleanliness of the room suggested the touch of a woman's hand.

Several doors led to other areas of the house, all closed. Ryerson figured most were sleeping rooms. Food and cooking smells emanated from behind one of the doors—obviously leading to the kitchen.

He had noticed riding in that Doan's house had a second story, or at least a floored-in upstairs loft. Now he studied the stairway up the side of the wall to a padlocked trapdoor in the ceiling. He couldn't even guess what Doan might be keeping secure up there.

Smiling warmly at Ryerson now—as warmly, Ryerson thought, as a cold-blooded killer and snaked-eyed outlaw could smile—Doan opened a solid-door cupboard near the weapons case and produced a bottle of whiskey and two glasses.

"You'll have a drink with me, Mr. Kenny Rollins."

"I guess you can see I ain't been near a saloon in a while," Ryerson answered. "Much obliged."

Doan poured stiff drinks for them into thick, deep, and

gleaming glass tumblers. Before Ryerson could walk to his, Doan had placed the rim of his glass against his lower teeth and with a deft toss of head and hand, sent the contents straight down his throat without so much as tasting the stuff.

"There," Doan smacked, "that there'll put a new light on the subject. Drink up, Rollins. Drink up!"

Doan poured himself another and sat down at the large and sturdy table in the center of the room under the wagon-wheel chandelier. Ryerson picked up his full glass and sat across from Doan. Looking at each other, they each sipped off a quarter of the contents of their glasses.

"Help yourself to more when you're of a mind," Doan said.

Ryerson flicked a glance at the boss-man. He was no stranger to the stuff, but for his style it was early in the day. Still he was committed to carrying off the charade of a free-wheeling, hard-drinking outlaw. The whiskey burned his gullet as it went down, but he smacked in disguised relish.

"You keep good stuff, Mr. Doan."

"Make it Jubal. I like your looks, Rollins. I didn't miss how you stared down the boys out front. Was you a greenhorn, they'd haze the daylights out of you. You put 'em straight right off that you're not a man to be trifled with."

Ryerson nodded at the statement. "And I ain't," he agreed, tempering his words with gruffness.

"Lots of these tadpoles," Doan said, speaking out of the side of his mouth and almost in a snarl, "drifters and saddle bums—we see our share of 'em—make lots of noises about wanting to hit the owlhoot trail but I send 'em packin'. They're the first ones to quit the bunch in a fight. I told Roy Chalmers never to send anybody my way that ain't first class."

Doan's fingers tapped a rhythmic tattoo on the tabletop.

Ryerson nodded again, more confident than ever that his bill of goods was being bought by Jubal Doan. He sustained the stern expression frozen in his features.

"My face and my line of work got too familiar over that way. Thought I'd better cool off in some strange territory for a while, and Roy wrote me that note to bring to you."

"Roy's a good man. I'm not long back myself from two years in Leavenworth because I slipped up. Just bein' Jubal Doan is enough to get myself salted away. I was makin' what you might call a moonlight saddle switch and a local dingbat constable east of here got the drop on me. To which they conveniently tossed in cattle thievin'. One of ol' Judge Winfield's circuit courts met about eight minutes and quicker'n scat I was on a train to the Kansas calaboose chained to a varmint with a badge on his vest and a hogleg Colt on his hip. Have another, Kenny."

Ryerson, determined to continue the Kenny Rollins charade but not really caring for Doan's rotgut, still reached for the bottle. A door opened suddenly across the room and in spite of himself, Ryerson stopped his reach in mid-motion, tensed to go for the Colt Navy at his hip.

· 6 ·

As fast as he paused in his alarm, Ryerson extended his reach for the bottle as the corner of his eye caught the entrance of a woman through the door he now figured opened into the kitchen.

"Ruby!" Doan called. "Come on over and meet our new hand, Kenny Rollins."

Ruby was hardly more than a girl, with red hair like Doan, but with even more of a coppery glint. Her hair, however, had become dull, stringy, and lackluster. Ruby would have been attractive, Ryerson thought, studying her, but time had not treated her too kindly. She looked tired, almost defeated, and her attempts to cloak the evidence under corn-flour face powder, touched-up eyebrows and lashes, and crimson rouge on cheeks and lips only served to deepen her shabbiness.

Ruby was without doubt Doan's cook and housekeeper, probably serving other of his needs as well. Ryerson wondered who she had been, where she was from, and how she came to be in the midst of a gang of one of the West's worst hardcases; maybe, he thought, she had come with the chaise lounge with its cathouse look.

"Kenny," Doan said loudly, intruding on Ryerson's thoughts, "meet Miss Ruby Montez."

Ruby Montez's disinterested eyes brightened as they fixed on the newcomer. The tension in her features eased and her expression turned bold and, Ryerson thought, mildly flirtatious.

"Howdy, stranger," she said, her voice throaty, and that in itself sent a message seemingly meant to be bewitching. "I didn't catch the name."

"Rollins," Ryerson reminded, getting up in traditional courtesy. He touched fingers to his hat brim. "Kenny Rollins."

"My, oh, my, Mr. Doan," Ruby cooed, not taking her eyes off Ryerson. "At last we have a gentleman in our midst. Pleased to meetcha, Mr. Rollins."

Doan appeared oblivious to Ruby's cordial reaction to Ryerson.

"Charlie and the boys are back in from their trail drive, and with Kenny here signin' on with the crew today, this'll be a good night for a frolic." Doan put veiled emphasis on "trail drive," and Ryerson suspected a herd of rustled cattle had been disposed of, or brought in.

The hard edge also had gone out of Doan's voice in chatting with Ruby. "You and the girls carve up a mess of steaks and roasts of that beef we butchered yesterday and put up all the fixin's for a feed, and make sure there's enough whiskey to go around."

At the mention of whiskey, Ruby Montez rummaged for a clean glass in Doan's liquor cabinet and poured herself a stiff jolt and came back to stand behind Doan's chair and sip along with the men.

"Time's gettin' on," Ryerson said. "Be okay, Mr. Doan, if I was to look to my horse and find a place to clean myself up a bit? Wouldn't want to come to your party lookin' like a seedy saddle tramp."

"You can call me Jubal," Doan reminded. As he spoke, he reached out for Ruby's hand. "Ruby," he commanded, drawing the woman close to him as if to underscore to Ryerson his right of possession. "Go out and see if Clute is hangin' around on the porch. He was there a minute ago. Get him in here."

The girl set her drink down and disappeared through the outside door.

"Clute'll get you situated, Kenny, and show you the ropes around here. Clute's an old-timer, don't ride much anymore. Mostly looks after things around the place for me. We'll kick up our heels tonight and tomorrow we'll see how good you really are with a runnin' iron. We're holding a good-size herd about five miles from here that'll be needin' a maverick brand. Got to get 'em out of the territory before some snoopy lawman outta old Winfield's jurisdiction gets in here and blows the whistle on us."

Ryerson hoped his grimace of apprehension wasn't evident. When it came right down to cases, he knew nothing about brand blotching. He only knew that a maverick brand was something cooked up, unrecorded, to throw the law or suspicious ranchers off the trail if a rustled herd was encountered.

Ruby strutted back with a provocative hip-rolling motion that seemed a characteristic of what Ryerson perceived was her normal profession. With her was the aging cowpoke Ryerson saw on the veranda when he arrived. The old-timer was still lean-hipped but his belly oozed over his belt buckle like dough rising in a breadpan. Even at the distance, Ryerson could see that Clute's eyeballs were bloodshot from too many years in the sun or the saloon or both, and his features were seamed and whiskery. He had the look of a devoted Doan follower whose meanness was on a par with that of the boss.

"This here's Kenny Rollins, Clute," Doan said. "Artist with a runnin' iron. Gonna be with us a while. Show him where to bunk and give him a look-see at our spread. Take him around to howdy with the boys."

Clute's tired but sullen-looking eyes regarded the newcomer suspiciously. He acknowledged the assignment with a glance at the boss and a small flick of his head. "Come on," he growled, sounding like it was an imposition. Clute bowlegged his way out of the house.

Ryerson got up, tossing off the rest of his drink and setting down the glass. "Thanks for the hospitality . . . boss." He started after Clute. "Miss Ruby," he called back, by way of begging her leave, and touched his hat brim.

"Nice to meetcha, Mr. Rollins," Ruby Montez called sweetly.

Clute waited for him at the door, scowling. "Said your name was Rollins?" Clute asked as they walked out onto the broad stoop.

"Kenny's good enough," Ryerson said. "But, yeah, Rollins. Kenny Rollins." They stepped off the stoop with Clute leading the way to what passed for a bunkhouse across a tawny stretch of weedless rammed-earth yard next to an ample building that served as barn and stable. On the other side of the barn a large corral of sturdy uprights and thick, peeled pole-rails baked in the harsh afternoon sun. Ryerson occupied his thoughts with reinforcing the tough, Kenny Rollins image.

As they strode across the ranch yard, Ryerson pivoted his head, letting his eyes rove the surroundings. Walking a step behind Clute, who trudged impatiently in front of Ryerson, he seized the opportunity to glance back over his shoulder at the big ranch house, imposing enough to serve as a fort.

Movement at an upper window, an opening without glass but larger than a rifle port, caught his attention.

In this split-second appraisal, Ryerson caught a glimpse of a bearded and dirty, anguished-looking face shrouded in the darkness behind the window. Before he could allow himself time to speculate on who might be locked above the ceiling trapdoor of Doan's front room, Clute's gruff voice intruded.

"Ain't hard even for these old eyes to see Miss Ruby makin' the calf-eyes with you. A word of advice, friend, just don't get took in by it. She's got the wanderin' eye and it'll damned near fetch a man, 'specially if he gets one or two under his belt. And she does under hers. She commences to start lookin' pretty good. Doan is so set on her, he don't see it. She's lamped that look on about ever' waddy ever come on the place."

"Don't worry about me," Ryerson said.

Clute's growl grew deeper. "I'm tellin' you somethin' to listen to, amigo. Just don't go cozyin' up around her. Doan's got a jealous streak wide as Black River yonder where Ruby's concerned. You'll learn mighty fast that Doan's guns'll come out blazin' if he sees anybody musclin' into his territory, cattle *or* women, and old Jube don't draw just for the hell of it. Besides, us boys got a good thing here and we ain't partial to anybody comin' in here and rilin' up our waters."

"Thanks for the concerned words," Ryerson said, almost facetiously. "And I told you not to worry about me." That decided, he figured to still play dumb and poke and prod some more. "What's Doan keep locked up in his attic?"

Almost at the bunkhouse stoop, Clute set his brakes and swung around to face Ryerson, eyes flashing. "See? There you go again. What does it take for you to keep your ideas to yourself and your mouth shut?"

Ryerson feigned innocence. "Just askin', for Pete's sake. No skin off me one way or the other. I saw the stairs and the padlock and just wondered."

"Just do your job and forget anything goin' on up at the big house."

Ryerson decided to try another tack. "Just let me say that I appreciate the warmth of your welcome, Clute. A man comes on a new spread, he's just bound to have a few questions. Sorry I stuck my nose in where it wasn't wanted."

Clute caught the sarcasm in Ryerson's tone. "You speak right out, don't you, boy? I told you, stick to learnin' about the operation and stay off what Doan does or don't do."

"I get it. Can I ask you one thing, and it isn't about Doan?"

"Fire away."

"You said something about the river. It comes through here?"

"Yonder side of the mesa, about eight mile. Opposite from where you rode in. But you won't want to fiddle around over there. Plunges th'ough a deep, narrow canyon and it's rocks and white-water rapids and falls till hell wouldn't have it. Anybody slips in there is dead meat right now. Nobody knows how far to where it smooths out again. Hell of a ways, anyway."

They entered the bunkhouse, a long, squat building perched on a low cemented fieldstone footer. "You'll camp in here," Clute said. "Down at the far end's a spare bunk. We lost a man in a stampede last month. You can claim that 'un."

The place reeked of sweaty clothing, tobacco smoke and tobacco juice, and tracked-in manure with just a whiff of gun oil, horse liniment, and latigo leather.

Ryerson wasn't particularly partial to sleeping in a dead man's bunk. He had no choice but to swallow and play it tough.

Crude wood cots lined both walls with enough room for a man to move between. On the wall beside the head of each bunk was a packing crate with shelves for a man's belongings and a butt can for soggy stubs from smokes or for tobacco juice if he took his ease in that fashion.

Wood pegs along the walls did for hanging Stetsons, trail coats, chaps, and such. Above the clothing pegs were more pegs for Winchesters or whatever long arm a cowboy preferred.

"Reckon you can meet most of the boys over supper," Clute said, summarily relieving himself of that part of Doan's assignment. "Prolly want to stow your gear by your bunk."

"Ain't got much. Travelin' light. Warbag and a bedroll about does it."

"None of us fixed much better."

"Like to unsaddle my bronc and rub 'im down," Ryerson said. "Maybe roust out some oats and grain. Then I'll move in."

Clute seemed to warm a bit more to the newcomer. "While you're about that, I'll chunk up the fire in the stove long enough to set some water to heating. Looks like you could use a shave and a whore's bath."

"Much obliged," Ryerson said, returning Clute's easier tone with a grin. "I prefer to call it a sponge bath even though I ain't got a sponge."

Clute dismissed Ryerson's wisecrack with a disinterested grunt. "Ruby said Doan's havin' a whoop-de-do this evenin'. Might be you'd oughtta put on your clean shirt, too."

"I'd been giving that some thought, too, Clute. Got time for a smoke?" Ryerson fished in his vest pocket for his cotton sack of flake tobacco and his papers and offered them to the grumpy cowhand.

Clute's callused palm came up in acceptance and Ryerson deftly tossed his drawstring cotton makin's poke to him. In moves that were marvels of efficiency, Clute fished out a paper, built a trough of it, sprinkled in the flake tobacco, spun it into a tube, licked it and parked it between his moistened lips at the far right side. He expertly snapped the head off a lucifer match with a long and thick thumbnail, cupped his hands around the orange-blue flame, and had his smoke going in seconds. Ryerson figured Clute could probably do the same thing from horseback at full gallop.

Clute led the way back to the empty bunk he'd assigned to Ryerson and parked his rear end on the adjacent bunk to use the ashcan. For Ryerson it was precisely the opportunity he needed to get a bit more of the lowdown. He sat across from Clute and rolled and fired his own.

"Guess you got me marked down for a nosy nuisance," Ryerson said.

"Some things you just don't trifle with around here." Clute's voice had turned companionable.

Ryerson perched on his new bunk across from Clute who, by contrast with Ryerson's first impression, now nursed his smoke like a man with all the time in the world. Clute stared at Ryerson through the rolling smoke of his cigarette clenched at the edge of his tight-clamped mouth.

"Clute," Ryerson began, "you're takin' on like I'm some kind of greenhorn kid not quite dry behind the ears. You got some kind of problem about me? I've specialized in re-markin' beeves since shortly after Appomattox. Before that I rode with Jo Shelby during the late unpleasantness. When Shelby vowed to ride into Mexico and keep on fighting, I petitioned for my discharge before he buried his Rebel battle flags and crossed the Rio Grande. Stayed in Texas and began helping round up maverick beeves for a livin'. Some 'mavericks' wore a brand and I got slick fixing 'em to whatever would fool the inspectors or some other rancher's tally man."

Once he got rolling, Ryerson relished building the shred of truth of his yarn into a believable whole-cloth lie.

Clute's limp cigarette sagged in the corner of his thin-lipped mouth as his jaw fell slack. "You rode with Jo Shelby?"

"Four years man and boy. Missouri to Arkansas and back into Missouri and Kansas a right smart of times on raids. You remember Shelby's raids, Clute?"

"Newtonia? In Kansas? Was you there, Rollins?" Ryerson could only guess he saw a glint of some admiration growing in old Clute's eyes.

"I guess you know I was. I said I rode with Shelby. In at Missouri, out at Texas after Pap Sterling Price and General Buckner and Kirby Smith and them sold the Army of Trans Mississippi down the river at New Orleans and old Jo swore to keep Shelby's Raiders fighting in Mexico."

"I took a Rebel Minie ball in the brisket at Newtonia

myself, Kenny," Clute said almost proudly. "Rode against you, son, with the Ninth Kansas volunteer horse calvary." A glow akin to comradeship burned bright in Clute's old rheumy eyes. "But I was tough and I made it through. Didn't so much as whimper when that butcher sawbones probed the bastard out. Not even a shot of whiskey to ease the pain. Still carry the slug in my warbag. I don't care a damn anymore whose side you was on or who won or lost. We was fighting bastards both sides no matter who was calling the commands or committing the troops. We was fighting bastards, Kenny, you and me!"

Clute's eyes now held a faraway look as he sat on the seedy cot in Doan's bunkhouse and looked across at Ryerson and across the years and the miles to Newtonia and the fields of valor of a dozen other cavalry battles and skirmishes.

"If it was a Minie ball it was from a musket. Couldn't've been me that laid you low, Clute," Ryerson said. "This old Colt Navy and a horse soldier's saber was all I had for four years of arduous service under Shelby."

"Warn't no calvaryman done it." Clute's eyes narrowed in grim reminiscence at Ryerson. "Foot sojer with a musket. I stayed in the saddle long enough to ride him down and take his head off with my sword. I still got his butternut cap. Wanta see it?"

"Maybe later, Clute. But you mean cavalry, don't you?"

"That's what I said. Calvary."

Ryerson grinned at the old man and got up. "I better see to my horse and spruce up for the whingding tonight."

"I'll set some shave water heating for you, Kenny." Clute paused, looking at Ryerson. "Sorry for bein' rough on you. If I'd've knowd you'd rode against me at Newtonia, I'd've never . . . well, what I'm sayin' is you're okay with me, Kenny."

Ryerson grinned down at Clute as the old man started to get up. "I'm glad at least one person here feels kindly to'ards me. I thank you, Clute."

"You'll do all right here," Clute said. "Anybody starts crowdin' you, you send for me. Doan'll back my plays anytime in keepin' these waddies in line."

Ryerson strode out to look after Rusty, feeling good about gaining Clute's confidence. He also felt a little sad that despite all that Clute had said, the old-timer was still the enemy.

· 7 ·

In the very midst of the brazen outlaws and cold-blooded killers he despised, Ryerson found himself—in spite of himself—getting caught up in the festive glow as he followed the flock of yammering cowboys trooping into Doan's crowded main lodge room. Dusk threw a gray cloak over the ranch yard. As he shouldered into the crowd, the delicious aroma of coffee reached him, reminding him of his hunger.

Every lamp was turned to its highest flame short of smoking the chimneys to fill the big room with the warm glow of light. Long tables and benches hauled in from the crew's cook shed groaned with the grand feed of steaks and roasts, fried and boiled spuds, cooked carrots and a fruit compote, gently spiced enchiladas, mashed Mexican *frijoles* and wafer-thin tortillas, cornbread and sourdough.

The meal itself was a chaos of commotion and chatter, the roar of thirty or more cowhands all talking and gesturing at once nearly drowning out even the closest conversation.

With Ruby Montez ramrodding the crew of cooks who doubled as servers, the plain but not unattractive Mexican girls skittered back and forth to the kitchen carrying away empty bowls and tureens and dirty plates, returning with more food anywhere it was called for.

Ryerson had no idea how the daily grub was for Doan's crew, but for this fandango, the rustler boss fed his men like royalty.

Clute sat across from Ryerson and alongside a grubby ox of a young man they called Homer who mowed away twice as much as the others, grossly stuffing food into his face and gulping it down half-chewed. Juice and saliva and bits of food oozed over his chin and stained the front of his grimy shirt. Homer's eyes held the unblinking, vacant stare of an imbecile, and his impassive, almost inanimate face did nothing to dispel the impression.

Homer had no shoulders to speak of, only a bull neck that sloped down to bulging upper arms and into his thick chest and a back humped with corded muscle. He had short-cropped brown hair, spiky, matted, and unruly, and with his large, protruding buck teeth put Ryerson in mind of an overgrown prairie dog.

Conversation with Clute, the only one Ryerson had much connection with, was virtually impossible, so they only glanced at each other occasionally and smiled.

After the grand feed was topped off with dozens of dried-fruit pies, two or more helpings for anyone who wanted them, Doan's cowhands cleared the room in under ten minutes.

They mobilized after the kitchen help mopped down the tables while a round of after-dinner drinks and cigars were savored by the revelers, standing in clusters around the room's perimeter.

With the tables cleared and cleaned, and on Doan's command, the men rushed in noisily, crews of four or five hoisting the long tables and heading them back to the cook shed. Pairs of others—Ryerson finding himself teamed with Clute—hauled out the benches. Ryerson noted grimly that the monstrous Homer headed for the door with a bench tucked under each arm, doggedly lugging them ahead of Ryerson and Clute across the yard, bathed in the rich silvery glow of a clear and full moon, to the crew's normal dining quarters.

As the hands walked back to the ranch house chatting merrily among themselves in knots of two, three, and four or more, Ryerson scuffed through the dark with Clute, the hulking Homer a dark clot of muscled might lumbering head down ahead of them. Ryerson could also sense an unreasoning meanness about the brute.

Ryerson itched to ask Clute about Homer but held back, knowing it was neither the time nor the place.

"That was some feed," he enthused candidly instead; it had been one of his most enjoyed meals in a long time.

"Another man's beef always tastes best," Clute observed laconically, his big boot soles slapping noisily on the yard's hardpan. "Now we get to run off our grub on the dance floor."

"Dance floor?"

"You'll see."

"But you need women to dance."

"You saw those Mex ladies that dished out the grub?"

"Yeah," Ryerson grunted.

"They're married to three of Doan's *vaqueros* from south of the line. But on frolic nights, Doan has 'em dance with the boys by turns. Some of the fellers get likkered up, too, and get to dancin' with one another. Just tomfoolery, that's all."

As they approached the ranch house, Ryerson could hear musicians tuning up. As they entered the packed, brightly lit lodge room, he saw at one end a fiddler, a banjo player, a man with a concertina, and two others, one with a Jew's harp, the other a mouth organ.

"When you get the chance, Kenny," Clute said out the side of his mouth as they shouldered into the din and the glare and wove their way through the collected cowpokes, "get a dance with Estella. She's the ugliest of them *señoras* but she's about as light and quick on her feet as any woman north of the line."

81

"What about Miss Montez?"

Clute stiffened beside him as they stood in a ring of cowboys launching into some two-fisted drinking. This time Clute's voice was friendly, fatherly.

"I told you, son, that's Doan's private stock. Play 'em close to your vest and grab Estella when you can, which won't be easy. I built me a dry hauling that bench out of here. Care to wet your whistle?"

Ryerson needed to stay sharp. "I'll pass for the time being," he said.

Clute moved off to the whiskey bar. Ryerson said "Fine evenin'" to a tall and lean cowhand next to him and got an indifferent grunt in response and Ryerson left it right there. Across the room from him, he found Ruby Montez's eyes fixed on him from the crowd. She stared steadily at him for a long moment before rolling her eyes and arching her eyebrows briefly. Ryerson couldn't grasp her meaning or message, if it was a message she sent.

He looked around quickly. No one seemed to have noticed, particularly Doan, who stood by his tabletop covered with whiskey bottles and glasses, working on a stiff one and chinning with a crew hand Ryerson had been told was Sandy.

The musicians, after a few tantilizing scrapes by the fiddler, who led the ensemble, launched into a fast-clip, chipper rendition of some tune Ryerson didn't recognize. Accompaniment was quickly supplied in raucous yips and hoots from the cowboys ringing the room, and much hand-clapping. Heavy booted feet shook the building with their foot-stomping.

From out of the ring of men, the three dusky Mexican women were led onto the cleared lodge-room floor and the dance was under way. None of the three cowboys waltzing the women about the floor was a particularly good dancer; the women's expressions held the same stoic and resigned indifference Ryerson had noticed about them when they served the food.

If the women were having fun, Ryerson thought, they sure had a strange way of showing it. It looked like to them it came more under the heading of duty.

Now and then a cowboy ventured out to cut in on his dancing saddle mate. It was apparent that the three women would be kept on the floor all evening; they had obviously worked most of the day preparing the food and then serving it. Ryerson imagined they were exhausted.

He spied the one who was probably Estella but since he'd never had much patience nor skill with dancing, he figured he'd be one of the crowd the poor *señoras* wouldn't have to put up with. Estella had a plain face with harsh, angular lines, abundant straight black hair, a comely figure, and a feather-light glide about her as she danced.

He sidled his lonely way to the whiskey table, deciding after all to fix himself a stiff one. He figured to nurse it most of the evening and stay alert.

It was becoming clear to him that these rustlers had worked together a long time and had plenty to talk about—with one another. He realized he was still the outsider and probably wouldn't be accepted into the clan until he'd ridden and worked with them a few days.

As the whiskey took over, the party became more boisterous. Cowboys began cutting in on the dancers more frequently. There were some arguments about it all that concluded short of coming to blows. Ryerson felt there might be an explosion of fists before the night was over.

"Havin' a good time, Kenny?" a familiar voice grated harshly behind him. He turned to find Doan walking up to him to refresh his own half-filled whiskey glass at the bar.

"Tol'able, Jubal, tol'able," Ryerson replied. Doan's normally flashing dark eyes were heavy lidded and glazed; Jubal Doan was well on his way to taking on a skinfull.

"I get it," Doan said, slurring his words. "The boys ain't warming up to you yet."

The band across the room lit into "Turkey in the Straw," the first of their numbers Ryerson could recognize. Somewhere nearby a shaky tenor, shamefully tone-deaf, started singing what few words he thought he knew, most of them wrong.

"I suppose you're right," Ryerson said loudly over the din.

From opposite sides of the room, two well-oiled rustlers in grimy trail duds got out among the couples and tried to show off their talents as crude clog-dancers, or what might be considered to pass for that, Ryerson thought.

"I've a hunch they'll sit up and take notice of you tomorrow when we get to a little branding business. You carry your own runnin' iron, Kenny?"

Ryerson thought fast. "The man who does that is looking for a hemp necktie if he's caught with it. Naw, Jubal, just about anything will do. Straight chunk of thin rod ought to suit me. I figured I'd find something in your blacksmith shop."

Doan took a healthy swig from his refilled glass. "You go look around by the forge in the east end of the big stable in the mornin'. Use whatever suits you best. Hear tell you're pretty good at your line of work."

Ryerson grinned inwardly and came up with an honest—but veiled—response. "There's those that say I am," he said, knowing they had altogether different lines of work in mind.

Ryerson also knew full well that before morning he'd have to have gleaned whatever information he was to get about Doan, his ranch, and his doings and somehow ride out of there. He grimaced inwardly. It'd be even more risky riding out than it had been riding in.

To top it off, in riding away so abruptly, he'd be exposed either as a spy or an officer of the law and fair game for any Doan man who got him in his sights from then on out.

He wondered only momentarily if he could pull off the facade as a brand-blotter and hold onto the disguise a while longer. Just as fast he knew he couldn't.

"Clute tells me you two faced off a few times in the war."

Doan's unpleasant voice intruded on Ryerson's important thinking. Doan had come up close to make himself heard over the raucous music and roar of thudding boots and loud talking and caterwauling of thirty celebrating, inebriated cow waddies.

Ryerson mustered a grin at Doan. "So he tells me. I suppose we must have. I rode with Shelby's brigade out of Arkansas and Clute was in the Yankees' Kansas horse regiments. We could have had one another in our sights a time or two, but I doubt it. I don't hold with slaughter. I only killed when it was me or him."

"Worthless trash got to be done away with," Doan spit out angrily, his whiskey-soaked mind turning angry. The fire came up in his hooch-dimmed eyes. "Like them cattle-breedin' nesters out south of here. I've got a plan to get 'em out of my hair and I want you to be a part of it, Kenny. In Berdan, there's a fella by the name of . . ."

Doan's words were cut short as a sudden hush fell over the room with the slam of the front door. The music trailed off, the dancers stopped abruptly as all eyes fixed on two men who had entered and posed in the doorway. In front of Doan's sentry, who held a cocked Winchester, stood a defiant short and stocky man with a rich, sun-cured complexion. His hat was gone and Ryerson saw short-cropped curly black hair circled by grizzled gray in the temples and in a wide ring along the back of his neck. Several days' growth of dark stubble darkened his cheeks and chin. He was grimy with trail dust. In the instant it took Ryerson to study the prisoner and assess him, he noted that the tips of two fingers were missing. Clearly he was an old cowhand who, at some time, had got his fingertips pinched off while roping cattle.

The man's features sent a dart of familiarity or recognition through Ryerson's head, a spurt of sensation that he'd known this man before, somewhere. But it was too fleeting, too vague, too nebulous to grasp. Was it through the eyes or the mouth that the face reminded him of someone? The inability to come to grips with it momentarily frustrated him. A name was on the tip of his tongue, but it eluded—and maddened—him.

The man was no spring chicken; in his late forties, probably, Ryerson surmised. His tanned features were seamed and twisted in anger, his jaw clamped in grim defiance.

From beside Ryerson, Doan's now all-business voice boomed, chopping a wedge in the hushed silence. "Whatta we got here, Sandy?"

"Caught this jasper sneakin' up the canyon in the dark, Jubal," the guard, Sandy, snarled loudly for all to hear. "I could've put a hole th'ough his skull and brought him up over his saddle. But since I had him dead to rights, I figured to let you have a few words with him first."

"Good thinking," Doan called, moving ominously toward the pair at the door. The now-silent, almost threatening cowboys closed ranks behind him, craning their necks to get a good look at the intruder, whose moments of life were clearly numbered as far as they were concerned.

"I'll attend to this," Doan growled, near enough to face the stranger. "Sandy, you go on back to your post. You'll be relieved in an hour and there's plenty of grub here to warm over and whiskey."

Sandy did an almost military about-face and ducked out of the room.

The stranger, seeing no escape, stood his ground belligerently, even leaning slightly toward Doan in rigid defiance.

"You got a name?" Doan rasped harshly, glaring into the stranger's eyes.

"Puddin' Tame. Ask me again and I'll say the same." The stranger's chin was thrust out arrogantly.

"You got a mouth on *you!*" Doan raged, impulsively bringing up his hand and cracking the man a mean, resounding slap across the cheek with the flat of his palm. The stranger's head snapped sidewise but it bounced right back to stare Doan straight in the eye, unperturbed, his own unblinking eyes darting sparks. The captive's hands hung

stiffly at his sides, the fists clenching and relaxing in spasms of fury.

Jarred by Doan's action, Ryerson moved close to the front of the mobbed rustlers who now backed Doan in a tight-eyed, half-drunk, hostile mob. The stranger's only escape hatch was the door behind him and to go for it spelled sudden death.

Out of the corner of his eye, Ryerson watched Homer muscle his way up to the front rank, a few steps away from where Doan's flinty eyes glared at the captive.

"You gotta be Doan," the man said, his lips tight in outrage. "You run off my stock. I'm here to claim it. Or collect a fair price."

"Mister, my ranch has branded mavericks all over this territory. If you think I or my men here have touched a one of yours, you got to be specific. This is open range. The man who plants the first brand claims the beef." Doan's voice was a snarl.

The stranger continued to glare at his inquisitor, silent now.

Ryerson still couldn't identify the man; obviously one of Sam Carson's and Rathburn's settler-ranchers. Moving into his field of vision, Homer detached himself from the crowd and stepped to the captive. The man swung his gaze from Doan as Homer reached out and with vise-like fingers and thumb, caught a pinching grip on the man's shoulder muscle above the collarbone. The victim grimaced in extreme pain and tried to flinch away.

"Mr. Doan done ast you a question what you doin' here," Homer demanded in a dull, bullfrog bass monotone, the first time Ryerson had heard him speak. Doan, grinning sadistically, had stepped aside for Homer.

When the man tried to wiggle out of Homer's agonizing clutch, the ox-size man drove his other fist into the stranger's vitals. Still held up by Homer's shoulder-hold, he slumped, finally slipping out of the big man's grasp to drop to his knees in acute pain.

Homer came off the floor with a haymaker that caught the older man on his blunt chin, driving him to his tiptoes to fly back, crash and slam against the ranch house door. He toppled over on his side, a doubled-up, leg-bent, twisted knot of agony, clutching his paralyzed gut.

Homer started the few paces to continue his battering only to freeze abruptly at Ryerson's shout. "Stop, god-dammit!"

Doan's head whirled in Ryerson's direction in astonishment, his mouth a perfect O in his face.

Ryerson's fury had turned his face nearly purple as he faced down the outlaw leader. "Look, Doan!" Ryerson shrieked. "I got nothing against fixing brands on another man's beef and I've done my share. Cold-blooded murder is something I'll have no part of and that's what you and your big-ox hand there have on your mind!"

"You stay out of this, Kenny!" Doan shrieked.

"I'm damned if I will!"

Homer forgot his victim to stumble closer as Doan and Ryerson faced each other. Homer's deep voice broke an uneasy silence. "You want I fix this 'un first, Mr. Doan?"

"Back off, Homer," Doan ordered in a growl. The hulking monster still held his ground and glared at Ryerson. At least now Homer ignored the pitiful, groaning wretch groveling in pain against the door.

"Kenny, this is none of your affair," Doan said, straining to return his voice to a level tone for Rollins's sake. "This party's part in your honor, but I'm telling you, don't crowd me."

Ryerson suddenly saw an out for himself, a way to ride away from Doan's camp without being shot out of the saddle. "I'm makin' it my affair, Jubal," he gritted. "I told you I don't hold with wanton savagery. I make my living changing cattle brands because that's what I'm good at. But I'll not stand by and see Homer pound the stuffing out of that creature there, which is what he's ready to do."

"Don't push it, Kenny," Doan cautioned again.

"I don't mean to, Jubal," Ryerson said, leveling his own voice now as well. He disliked using the beaten captive as his pawn, but it was the best thing he could do, and worth the risk. "But if it's all the same, I'll pack my gear and ride on out of here before you turn that brute loose again. I'm sure Roy Chalmers has other friends not quite so bloodthirsty."

The characteristic flinty glare in Jubal Doan's eyes softened. "Kenny, Kenny. Let's not destroy the start of a beautiful friendship."

Doan turned away. "Homer!" The giant swung his blank gaze on Doan who fished in his pockets.

"Here. Here's the key to upstairs. Haul that jasper up there and lock him away. We'll deal with him later."

Homer took the key from Doan, his listless stare boring into Ryerson's eyes. Homer, clearly, had relished the idea of pounding the life out of the captive by slow degrees. The new man had deprived him of being the talk of the camp for days to come after he whaled the bejeebers out of the intruder.

Homer's look at Ryerson suggested he'd settle with Ryerson on that score later when Doan wasn't around. He glared at Ryerson a long time, a killer light in his emptyheaded, unreasoning eyes.

"Homer!" Doan roared. "I told you to do something!"

Like a man coming out of a daydream, Homer snapped alert. "Yessir, Mr. Doan," he grunted. Homer went to crouch over the still groggy captive. He lifted the unprotesting man by an arm and a leg, draped him over his shoulder and headed up the stairway built against the wall.

Doan watched his progress for a moment, then turned to the hard-eyed hands behind him. "Well! What are we waiting for? Fiddler! Saw us a tune!"

With Doan's command, the music picked up, as did the slow start of the return to the roar of men's voices and the tempo of the festivities.

Ryerson watched Homer unlock the trapdoor, fling it up and shove his load like a discarded rag out onto the second floor. The door slammed shut again; Homer snapped the padlock on the hasp and started back down the stairs.

Ryerson looked at his half-filled whiskey glass still clutched in his hand and tossed the contents down his throat. He was far from out of the woods in getting away from Doan's clutches. To top it off, a confrontation with the monstrous bully was almost assured.

· 8 ·

Despite Doan's uncharacteristically bland decision about the aging intruder and Homer's reaction to Ryerson's butting-in, Ryerson knew that Doan would let nature take its course when the crew—Ryerson and Homer included—returned to the bunkhouse after the evening's festivities.

As he plodded the fifty yards from Doan's house across to the crew's sleeping quarters, Ryerson felt that Doan would now let Kenny Rollins do his own fighting. The results would cast the dice in deciding if Rollins earned the confidence of Doan's crew or was beaten to a bloody pulp in the process.

A half a dozen men were already in the bunkhouse when Ryerson strode in and made his way back to where his bedroll was spread.

As he walked the alleyway between the bunks, he heard one voice call out, "How you doin', Ken?" Ryerson merely nodded and waved in acknowledgment as he passed. At his bunk, he hung his hat and vest on the peg that supported his belt and holstered Colt Navy. He sat on the edge of the bunk to roll and fire a bedtime smoke.

Still, there was unfinished business to be settled before he could roll up in his soogans this night.

He was also aware of a hushed anticipation in the air, bright and crisp as lightning before the storm, as other cowboys drifted in; nobody, it seemed, was quite ready to skin down to his union suit and crawl into bed.

Somehow the word had passed; Homer was spoiling to clean the newcomer's plow and the yearning to see blood spilled oozed out of Doan's cowboys like a smell.

Ryerson felt his heartbeat picking up the pace and the throb of blood pulsing through his temples. Homer had sledgehammers at the ends of both arms. If it came down to a bare-knuckles free-for-all, Ryerson was not altogether certain how he'd handle it and come out the other end on his feet.

Still, whether he was Kenny Rollins or Cole Ryerson, he'd not back away if pressed to a confrontation. Ryerson looked down at his own hands, good-size mitts that they were, and wondered if they'd pull him through this one. He'd done his share of fist-fighting and brawling, but never against such a mountain of might as Homer.

The usually clumsy man on Ryerson's mind must have entered the bunkhouse with an extremely light step. When Ryerson looked up from his hands, the giant stood a few paces away from him, a glare in his beady, prairie-dog eyes. Just now, Ryerson thought, his mind taking weird twists, Homer looked more like a prairie dog crossed with a wolverine and a little touched with grizzly bear. Homer studied his intended adversary malevolently.

Ryerson felt his breath catch in his throat. Homer sure enough had it in his mind to make a finish of the confrontation that started in Doan's lodge room.

Ryerson figured his best defense was a good offense and that offense should be to take the brutal emptyhead off guard. He took another draw on his cigarette and let the smoke out slowly. "Hahdee, Homer. You have a good time this evenin'?"

Homer's eyes, narrowed in anger, opened, rolling and

unblinking in confusion. His brows knit in bewilderment; he'd expected a quite different greeting from Kenny Rollins.

Clute sidled past Homer to take a spot in the dark at the far end of the bunkhouse. The others sat or stood expectantly behind Homer. Ryerson wasn't altogether sure some of them hadn't egged Homer to goad Kenny Rollins into a fight.

Homer's brows continued to be knit in thought and question. He took two steps closer to Ryerson, his fists clenched. Ryerson decided it was time to take the initiative and speak again. "You got something stuck in your throat, Homer? Cough it up. You'll feel better."

Homer found his voice at last. "You . . . you got Mr. Doan to stop me from . . . from takin' care of that guy."

"You think that was wrong of me, Homer?" Ryerson kept his voice level.

"You . . . you fixed it so I couldn't take care of that guy."

Ryerson forced a laugh out loud. "You weren't figuring to take very good care of him, Homer!"

Again Homer's brows knit in bewilderment; he wasn't all that sharp when it came to semantic sparring. Ryerson figured it was high time to bring it to a head. "So you figure that if you couldn't take care of that guy, you'd take care of me now." Ryerson stood up and closed the gap between them to come to within swinging distance of Homer.

"I'll . . . I'll . . ." Homer started, his fisted arms slightly bent at the elbows. Ryerson grinned inwardly; poor dumb son of a bitch doesn't even know how to put up his dukes, he thought, but he'll kill me with them if I give him the opening. He decided not to give Homer the opportunity.

"Hey, Homer," he called loudly. "Your fly's unbuttoned!"

When Homer's head bobbed down to check his pants buttons, Ryerson pulled a right from low down that caught the big ox on the chin, bringing his head up, but the giant wasn't fazed. When Homer had sent Doan's intruder an uppercut like that earlier, it piled him in a paralyzed heap against the doorway.

Ryerson's heart sank; he might as well have taken a poke at the granite cliff behind Doan's house. Homer's lips folded back from his yellowed fangs of buck teeth to make a savage mask of his face.

Ryerson was caught off guard as a lightning blow from Homer's barn-beam-size arm came from behind him and took Ryerson beside the head, sending him reeling along the aisle between the bunks. He quickly recovered and bounced back to smash another right to the big man's rocky jaw.

Ryerson's opponent, it was now confirmed, was big and tough and filled with furious strength. With the blow, Ryerson saw rage darken Homer's dimwit face.

Ryerson now knew his advantage lay in his agility. He began crashing in, never letting the burly Homer gain his balance. Homer didn't need balance; like a big rock, he was fixed to the floor. Despite Ryerson's telling pokes, Homer lunged in with a wild and mindless advance. Ryerson ducked to the right of the intended blows and slashed in with a fist that connected with bone over Homer's right eye.

Blood bubbled out of an eyebrow split against the bone to stream into Homer's eye and set him blinking against its sting; Homer bellowed a maddened scream of rage and fury and ferociously waded in at Ryerson again.

Ryerson's fists came up defensively to protect his face but the sledgehammer force of Homer's blow knocked them away to smash Ryerson a solid clip to the jaw; flying sparks as from a blacksmith's forge showered in the marshal's head.

He staggered backward and by the time he'd caught himself and waded back at the brute, he was in control. Ryerson ducked under three more wildly swinging blows, a right and a left and another right. He came up on the tail of the three misses with a left to Homer's crimson-gushing right eyebrow; the wound opened more, the blood flowing more freely.

The eye was already puffy and taking on a sickly purple hue.

By now Ryerson had felt Homer's supernatural strength in several blows and knew that his hope lay in avoiding a straight give-and-take. Hit from the right angle by the giant's fists, his head could snap, breaking his neck. He had to win with footwork or Homer would beat him to a pulp. His own strength was no match for Homer's power blows.

Keeping up his evasive tactics, Ryerson went flashing in with quick one-two blows, retreating from Homer's wildly swinging powerhouse punches. He bore in relentlessly, now trying to work on the other eye, hoping to blind the big Goliath and finish him off when he couldn't see.

Homer's vision appeared to fade as each blow to his head puffed the eyebrow skin higher to loosen fresh blood. The big man's swings became wilder and Ryerson turned more skillful in ducking them. Homer wasn't seriously injured, but he could scarcely see. Infuriated at the pain and his inability to land one on his opponent, Homer lifted his great fists and charged.

Moving fast and hitting hard, Ryerson landed a left that cracked against Homer's chin, tipping him backward.

Now Homer's fists only whistled past Ryerson's cleverly ducking head. He kept to lightning moves on his feet; he was never where Homer thought he would be and Homer missed many potentially stunning blows. Ryerson lifted him after each miss with a thudding uppercut or jarred him with a violent jab at Homer's rock-hard midsection.

Like a grizzly or a buffalo bull, Homer would take a lot of punishment before he went down.

Wading in again, Ryerson threw a long hard looping left that caught Homer on the jaw and at last dropped him on the floor to lie like a dead man; Homer's labored breath whistled through his teeth.

"You kilt him, Rollins!" a voice screeched from out of the crowd as Ryerson danced to bolster his sagging stamina and waited to see if Homer would stay down for good.

The brute struggled to lift himself on hands and knees, shaking his head to clear the cobwebs. Homer's blood splattered in the dust of the bunkhouse floor. Then he was up, more enraged than before, and lunged back with a roar at Ryerson who was nearly played out himself with agony and exhaustion.

The interlude on the floor was all Homer needed. Bellowing like a wounded elk, he weaved in at Ryerson with strength flowing back into him. Ryerson's face was grimly set as he sidestepped Homer's renewed charge.

As Homer neared him, Ryerson summoned the energy of every pound of his lean form to send it zooming along his muscles as he lashed out to take Homer square on the bridge of his nose, shattering it like a brittle chicken bone. Blood from his nostrils gushed over his upper lip and down his chin; Homer's face was a battered, bloodied mess.

Now Homer seemed to stand there, incapable of swinging his fists, incapable of being floored, still daring Ryerson to put him down. Dazed himself, but determined to the end, Ryerson settled on his heels to punch at the face and to plow both fists violently into Homer's gut.

Ryerson's arms and legs were heavy as stone. The two stood, squared off; Homer was blinded and battered into insensibility but refused to fall. Ryerson weaved on his feet, too, knowing he'd won, but sensing little gratification in the victory and wishing to Christ Homer would be finished soon.

Ryerson mustered the strength to draw back and cock his right arm and clench a supremely aching fist one more time. He stood there a long moment, searching for the strength to pour into his arm for the final, telling blow.

Homer's hands came up, stubby fingers extended, groping in his blindness for a grip on Ryerson's throat. Ryerson's last arcing swing came out from behind and beside him as Homer caught hold of Ryerson's shirt collar.

In a movement that seemed to take forever, Ryerson's blow whipped in as Homer tugged at his shirt. Ryerson's final desperate haymaker caught the big man on the left cheekbone and eye.

Most of the front of Ryerson's shirt ripped away from him as the blow stiffened Homer and he reeled away from Ryerson to fall over on his back with his buck-tooth mouth slack. Blood oozed from his mouth and nose. Homer's open, glazing, unconscious eyes stared up at the bunkhouse rafters.

In the action as Ryerson's shirt tore, something silver spun past Ryerson's blurred vision to clatter on the floor. Ryerson swayed back, gulping for air, his legs none too steady.

"Jumpin' Jesus!" a voice near him shrieked into his dimming consciousness. "The son of a bitch is carryin' a badge!"

Ryerson turned stiff with shock; he'd forgotten the badge in his shirt pocket.

From behind him Ryerson heard the sinister, metallic chatter as a cartridge was jacked into the breech of a Winchester.

· 9 ·

To Ryerson's total astonishment, faces fell in fear among the cowhands crowding close to the inert Homer. Wide-eyed, they shrank back farther into the murky bunkhouse gloom.

The glint of the blued barrel and magazine tube of a Winchester poked past him, and as he looked, Clute appeared in his side vision, holding the menacing rifle on Doan's crewmen.

"Clute!" somebody yelled out of the crowd. "What the hell's the matter with you? He's a damned lawman!"

"Ya'all just keep back!" Clute commanded. "Kenny! Pick up your badge. We're going out of here. You fellas back off."

"You're out of your head, Clute," a voice called from out of the darkened faces. Still none of them challenged Clute's trigger finger. "Doan'll hunt you down and kill you."

No one in the room was more surprised than Cole Ryerson. In the urgency of the moment, his pain and exhaustion from the fight with Homer was set aside.

"Get your weapon and your gear, Kenny," Clute commanded coolly, a distinct glint of determination in his old eyes. "Then catch up my bedroll and warbag."

Still bewildered at the astounding turn of events, Ryerson

deftly buckled on his Navy, assembled his gear, and, with Clute waving back the crowd with the Winchester, pulled the old-timer's outfit together.

Holding the Winchester straight out, Clute barked his commands.

"Kenny, you get on down to the corral and saddle your horse and the only paint that's in there. That's mine. I'll make sure these fellas stay inside till we've had a head start."

Clute's lever-action continued to hold off the dumb-founded cowboys. Behind them, as Ryerson and Clute backed through the bunkhouse, Ryerson heard Homer's groan and saw his hands come up slowly toward his battered head.

"Boys," Clute called loudly, "I'm goin' out and closin' the door. I'll be out there while Kenny's down getting our mounts. I see a flicker of movement around the door or windows and you'll be saying sad words over somebody in the mornin'."

Ryerson had no time to question Clute. The fat was in the fire and smoking. He only knew that Clute was setting them up for a hell-bent ride to freedom down the canyon in the pitch dark. Questions would have to come later.

Outside the full moon had retreated behind a cloud bank; it was hard even to see where he put his feet.

"Go!" Clute roared. "Till we get out of that canyon, I'm calling the shots. Now git!"

As he hurried toward the horse pen, Ryerson momentarily wondered about Doan. He hoped the rustler chief was stupefied by his day's drinking or aware only of the charms of Miss Ruby Montez just now.

With difficulty and a waste of precious seconds, he singled out Rusty in the milling remuda and got him saddled and bridled. Diffused moonlight briefly broke through the gauze-like fringe of clouds and he spied the pinto; the horse turned its head and surveyed the man coming toward him, but without alarm.

Commanding Rusty to stay put, Ryerson grabbed for a nearby saddle and bridle and swiftly rigged Clute's horse. Almost as fast, he tied their bedrolls and gear behind the cantles.

A short distance away he could see Clute through the dark, a stiff resolute shape against the moonlight, Winchester at the ready, his attention fused on the bunkhouse door and windows. Ryerson quickly led their mounts down to him.

Before they mounted up, Clute cupped his hand beside his mouth to speak softly in Ryerson's ear. "When we hit the saddle, they'll come boilin' out here, guns blazing. They'll be blinded a bit from the light and as dark as it is, they'll be blasting away at shadows."

"Yeah," Ryerson said.

"Sandy's down the canyon on guard and I know where. He'll hear some shootin' and I've got a story all fixed up, so let me do the talking."

"You're in charge, amigo," Ryerson whispered.

"You in shape to ride, son? That bastard lambasted the tar out of you."

"Well, let's say I'm not about to go back in there and go to bed."

"Then we're off like a calvary charge at Newtonia!"

They hit their saddles and spurred out at a dead run across the yard toward the cleft in the surrounding hills. Their thundering hoofbeats drowned out the roar of angry cowboys filling the night behind them. All hell broke loose back there. Ryerson concentrated on using what moonlight there was to guide his horse safely. This was sure no time for a spill.

Guns roared from the ranch yard but the bullets twanged harmlessly through the dark around them. True to Clute's word, none of the cowboys could see well enough to take careful aim. Their rifles spewed lead recklessly.

Ryerson bent low over the roan's neck and rode for his

life. The shreds of his torn shirt flapped around his bare arms and shoulders.

Once in the canyon, they had to slow their pell-mell pace because of the precarious footing for the horses. At least gunsights couldn't find them. When they were near the sharp turn in the canyon and the sentry's outpost where Ryerson had been challenged, Clute held up his hand for silence.

"Sandy!"

A voice broke out of the black stillness. "Yeah! What the hell's going on? I heard shootin'."

"It's me, Clute, and one of the boys."

"What's up?"

"They want you back there. The boys got to drinking and got rowdy. There was a fracas and gunplay. Doan's bad hurt. We figure them nesters got a doctor in town. We're ridin' for him."

"Anybody else get hurt, Clute?"

"Homer's not in very good shape. We got to ride. See you in the mornin', Sandy." Ryerson grinned in the dark in amusement at Clute's veiled reference to Homer's condition.

As the two of them resumed their way down the trail, Ryerson heard Sandy scrambling down from his perch to hunt up his horse.

"Let's ride, amigo," the old-timer beside him said softly. "We'll talk when we're out on the flats." In the dark, their horses leaped down the steep drop of canyon.

When they finally hit the low ground and wormed their difficult way out of the thicket, starlight lay pale on the desert; the moon had set. Night's thin chill clung to the land.

Around them the broad valley was a dull pewter-colored bed under the night sky. Out of it, down close to the land, came the soft rustle of wind-stirred grass. Nearby clumps of sage, bulkier mesquite bushes, and the far-off hills were but black-clotted reminders of their daytime shapes.

Clute was the first to speak. "We can slow up. Doan won't mount a chase tonight. Lost too much time. Maybe Doan figured Sandy might drill us as we came by."

"You foxed old Sandy in pretty good shape."

"Believe I did at that," Clute gloated.

"Let's stop and I'll get into my other shirt. This one leaves a little to be desired."

"Yeah, you don't exactly look togged out for a cotillion." Clute leaned off his horse as Ryerson rummaged through his warbag. "Doan'll know fast enough you're a lawman."

"What'll he do?"

"Hard to say. He's got a lot invested in this country. He also knows you could bring in a militia against him and his goose would be cooked. But that'd take weeks maybe. So he's savvy enough to take plenty of time with his decisions. Don't figure Doan to bull into something without a lot of consideration."

"All right, Clute," Ryerson said, mounting up again. "Out with it. What gigged you to stand up for me like that?"

"First, where we headed?"

"To Berdan. To alert them. And to get answers to a hell of a lot of questions."

"Then let me answer yours. You may have had Doan buffaloed, but not me. I been around too long, son. A whole lot of things were done and said that told me you were too decent to have ridden the owlhoot trail with the likes of Roy Chalmers. Then you fought Homer too clean. I knew that fight was coming after you faced up to Doan when they dragged that outlander in. I knew I'd get your measure when you squared off with Homer. That's why I went and stood away from the rest."

"But why stick your neck out?" The question turned Clute silent again.

The jolt of Rusty's walk over uneven ground drove spasms of pain into muscles and bones bruised in the fight. Occasionally Ryerson shifted Rusty's reins into his right hand to ease tense, aching knuckles and finger and wrist joints. But there was still a euphoria in being out here, away from his short stay in Doan's evil domain; it had not been an easy, relaxed time.

At least he could balance his freedom and being in one piece against his discomfort. Even the chill night air had a fresh, free zest. Ryerson felt good despite his exhaustion and aches, though there were still a lot of unanswered questions about the uncommon ally who rode beside him.

"It's a fine night, ain't it, Kenny?" Clute said, a strange, relieved-sounding tone in his voice.

"Free air has a tang all its own, Clute," Ryerson responded, giving Clute whatever time he needed as they jogged quietly through the starlit, solemn night toward Berdan. They distanced themselves from Doan and it seemed evident that the rustler-boss wasn't coming after them . . . yet.

Doan would be a menace as long as Ryerson stayed in the Ramirez Plateau country.

"With me, maybe it's like smelling it free for the first time in a long while," Clute said with a kind of unabashed relief. Another deep silence passed between them and Ryerson guessed Clute was rebuilding the past in his head.

"I lived in Lawrence—that's in Kansas—for twenty years before the war. Came out from New York State before I was twenty. Was a carpenter. Then for a time I was a storekeeper, a decent man, law-abiding, God-fearing. Married and had a boy. He was fifteen when the war came along, too young for service and too young to be left alone. But I believed in my country and my new state and what it stood for. When they called for volunteers, I told my son to look after the store and his mother. I went over to Fort Leavenworth and enlisted for three years."

Clute turned silent again; Ryerson said nothing, allowing Clute room to mull his thoughts before proceeding.

"Well, we did some fighting. Then Quantrill sacked Lawrence . . ."

"I met Quantrill once," Ryerson interrupted. "Never approved of him."

Clute scarcely heard him. "Matthew Mills was sixteen years old. Quantrill's guerrillas shot him down in cold blood, Kenny." Clute said it with a catch in his voice.

"God, I'm sorry, Clute."

"I was away. Didn't know it for eight months." Clute's voice wavered. "My home and my store were burned to the ground. First his mother, bless her soul, lost her mind and three months later the shock and my not being there to support her in her grief . . . well, it killed her."

Ryerson was momentarily reminded of the grief of Sam and Nora Carson. In his own life was the bitter loss of his best friend who died in battle saving Ryerson's life, and his sadness over his unfulfilled love for Dan Sturgis's widow. "I'm awfully sorry, Clute," he mumbled.

"Yeah," Clute said with a choked sigh.

"Mills, you said. That your last name?"

"Yeah. Mills. Clute Mills."

"You must've figured by now my name's not Kenny Rollins."

"Yeah. Guess so." Clute spoke like a man coming awake. "Haven't had much time to think. Who are you?"

"The name's Cole Ryerson. Federal marshal representing Judge Isaac Winfield. You may have heard of me as Boot Hill Cole."

Clute looked at him with widened eyes. "Boot Hill Cole! Swear to God? Guess I saved a pretty important lawman from that gang up the canyon."

"Whatever my reputation, I'm mightily obliged, Clute."

Clute turned silent again and they rode several minutes through the dull-silver prairie night before he spoke. "When I learned what happened in Lawrence, and to my family, I guess I went kind of crazy. Had my nose in a jug a lot of the time. Stood a lot of company punishment, court-martialed and reduced in rank once. For a time I wanted to kill anything that rode under the same flag as William Clarke Quantrill. Then I got hit at Newtonia and when I was back on my feet, they turned me loose. Surgeon's certificate of disability."

"After Newtonia?" Ryerson asked.

"Yeah," Clute responded. "But I was still fighting. Fighting a heartless world, I guess. Maybe I was fighting myself . . . in my head . . . feeling responsible . . . guilty maybe . . . for not looking after things better. I bummed around the West, maybe looking for another bullet to do what that Reb Minie ball did only a half a job of. I suppose I tried like hell to see if the hootch would do it, too. I rode with a lot of owlhoot gangs. Soon after all that I met up with Doan here some years back. I was too old to keep fightin'. He kept me on at the place—oh, I did my share of the work—and then yesterday you walked in."

"You had a good thing going. I still don't see why you took my side in the face of such uneven odds. Though I'm glad you did."

Clute rode in silence more minutes, probably still reflecting on the past.

"Sometimes, Kenny—I mean, Cole—sometimes a man runs smack-dab up against a situation he can't stay out of. Like you did against Doan and Homer and that stranger. I had to take sides. Couldn't see standin' by and watching you take it alone. Didn't really have time to think it over, though. I told you once I was a decent man. Still think like one in spite of everything bad I've done. But for the first time in a long time, I believed what I was doing was right."

"Regardless of the consequences?"

"Regardless of the consequences . . . until just now."

"What do you mean by that?"

"I've run with outlaws, Cole. That makes me an outlaw. I've had time to think about it now a little . . . since we've been riding."

"What?"

"I want to ride back with you when you're done here. Help you till then. I want to appear before Judge Winfield, tell him how I've lived, what I've done. And, by God, take what I've got coming."

"When he hears what you did tonight, I'm sure he'll deal gently with you, Clute."

"I ain't asking no favors." A familiar growl was in Clute's voice and Ryerson felt his heart lift a bit in his chest. The old owlhoot had grit.

Dawn glorified the sprawling clouds of night in tones of pink, salmon, and rose. A bland early warmth promised heat by midday when Clute and Ryerson paused on the hilltop overlooking Sam Carson's spread.

"This time I'm calling the shots, Clute," Ryerson said as they paused on the knoll before riding down. "Did you ever know, or meet Sam Carson? Or see him?"

"Never seen any of the nesters, Cole. My work kept me mostly around the ranch. I think you know Doan shot one of 'em."

"That's why I'm here. Among other things."

"Yeah," Clute said, almost abruptly.

"The killings. You say Doan killed one?"

"Yeah, an old-timer. Then rustled some of the man's herd."

"Only one killing, eh?"

"All I heard of in this latest to-do."

"You never heard of them killing a young man?"

"Huh-uh. Why?"

"Sam Carson's boy has been missing since a few days after that rancher was shot."

Clute looked Ryerson straight in the eye. "I don't know whose boy he is, but Doan and some of the men dragged in a youngster late one night. They'd been to town. I know there's some kind of deal going on, but nobody around there is saying much. Doan's close, sometimes, about his dealings."

"Wait a minute!" Ryerson rasped in sudden awareness. "Not the man in the attic?"

"The very one. Course, you know, now there's two of 'em up there."

"The younger one would have to be Jim Carson! I was so busy playing Kenny Rollins that it didn't occur to me it could have been Jim Carson!" Thoughts ricocheted through Ryerson's mind like gravel flung on a tin roof.

"Never heard the lad's name, if any of the boys knew it."

Ryerson collected himself, and took a deep breath. Things were happening almost too fast to respond to appropriately. He spoke softly to Clute.

"For the time being, let me do the talking when we get down there with the Carsons. If it is Jim back there, he's still not out of danger. I want to pick the right time and conditions to open it up with Sam Carson."

As they watched, the back door of the house opened from the kitchen and Sam Carson stepped into the yard, shading his eyes with his hand against the morning sun to make out the riders on the nearby hilltop.

"That Carson?" Clute asked.

"Yeah. We'd best get down there." They urged their horses off the knoll.

"Kenny!" Sam yelled as they rode across the ranch yard toward him. "Glad you're back. Any news?"

"Plenty, Sam, plenty."

"Come on in. Had breakfast? Who's your friend?"

"No to the first question and if that's an invitation, yes. As to the second, this is Clute Mills, a rider I picked up along the way, and he's been helping me out."

"Nora and Mrs. Douglas are just about to put the food on the table. Come on in. Mr. Mills, come on along."

As Ryerson and Clute got down and prepared to tie up their horses, a woman's voice, familiar to Ryerson, came from the open back door.

"Mr. Carson, your wife says to come in to eat."

Ryerson looked up at the comely features of pretty

Melissa Douglas in the doorway and he froze, wide-eyed. His astonishment was almost greater than when Clute stepped in to rescue him.

The eyes, the mouth, and the facial structure were nearly identical. He recalled it instantly; wondering why the face of the stranger at Doan's was so familiar and yet so perplexing.

My God, Ryerson thought, that stranger is Melissa Douglas's father!

· 10 ·

Ryerson watched Clute clump eagerly up the two crude plank steps to the stoop and into Nora Carson's kitchen. As Sam Carson moved to follow Clute, Ryerson reached out and dropped a mild, restraining grip on Sam's forearm.

"As far as the folks in there know, Sam, I'm still Kenny Rollins. Clute knows better."

Sam Carson's eyes were bright with anticipation. "You know anything, Cole? About our Jimmy?"

"Maybe. I'd as leave for now go in and keep things cheerful and light. You and I and Clute can go out to the barn right after we eat."

"Is Jim all right?"

"I'd rather wait and give you the details later, Sam. Trust me. For now, let me say I think he's all right." Things were so dicey out at the Doan place that Ryerson wouldn't commit himself further to Sam Carson.

Sam sighed deeply, and his remark made Ryerson cringe thinking he'd been too optimistic. "Thank God! That's what I needed. All right. I'll go along with you. We'll talk later."

Over their meal, abundant and spread out on the Carsons' dining table with all the leaves in to accommodate the crowd, Ryerson's eyes roved the faces around him. He knew

109

he had both encouraging and discouraging words for all of them later on.

He had especially surprising and distressing news for the Douglas family.

As he ate, he found it difficult to look at Sam Carson, who watched him expectantly each time Ryerson glanced his way. Ryerson's eyes also frequently sought out the face of Melissa Douglas.

The brew was thickening too much and too fast for his taste.

Sam Carson had said that George Douglas had headed west to scout out a new homesite for his family after foreclosure of his Berdan ranch claim. He continued studying Melissa's face while he mowed away a cowboy's breakfast of eggs, ham, and fried potatoes; her expression told him something else.

Her eyes, for anyone shrewd enough to see, spoke of a young woman in anguish, or at least suffering grave concern. It was there, too, in the sad set of her pretty mouth and the barely perceptible sag in her normally strong chin.

Melissa's concern for young Jim Carson, Ryerson thought, went a great deal deeper than merely that of a good friend; she grieved for a love lost or threatened; a love that, because of social conventions, had not been—or couldn't be—fully expressed.

Ryerson cut a chunk of thick, sunny egg yolk with the side of his fork; in scooping it up, he skewered a tender disk of fried potato. He slipped the tasty morsel into his mouth behind pursed lips, letting his mind roam free on the past and on personal tragedy. Watching Melissa and thinking of her feelings for Jim Carson, he remembered the one time he had known love and lost it. Within a year he also lost the best friend he ever had; his grief was compounded by the fact that Dan Sturgis was the husband of Ryerson's first true love.

The gleaming upturned tines of the dinner fork in his hand resembled too much the gallant sweeping curve of a cavalry saber. Clute's talk the night before of the days of combat had brought the ugliness rushing back, rasping emotional scar tissue still tender despite years that should have effected a healing. The grief in Melissa's eyes only reinforced the poignant sadness building inside him that he had managed—for a long time—to keep behind a brick wall of stoicism and self-reliance.

Dan Sturgis was of easy smile and disposition; tight waves of red hair added to his amiable appeal. Maybe, Ryerson mused, munching his breakfast, Jubal Doan's brick top and wire-brush mustache of red had helped bring the past sweeping back like a bitter flood. Red-haired men had always reminded him, sadly, of Sturgis.

A fleeting hint of pain in the eyes of Doan's woman Ruby had also made him think of Ruth. His mind turned to St. Louis, May, 1862.

The balminess of a Missouri spring night was complemented by their joking and companionship under the spread of a full moon on the eve of Dan's wedding. The dim coolness was delicious inside the church next morning as he and Sturgis, both standing tall in Confederate cavalry gray with gold piping, waited expectantly and watched as Ruth came down the aisle.

Soft breezes through tipped-open stained glass windows brought the cloying scents of spring blossoms to add to an intoxication heightened by soft, traditional organ music. Ryerson felt clean and militarily crisp, proud, vital, and jubilant. So much joy swelled in him that he found it hard to breathe.

Ryerson, the happy loser, stood up for Dan when his comrade-in-arms wed the only woman Ryerson had ever loved. Loved her so much, so completely, that when she confessed her intention to wed Dan Sturgis, Cole Ryerson took time to set his mind in order. Deciding that happiness for the two people he cared most about was preferable to losing both of them completely, Ryerson took a step backward, out of the picture, except as a friend to Dan as well as to Ruth. For Cole Ryerson, it was a time of intense understanding. And love.

Four days later, Captains Ryerson and Sturgis rode west to rejoin Brigadier General Joseph O. Shelby—the redoubtable Jo—and his command under Major General Sterling Price and coming campaigns in Missouri and Arkansas.

Helena, Arkansas, July 4, 1863.

Eyes red-rimmed and aching from sleeplessness, exhaustion, and the dust of cavalry combat, Ryerson rode in the early morning light along the ranks of his command. The grimy faces he saw under gray kepis were also grim. His own stamina flagging, he encouraged them with words of discipline and valor, mentally girding them for the combat to come, his own naked saber carried blade down along his right stirrup. He reined around then to face the enemy position. Price's orders: Take Graveyard Hill.

What a hell of a name! Ryerson thought years later at the Carsons' breakfast table. Too dismally prophetic.

Down the straight gray regimental rank, cavalry chargers were held by riders in a virtual posture of attention. Through the mists of dawn, twenty yards down the line, Dan Sturgis, like Ryerson a few paces ahead of his mounted troop, faced the enemy with determination; as their eyes met, Sturgis brought up his saber to touch it to the black visor of his kepi in a salute of comradeship. Swelling with their rare kinship and Dan's strong grin, Ryerson easily swung up his own steel-gray blade to return the gesture. And the grin. Behind him, a horse stamped and whickered in nervousness or impatience; Ryerson swung his head around to glower at the trooper's inability to keep his steed controlled.

Leading a cloud of dust, hooves thundering, Price's courier slid to a stop beside Shelby, an imposing tower of dusty gray uniform and chest-length dark beard. Shelby checked the lines of his brigade and waved his saber. Forward! At the gallop! Horses leaped and bellowed. The screech of Rebel yells rose behind Ryerson. His lust for combat suddenly overwhelming his fatigue, Ryerson spurred his horse forward as the crest of Graveyard Hill sprouted a field of ominous dark-blue forms of Federal cavalry pouring down the slope like a tide.

In what seemed seconds, the mounted combatants were engaged with thunderous impact. In the swirls of dust, pistol shots and shouts rang out, mixing with the whacks of sabers and the shrieks of men and horses. In the melee, Ryerson whipsawed his gray, seeking blue-uniformed targets for his blade as he screamed encouragement and orders to his command. "Charge! Take the hill!" Parry! Thrust! Fend off the enemy swordsmen.

From ahead of him, Ryerson heard the shout of a familiar voice; Dan Sturgis riding straight for him out of the golden haze of dust, arm locked, saber extended in the thrust position. "Behind you!" Dan screamed. Seeing it now, in agonizing slow motion, Ryerson cranked his head around as an enemy rider bore down on him, saber poised for the thrust at Ryerson's back. The Yankee deflected his aim as Dan Sturgis pounded past, the two riders on collision course. On impact, Sturgis's blade lanced through the enemy's midsection as, with horrified eyes, Ryerson saw the gory tip of the other's saber emerge out the back of Dan's gray tunic. The two plummeted from their saddles, fists frozen around their saber hilts, each impaled on the other's blade.

Ryerson's attention was diverted by the frenzy of combat and the need to hasten his unit's valiant advance up Graveyard Hill; at ten in the morning by Ryerson's watch Graveyard Hill was secured by troops under Price and Shelby. Other Confederate forces were not as successful in other salients; at half past ten Price obeyed the order to withdraw. An exhausted Ryerson reluctantly commanded his troops to retreat.

In the confusion that followed the early-morning battle and subsequent Confederate withdrawal, Ryerson, to his eternal dismay, was unable to find Dan Sturgis's corpse and pay a comrade's final respects. Ryerson rode away from the Helena battle blinded by grief.

Around him, the breakfast table chatter was good-natured and lively. Maybe too much so. Beneath it, Ryerson perceived, lingered an undertone of great care and concern—on the part of all those around the table. Shattered dreams, he had learned from his own bitter experiences, were hard to mask under forced cheerfulness, but with the pluck of their kind, the Carsons and the Douglases tried very hard.

It struck him then that all of them were somehow being cheerful for the benefit of others and the sum total was that they were weathering their mutual travail.

That was what, he thought, close friends and family were all about. Pillars to lean against, shoulders to cry on when the going got rough. He himself had no family left that he could recall; the transient nature of his work provided him few lasting friends. His sources of strength and support had always come from within.

Ryerson also studied the face of seventeen-year-old Vic Douglas who, to Ryerson's near amusement, darted furtive looks across the breakfast table at Penny Carson. The sap of vigorous young manhood without doubt ran warm in Vic's veins. Ryerson sensed Vic harbored sweet thoughts for the young daughter of his host family.

The young woman also regarded Vic pleasantly, though shy and guarded; another love-match a-borning, Ryerson thought. It was a happy prospect in the face of all the evil forces at work in the lives of these people.

Sam Carson finished his breakfast and got up abruptly, almost too eagerly to suit Ryerson. Sam was anxious to get to the barn and the details of Ryerson's findings. Ryerson hoped nothing alarming would telegraph to the women.

"Kenny's got something to tell me about his trip out into the prairie," Sam announced. "Let's us men go down to the barn so the ladies can get their housework done."

Ryerson quickly scraped up the balance of his breakfast shreds with his fork, hurriedly crammed it into his mouth, and gulped.

Clute was on his feet almost as fast as Sam Carson, reaching behind him for his hat on a wall peg. "Miz Carson," Clute said, "I want to thank you ladies for that fine, home-cooked breakfast. I hope you'll think up some chores I can help out with by way of showing my gratitude."

Nora Carson fairly beamed. "Thank you, Mr. Mills, but no need for that. It was a pleasure having you."

For Ryerson, it was time to take command. "Clute, come on down to the stable with Sam and me." He looked at Vic Douglas and Rick Carson eyeing him. "If it's all the same to you, Sam, I'd like your boy Rick and Vic Douglas there to be in on it too."

Sam Carson looked at Ryerson quizzically and shrugged. "Let's go then."

"Ladies," Ryerson said, getting up, as if to beg their leave.

"You men go along, Mr. Ryerson," Nora Carson said. "There's nothing worse than having men underfoot when a woman's trying to get her kitchen work done."

Ryerson and Carson led Clute and the two young men across the hard-packed ranch yard to the barn-like stable.

"Let's go out back," Ryerson said as the five of them started through the tall and wide stable door toward the horse stalls. "I don't know about you fellas but after a fine breakfast like that, I need a smoke. And I make it a practice never to smoke in another man's stable. Don't need to be responsible for a fire."

In the cool morning shade behind the stable, Ryerson crouched and hauled out his makin's, rolled one and handed the sack to Clute. The others hunkered down in a crude circle.

When Clute had built his smoke, he passed the cotton tobacco sack to Rick Carson. Rick held the pouch a moment, looked suspiciously across at his father and studied his expression as though wondering what he'd say if he rolled a smoke. He thought better of it and reached past Vic to hand the sack to his father.

"Never use them," Sam said, offering the sack back to Ryerson.

Ryerson held his glowing cigarette in his lips, eyes squinted against the curl of smoke along his cheek. He picked up a stick thoughtfully and traced a few random lines in the dirt as he thought how to open up to his subject. At last, he tossed down the stick and cleared his throat.

He looked around at the men circling him.

"I wanted Vic Douglas in on this because he's the man of that family for now. Rick's got a stake in this, too. I hope you understand, Sam."

"You've got your reasons, I suppose. Get on with it."

Ryerson tried not to find antagonism in Sam's words but it was there.

"First off, boys, my name's not Kenny Rollins. I'm a Federal marshal. Cole Ryerson. Some people know me as Boot Hill Cole, but I'm not much of a hand to particularly brag on it."

Vic and Rick's eyes met and their eyebrows arched; they'd heard plenty about Boot Hill Cole Ryerson.

"I came in here to look into the murder of Mr. Moseley. I guess both of you knew him."

Rick answered for both of them, and his tone was reverent. "Very well, Mr. Ryerson."

"I'm also here to find out what happened to Rick's brother, Jim. And to look into whatever happened to cause Mr. Douglas to lose his land claim."

Ryerson looked at Sam Carson a long moment before continuing. "Don't know how to begin this, Sam. Clute here rode with Doan but last night he came to my aid and helped me escape. I've him to thank for my life."

He noted Sam Carson eyeing him suspiciously.

Ryerson looked Sam in the eye, but spoke to all. "As far as

I'm concerned, Clute's past is bygones. But he knows just about everything about Doan."

"What about our Jimmy?" Carson asked, a bright eagerness replacing the questioning look.

"I guess something went on in town the same night Jim disappeared. Clute here isn't privy to the details, but it's quite evident that your Jim—if it's him—is being kept prisoner in a big attic at Doan's house."

"Thank God!" Carson exulted. "Our prayers are answered."

Ryerson looked quickly at Rick Carson and Vic Douglas. Their eyes were locked on each other's, but saying nothing. Ryerson interpreted their expressions as less jubilant than the elder Carson's. Both young men appeared to have a more realistic reaction; more aware of the hazards attached to Ryerson's revelation.

"What do we do, Cole?" Sam asked. "How can we get Jim out of there?"

Ryerson paused long enough to stare at Carson several moments before responding. "By moving very, very slowly, Sam. There's a lot more needing to be considered. The whole thing gets very, very sticky."

"Looks cut and dried to me," Sam said. "We get up an armed force of Berdan men—our settlers—deputized by you and ride out there and get him."

Ryerson turned loose a mildly emphatic tone. "I said we proceed very, very slowly, Sam."

"You'd best listen to the marshal, Mr. Carson," Clute added.

Despite Sam Carson's very apparent impatience, Ryerson paused again to study the faces watching him. "I'm going to ask Clute what will seem a very mysterious question."

Sam Carson's anxieties were still written all over his face.

"Clute," Ryerson asked, "did you get a good look at everybody at the breakfast table just now?"

Clute studied Ryerson a long moment and abruptly said, "Yup."

"Anything come to your mind?"

"Yup."

"Miss Douglas?"

"Yup."

"You thinking what I'm thinking?"

"Yup."

Impatient insistence rang in Sam Carson's tone. "All right, Ryerson! What's this all about? You're evading the issue! Why do you keep dragging this out?"

Ryerson's eyes narrowed on Sam Carson. "Sam, I've been trying to ask you since I rode in here this morning to please bear with me. I was nearly killed out there last night. We're dealing with a vicious man in charge of a pack of equally savage men. No one wants your son out of there more than I do. But we've got to take it one step at a time." Ryerson's "one step at a time" was uttered with an emphatic pause between each word.

"Get on with it," Carson said, "but for Lord's sake don't leave me hanging. I've got to get my son out of harm's way!"

"There may be even more to it than that. Vic?"

Young Douglas looked up at him intently, questioning with his eyes.

"Your sister Melissa. Does she resemble your father?"

"Spittin' image, Mr. Ryerson. Most folks notice it right off."

"Does he have a couple of fingertips missing on one hand? And a nose that looks broken?"

All eyes locked on Ryerson. Vic Douglas's face was ashen. "Yessir. He does."

"That clinches it, Clute," Ryerson said. "Sam, Doan has another prisoner out there. They dragged him in last evening. I don't think George Douglas is out west hunting a new homesite. I believe he doubled back to get even with Doan and nearly got himself killed. Would've if I hadn't been there to step in."

"Daddy!" Vic cried, his face and eyes mirroring his shock.

"Easy, Vic," Ryerson said. "Everything's going to be all

118

right. Sam, that's why I wanted these young men to hear me out, too. We've got a first-class crisis on our hands."

The now-unpredictable Sam Carson leaped to his feet. "Our Jimmy and George Douglas out there? We'll call the ranchers together with their guns! We'll storm the place. Got to get them out of there!"

"Sam!" Ryerson called loudly, standing up himself. "Set down! We go bulling into things like that and we'll wind up with your son and Vic's dad dead and God knows how many ranchers who know little or nothing about fighting."

"You can organize them, Cole, drill them."

"How long would that take, Sam?"

Carson regarded Ryerson suspiciously again. "You were out there. You saw Jim, at least knew Doan had a prisoner, and you should have put two and two together. You made no move to rescue him or George Douglas. But you rode out with this man, this Clute, one of Doan's outlaws."

Rick Carson spoke up. "Dad, calm down. You're not even sounding rational. Mr. Ryerson here is as concerned as we are about getting Jim and Mr. Douglas out safely. He's doing the best he can."

Sam Carson looked from his crouching son to Ryerson standing across from him. Sam regarded Ryerson a long time, the anger draining from his face. The look of anxiety remained. "I guess you got to forgive me, Cole. You can't imagine what the strain of these past weeks and months can do to a man."

"I *can* imagine." Ryerson glanced at Clute and saw him studying Rick and then Vic, a sadness prominent in his eyes; Ryerson was certain he was thinking about his own dead son and wondering if he'd have turned out like these two fine young men.

Sam Carson slid back into his crouch around the circle again and Ryerson followed suit. "Now," Ryerson said. "We go in there with a gang of armed ranchers all horns and rattles and the least we can expect is that Doan will use Jim and George Douglas as human shields to buy his way past us

119

to freedom while we stand by helplessly with our fingers in our . . . mouths. That method of approach simply won't work."

"I understand that now." Sam's tone was soft, resigned. "You must have some other kind of plan."

"Somethin's hatching. I don't think trying to bargain with Doan would work. His freedom for Jim and Douglas. In that kind of deal he's holding all the cards, knows that once he turned them over to me that I'd hound him to his dying day. He'd never agree to the terms. The only other way to pull it off is stealth. Just Clute and me."

"No, too much chance of your getting caught with all Doan's men around. Then all four of you would be dead. Naw, Ryerson, that don't scour," Sam said.

"If Doan and his owlhoot army were suddenly called away, we wouldn't have that much threat."

"How'll you do that?"

"That's why I want Rick and Vic to go along."

"These boys?" Sam countered, aghast. "You're out of your mind, Ryerson!"

"Sam," Ryerson said, "you're having a lot of trouble finding much faith in my methods lately."

Sam Carson's face now turned livid. "You can't be serious in thinking of declining an armed force of a goodly number of our ranchers in favor of using these young men on some harebrained night-time attack on Doan's gunslingers?"

"Well, not that exactly. But I can use them in my scheme and I can almost guarantee that their safety and welfare won't be threatened in the least. And they may have an adventure to tell their grandchildren about."

"Poppycock!" Sam Carson's outburst was like an explosion. Again he stood up. "Exactly how do you propose, Mr. Ryerson, to balance these boys' lives against a cold-blooded killer like Doan and those of his stripe?"

"Well, I'll tell you, we aren't exactly goin' skylarking like you seem to suggest. This is dead serious business, rescuing one of their brothers and the other, his father. Clute, let me ask you something."

Clute suddenly showed considerable interest.

"If we could get back in there, could we get up on the rimrock above Doan's house? I mean in the dark, unsuspected?"

"Tough, but it could be done."

"And if some ruse was managed to send Doan and most of his boys down the canyon, could we get onto his roof and then drop a rope down to the attic window?"

"You're talking about risky business, Cole. Risky business."

"I know that. You know anything in this life that's easy, Clute?"

"I could think of a few. This ain't one of 'em."

"We're working on a scheme to snatch those two men out from under Jubal Doan's nose. Maybe I don't have every step mapped out. I'm doping out the overall plan, the framework."

The eyes of the young Carson and Douglas men as well as of Sam Carson were on Ryerson and Clute. Clute tried to plumb Ryerson's thinking.

"You're figuring, Cole, on havin' these boys do something down the canyon that'll send Doan and the crew skallyhootin' down that way. That'll leave the ranch unguarded so you and I can get in and get those two jaspers out with their scalps."

"You're a jump or two ahead of me, Clute, but right. After we leave them down in the thicket, in the dark, these boys'll wait an appropriate time before they set fire to the brush and run around shooting off their rifles, maybe even blow up some containers of powder, anything to raise a ruckus. Then they'll hightail it off into the dark long before Doan gets there to find out what's going on."

Again Clute tried to anticipate Ryerson's thinking out loud.

"You're figuring Doan will be skittish anyway after what happened last night and none of Doan's boys'll want to be left out. Everybody'll go tearin' off down that way, leaving the ranch clear for us to make the rescue."

"You thinkin' they won't, Clute?"

"If Doan sees he's attacked, there's not a man in that outfit that'd miss chargin' down that canyon to get into a good scrap."

"You think the boys here firing the thicket and making some explosions and rifle fire would do the trick, Clute?"

"After last night, Doan'll shoot at anything that moves. I don't think he'll figure it's a trick right off. Not until he gets down there."

"And just to reassure Sam here, how long do you think it will take for Doan's boys to get organized and get down there, especially if we pull it off after midnight."

"They'll be fallin' all over one another getting their guns and their gear and roundin' up their mounts." Clute chuckled. "Dang, how I'd like to be there to see that! I'd bet it takes 'em an easy twenty minutes. Half of an hour would be more like it."

"Plenty of time for Rick and Vic here to get a head start on losing themselves in the night."

"One thing I hadn't thought of, Cole. If you fire that thicket, that'll hold Doan up too, and some additional powder charges set to go off later—maybe when the fire gets to it—will give these boys plenty of time to almost get home before Doan realizes he's been taken in."

"See, Sam?" Ryerson said.

"I still don't like it."

"You got any better ideas for getting your son and your good friend out safely?"

"No," Carson said, sighing. "I guess it will be all right. But if anything happens to these two boys, I'll never forgive myself. Or you."

Ryerson turned to Vic and Rick. "I haven't bothered to ask you fellas. Want to go along?"

Their eyes gleamed along with their teeth. They almost chorused, "Count me in!"

Ryerson looked at Clute; the old-timer watched Ryerson with narrowed eyes.

"Something wrong, Clute?"

"Just one slight detail."

"Which is?"

"You're at Doan's place. He's down at the bottom of the canyon finding out he's been tricked. He's madder'n a hive of hornets. You ain't taking them two men out that way, mister, let me assure you."

"I never intended to, Clute."

"Well, how the hell you figure to get out of there."

"You're going to think I'm nuts again. We go out the way Doan least expects. Down the rapids of the Black River gorge!"

Clute rocked back on his heels, his mouth gaping in astonishment.

"You *are* out of your mind, Cole!"

· 11 ·

There must be a way over land out of there," Sam Carson protested. "I've heard of the gorge. Haven't seen it. But what you're planning, Cole, is idiotic."

"Ain't no way on land. Ain't no other way out," Clute said laconically but emphatically.

"But there's a way to the river," Ryerson insisted. "You told me yourself yesterday, Clute."

"Yeah, I been there. There's no possibility you can scale those cliffs. Only safe way out's by the canyon and Doan's boys'll have that stoppered up. Only other way is down the rapids and before you chance that you might as well put a gun to your head."

It was Sam Carson's turn to speak out again in protest of Ryerson's scheme. He looked at Ryerson with stern eyes. "I'll not allow you to put Jim's life, or George Douglas's, in jeopardy that way, Cole! I simply won't permit it."

In contrast, Ryerson's eyes squinted at Carson in determination.

"You seem to forget, Sam, that if I put Jim's safety on the line in going down the river rapids that I won't be sending him off alone. If he's lost, I'll go down the drink with him."

"Maybe I had you figured wrong, Ryerson. You're a fool."

"Sam," Ryerson started, and then paused, thinking, nibbling at his lips, trying to find the words. "You gotta quit crowdin' me. We're up against a gang of killers in about as foolproof a setup as there is in the West. My assignment, as it shakes out, is to get your boy and your friend out of there alive and by God—no, let me put that a little stronger— with God as my witness, I'll do it!"

Sam's mouth firmed with emotion. "It can't be done. But go ahead. I'll try to hear you out."

"Now, Clute," Ryerson asked, getting back to the business at hand. "Anybody ever take on the rapids?"

"If they did, they never lived to put it in the history books."

"Any timber that way? To build a raft?"

Clute was silent a long moment, eyeing Ryerson. His eyes brightened. "Yeah, I was to such a place. Found it when I was out huntin'. There's a narrow ledge along the cliff to a flat area along the bank, an acre, maybe two, with some leggy trees. Always thought it'd be a proper place to get away to and make a camp for a couple of days. Where a man could hide out, find himself again. Only way in and out's by that ledge. It's a fifty foot drop straight down to the rocks and the water churnin' below, and she's so narrow in some places you got to grip with your toenails and you daresn't slip."

"Does Doan know about it?"

"Nah. Huh-uh. Not him. Nor any of the others. It was kinda my secret."

"So he'd have a tough time comin' after us."

Clute chuckled. "He might try, but you take and knock a couple of his boys off with a Winchester down into the water and the rocks and any of the others'll ask for their wages and ride out before Doan persuades any of 'em to try it again." Clute grinned broadly.

Clute's glimmer of enthusiasm warmed Ryerson. "This is all getting better and better. Then we're not likely to be harassed while we're building a raft."

"Not so's you'd notice."

"Cole?" Sam inquired. Ryerson looked at him. "I've been thinking, too. Why not let me and one of the other ranchers handle that chore in the thicket that you want Vic and Rick to do."

The faces of the two young men in question suddenly fell.

"Well, that'd be just fine, Sam, except I've got a pretty important job for you. Maybe even more important than what I've got cut out for Vic and Rick."

Carson looked at Ryerson questioningly.

"There's a strong possibility that Doan has a spy somewhere in your midst. Clute thinks there's some kind of shady deal going on in town and Doan almost told me his name last night. Just before Doan's guard brought in George Douglas."

"I can't imagine who that would be," Carson said.

"Somebody knew that George Douglas had spread himself pretty thin and stood to lose his place if his cattle were taken."

"Almost anybody around here would know that."

"And could spill the beans to Doan," Ryerson said.

"Yeah, but where do I come in?"

"Doan knows I'm a lawman on the side of the settlers. He doesn't know what to expect now, but his hunch will be an armed attack. He knows it'd take forever for me to ride back to Fort Walker for a posse, so he'll expect us to organize the ranchers. The very thing you suggested at the start, Sam."

"I see one of the reasons you said that wouldn't work. They'll be expected."

"We keep the element of surprise. We're all—all of us here—sworn to secrecy right now. Are we agreed, gentlemen?"

Murmurs of assent and nods went around the four men with Ryerson.

"I want you, Sam, to organize the ranchers, get in some target practice, hold some meetings. Don't even try to keep it quiet. Let it be known that I'm out scouting an attack plan. You're the chief organizer of our little army. I want the word to leak to Doan that we're coming in just the way he expects. But he won't know when. Tell everybody to keep it a secret. That way it's sure to get back to Doan, and convince him that an attack is brewing."

Sam Carson's pessimism was written all over his face. "Won't that put Jim and George in jeopardy?"

"I don't think so. He's shrewd. As long as he has live prisoners, he has bargaining power. If they turn up dead, he knows he's a dead man, too. It's in his best interests to make sure nothing happens to them. Agree, Clute?"

"Yeah. And then . . ." Clute paused and the circling men looked at him. His old, faded blue eyes crinkled in glee and his grin was broad. "And then we do what Doan least expects!"

Ryerson grew angry with himself. At a time when he most needed to narrow his thinking to the problems at hand, he had allowed the past—the war years and the death of Dan Sturgis—to come out into the open of his thoughts and grow sharper. Riding out the next morning for time alone to clear his head, his thoughts annoyed him by circling back to Ruth Bascom Sturgis.

At war's end, stranded and broke in Texas when General Shelby took the survivors of the old brigade into Mexico, Ryerson rounded up a few mustangs to sell, branded and sold a good-size herd of maverick cattle, and increased his holdings at the poker table. When he had enough money to travel in a degree of style, he made his way to New Orleans and a steamer bound for St. Louis. Before he could get on with his life, he had to see Ruth Sturgis; secretly there was a hope in him that sad as it was with Dan gone, there now might be room in her life for him. Together they might recapture some of the gaiety and luster of those innocent adolescent years; the war had robbed him of so much.

Regardless of those feelings, propriety dictated that he visit the widow of his best friend, even if it meant traveling nearly halfway across a continent. Besides, he thought, in those glorious days they now called "antebellum," the three of them had been inseparable in the St. Louis of their young adulthood; he and Dan had individually called on Ruth Bascom. For Cole, it was a head-over-heels love that, because of what he considered his lowly station as a gunsmith's apprentice, and a tendency to become tongue-tied where pretty young women were concerned, he was altogether incapable of expressing or demonstrating his feelings for Ruth.

The fall of 1865 was well along when Ryerson wrote her of his coming. On arriving in St. Louis, he sent around his calling card and note suggesting a mid-afternoon visit at her home the next day.

As the last man who saw her husband alive—the man who had died saving Ryerson's life—and with the sting of his own personal loss still smarting, he knew it would not be an easy meeting for either of them. Another compounding—and confounding—element was little Cole Bascom Sturgis, born three months after the tragic Helena fight.

In her presence, Ryerson suddenly felt less sure of himself and less able to say what was in his heart. "He's a beautiful child, Ruth," Ryerson said, handing little Cole back to his mother. She had taken several rooms in one of the better St. Louis boarding hotels. Though the baby had Ruth's incredibly expressive eyes, in all other respects he resembled Dan—the puckish grin that invariably brought smiles to others, and that unmistakable red hair. Ryerson bit his lip and squinted against emotion at seeing the little fellow's topknot.

"Dan wanted him to have your name if it was a boy, Cole," she said wistfully. "And my maiden name."

"I'm deeply honored," Ryerson said. "I knew you were . . . in a family way soon after Dan came back from his last furlough. But he said nothing about names." To Ryerson, his words sounded stiff and unnatural with her; not the easy, carefree banter of years gone by. Something had changed. Maybe, he thought, it was both of them. Still he would try.

"He wanted to surprise you and hoped that somehow you both could get time off to be at the christening. You and I were all he had."

A lump rose in Ryerson's throat. "That works both ways, Ruth." He looked around at Ruth's clean but simple quarters. She could have gone back to her parents, the well-to-do Sylvanus and Martha Bascom, leading lights of St. Louis society; only Ruth's need to accept responsibility for her own adult life and decisions kept her from it.

Four years of horse soldier command had helped teach Ryerson how to come straight to the point; and he remembered she *had* been strong enough to hear from him the details of Dan's heroic death. "It's all over now, the war and the hell of it. It's time, they say, to pick up the pieces and get on with life. A lot of others lost true friends and lovers. What will you do now, Ruth? With your life?"

"That ought to be evident," she said with astonishing candor. "Raising the baby alone is going to be a big responsibility. But with the love I have for him, it will be joyful and fulfilling."

"You wouldn't have to . . . do it alone."

Ruth Sturgis looked him in the eye. "Are you suggesting I remarry, Mr. Ryerson? As a matter of fact, I've thought about it. I've passed a reasonably respectable time of widowhood."

Now more than ever, Ryerson felt it was time for him to be direct. "I've always loved you, Ruth. Come with me to Texas. It's beautiful there. We can have a fine life."

"What kind of life, Cole? You're not a soldier anymore."

Ryerson brightened; she seemed interested. "I've applied for a deputy sheriff job in Abilene. They want me. All I have to do is say the word. I'll report there as soon as I go back." He started to feel enthusiastic. "You and little Cole can come on later. I'll get us a nice house . . ."

Ruth watched out the window, but without seeing anything. "You're a dear, sweet man, Cole Ryerson. I've always cared for you deeply. But I married and lost the only man

I'll ever love. I can't say with conviction if I'll ever love or marry again."

Ryerson's heart sank. "Doesn't it matter that I love you, Ruth?"

Her chair was close enough to his for her to reach across and lay the palm of her hand affectionately over the back of his, resting on his chair's arm. "Dear Cole. We both learned bitter lessons with Dan's death. He perished by the sword and I'll not risk investing my affections in another who puts his life on the line the same way. And . . . I couldn't leave St. Louis. All of my life, everything, is here. Civilization. The savage West would be foreign to me."

"And my life, my freedom, room to grow, and to be myself and make something of myself are all out there. One of my reasons in coming was to try to persuade you. Now I see it won't work. I couldn't stay here. This place is too confining for me now. I'd suffocate in a week."

Ruth came over to him, leaned over and kissed him on the cheek. "I love you, too, Cole Ryerson. I hope we'll always be dear friends."

Coming back to reality three miles from the Carson ranch on Rusty's back, Cole Ryerson looked out over the rolling grassland, the distant mountains an outline of soft purple haze and a sky that was uniquely higher and wider, clearer and bluer than any other place on Earth. "She doesn't know what she missed," he mused.

The settling of full darkness had prompted Martin Rathburn to rouse up from his paperwork and light his office lamps. Highly polished concave reflectors bracketed behind each chimney bounced the light into the room to turn Rathburn's work area almost as bright as day.

A tapping against the windowpane at the rear of his office brought Rathburn instantly alert. He held a lamp up, directing its reflected light toward the darkened window. The frowning features of two of Doan's confidants, Chris and Sandy, materialized outside the window in the murky glow cast by the soft reflected light. Sandy's mouth exaggerated his silent words. "We got to see you." Rathburn immediately surmised that something was amiss.

Impatiently, he waved them around to his front door. He went to it, opening it a crack as the two shadowy figures materialized out of the night's gloom. He looked around at Broad Street. Light from the saloon windows across the way cast rectangular patches of yellow on the rutted street but the rest of the town was dark and silent and apparently empty.

Three or four horses were tied up in front of the saloon, and Rathburn hoped Sandy and Chris were smart enough to tether their mounts away somewhere in the dark. The two slid into the light of his office and he felt relieved that no one had seen them enter.

"What are you men doing here?" Rathburn demanded. "Dammit, Doan knows how risky this is!"

"That's why Doan had us come at night," Sandy said. "And come in here careful. We made sure nobody saw us."

"Got bad word from Doan," Chris added. He was a tall, rope-thin cowboy with the hard, pinched features that went along with men who operated outside the law. The face of his shorter companion was similarly tight, his complexion holding more of a ruddy cast. Sandy wore his wide-brimmed Stetson on the back of his head, a curling lock of sand-colored hair showing under the brim.

The weight of sixguns with full cartridge loops made their gunbelts sag below their waists.

"Some lawman has sneaked in here," Sandy said. "Got clear to Doan. Was carrying a letter from a friend of Doan's telling Doan to give work to this guy calling himself Kenny Rollins."

Rathburn was bewildered. "Wait! I know Rollins! Sam Carson brought him in the other day. He's a lawman? He's supposed to be somebody interested in investing in a cattle spread."

"Well, he showed up at Doan's," Chris said. "Hung

around there most of a day. Probably figuring to get the lowdown on Doan's setup. He'd be there yet but for a fistfight and his shirt got ripped. He had his badge hid in his shirt pocket. It fell out and the boys saw it."

Rathburn's face reddened. "What'd Doan do? Just let him walk out of there? Of all the . . ."

Sandy spoke up. "This feller Clute, an old man Doan kept around the place to do the odd jobs and kind of look after things when most of us are away . . ."

"What about him?" Rathburn interrupted impatiently.

"Grabbed a rifle and took this Rollins's side. Just like that!" Chris explained. "Held the boys off, his own friends and saddle pards. How do you figure that one?"

"Doan wants both their scalps," Sandy said. "Clute held the gun on 'em while this Rollins got their gear and horses together and they hightailed it out of there in the middle of the night. I was on guard, heard a bunch of shootin' and Clute and this Rollins came hellbent down the canyon with a cock-and-bull story about Doan gettin' shot and rode right by me."

"Where the hell was Doan in all this?"

"Up at his house," Chris explained. "Hell, it was past midnight. We'd've all been in bed except that one of the hands, an emptyhead named Homer, got gigged to take on Rollins in that fistfight."

"Sam Carson knows about this, I'll warrant," Rathburn said. "I'm betting Rollins is out at Carson's place right now. What's Doan figuring to do?"

Sandy turned reflective, not knowing exactly how to explain the situation to Berdan's financier. "Doan's kinda got a bull by the tail. He's got a couple of prisoners . . ."

"Prisoners? What prisoners?"

"Well, you remember that young jasper we caught the night Doan came to see you a long time back."

Rathburn was incredulous. "That's young Carson! I told Doan to get rid of him! Good Lord. Jim Carson knows everything! Who the hell else is he keeping out there?"

"The night Rollins was there," Sandy said, "I was down the canyon on first night guard. Got the drop on this waddy ridin' in. Doan thinks it was that fella whose herd we run off and you called his note."

"Douglas? You got George Douglas too?"

"If that's who it is."

Rathburn's mind ran at top speed. Sam Carson knew from the start that this Rollins was a lawman and kept the information from him. That, in itself, outraged him. Rollins and this Clute were probably at Carson's ranch this very minute plotting. Rollins had to know that young Carson was Doan's prisoner and that George Douglas was out there too.

"Gentlemen," Rathburn said, and in not too kindly terms. "This is a fine mess. We're up to our necks in damned serious trouble. I'd leave town right now if my entire future weren't riding on what happens here. No, we've got to stick and work it out. What's on Doan's mind? How does he expect we're going to handle it?"

"First off, Doan ain't going to budge. He's staying, too, for now anyway," Chris said.

"Doan figures Rollins will be back," Sandy offered. "Probably they'll try an attack on the ranch to get those men out, particularly after Rollins was out there and saw 'em stuff that man I brought in up in the attic. And Doan knows that Clute knows about the young man who's already been penned up there quite a few weeks. Doan figures somebody from town, probably this old man Carson, called in the law and that Rollins and Carson probably got it figured that it's Carson's son up there, too."

"My name's got to be kept out of it," Rathburn said angrily. "I was afraid something like this would come along and foul up the stew the night your men dragged young Carson in here. Doan's too stubborn, too bullheaded. I knew right then it was Jim Carson or me, and I ordered Doan to get rid of him. Now you go back and tell Doan I want those two eliminated! And I mean right now! Do I make myself clear?"

A half-full brandy bottle and thick gleaming tumbler on Rathburn's desk jumped with the thump of his fist on the desk to emphasize his order.

Sandy and Chris looked at each other. "We'll tell him, Mr. Rathburn," Chris said.

"If Doan had done as I told him, we'd probably still be in some kind of a fix with this Rollins in our midst. But there'd be no way to prove anything. As long as young Jim Carson is alive, it's risky for both Doan and me. Tell him that."

"We'll tell him, Mr. Rathburn," Chris said again.

"You tell him to get rid of Carson and Douglas. I'll take steps to handle the situation with our Mr. Rollins. Once those things are done, we'll be on our way to getting things settled down again. It'll take some doing with what Sam Carson thinks he knows, but I believe I can deal with him. I think we can still get the ship back on even keel."

"What're you gonna do about Rollins, Mr. Rathburn?" Sandy asked.

A cold and calculating look was in Rathburn's eyes as he regarded Sandy. "You just get Doan to do what I said with Carson and Douglas. I'll manage our Mr. Rollins."

Chris grinned. The grin was more of an animal leer. "If Rollins rounds up the ranchers to attack Doan, Mr. Rathburn, you better dedicate a big piece of ground to start you a buryin' place."

Sandy grinned, too. "You might likely lose a few customers, Mr. Rathburn. But then you could foreclose without having to rustle their steers!"

Rathburn was having no part of their crude jokes. "One of you slip back into town after dark in two days and give me a report on what's going on with Doan. I'll find out what Rollins and Carson have up their sleeves by then, too."

"Well, Chris," Sandy said, "reckon we ought to be getting back."

First thing next morning, Rathburn bustled down to Berdan's recently opened telegraph office, his notes all prepared. Even if the telegrapher sneaked a copy of the wire to Rollins or Carson, there was nothing they could pin on him. He found the operator at his machine furiously decoding a message clicking and clacking dots and dashes through his receiver. When he finished, Rathburn dictated his wire to the telegrapher.

"Jack Reno stop Paso del Norte Hotel stop El Paso stop Have work here for you stop Come immediately stop Report to me stop Martin Rathburn stop Berdan stop."

Rathburn walked away from the telegraph office gloating, his face wreathed in a smirk of minor victory. He'd used Jack Reno's hired gun before.

· 12 ·

Under the bright aura of a glorious morning sun flooding the Carson ranch yard, Ryerson stood by a wagon drawn by a handsome span of bays, looking up at the eager faces of Rick Carson and Vic Douglas on the wagon's spring seat. Rick leaned forward easily, elbows on knees, clutching the reins lightly between his fingers. Beside him, Vic was bright-eyed with anticipation, both hands gripping a Winchester between his knees, muzzle skyward.

"You've got enough money for about ten pounds of powder," Ryerson told them. "Remember now, don't go out of your way to announce it. On the other hand, don't hold back if you're asked. We're getting ready to reload a bunch of cartridges for the ranchers. Nobody needs to know more than that."

"We got it, Mr. Ryerson," Vic said.

"Boys, I got nothing against showing respect for your elders, but as far as I'm concerned, you can call me Cole."

Rick beamed with the acceptance of his adult equality, especially from none other than the celebrated Boot Hill Cole. "Thanks . . . Cole."

"You can depend on us, Cole," Vic said.

"Just be casual, matter-of-fact about the whole thing.

That's the way gossip travels best. We go to overstatin' our case one way or the other and the prey we're after is sure to catch a bad scent and we may wind up gettin' neither hide nor hair."

"We got other things to get at Estevans' store. We'll make it look natural as any other trip to town. You can depend on us, Cole," Vic repeated.

"See you when you get back, fellas," Ryerson said as Rick flicked the reins and clucked at the team. The wagon rattled off toward the lane to town.

Ryerson turned around to find Penny Carson standing on the back stoop shading her eyes against the early-morning sun as she watched the departing wagon.

"Mornin', Miss Carson," Ryerson called, heading for the stable to look in on Rusty before going out behind the barn for a smoke and some meditation.

"Morning, Mr. Ryerson. Fine day, isn't it?" Her eyes quickly switched away from Ryerson to the disappearing wagon.

Ryerson looked around at the ranch yard and at the sprawling prairie beyond and then up at the powder-blue morning sky. "Your presence helps make it so, Miss Carson."

"They'll be all right, won't they? Vic, I mean. And my brother."

"Penny, if I thought for one minute they couldn't measure up to the job, I'd not have asked them."

Three nights before, after supper, Ryerson gathered the Carsons and the Douglases in the living room and took the lead in briefly revealing his astonishing news about Jim Carson and George Douglas. He also told the women the essentials of his planned strategies.

The women took the news with shock and then with guarded acceptance. Hanna Douglas was the most shaken by the revelation that her husband, indeed, had not traveled West, but had become a prisoner at the rustlers' ranch. Still she listened quietly and intently to Ryerson's and Sam

Carson's proposed tactics with appropriate questions; Ryerson was relieved that there was little of the stubborn protest he had encountered with Sam in their early-morning conference behind the stable.

Ryerson was again impressed with these pioneer people, sturdy in strength as they were in moral fiber, and he was glad to be among them. Though he did not regard himself as a particularly spiritual man, he was deeply moved when, before the family members went to bed, they held hands in a circle in the open center of the living room as Sam Carson offered a prayer for the success of their quest and for God's blessings on those taking part and those in captivity.

Ryerson held Vic Douglas's hand on the one side and Penny Carson's on the other. With the "amen," he gave both their hands a quick and gentle reassuring squeeze. Each looked at him in acknowledgment before their eyes swung away to meet each other's.

"You're both fine people," Ryerson whispered so softly that only Vic and Penny could hear. They understood and smiled at each other. Ryerson was more certain than ever that these two young people had made a commitment in their hearts that had yet to be expressed aloud; and, he felt, each knew of the other's feelings. To Boot Hill Cole Ryerson, it was a heartwarming thing to witness.

Watching Penny now as she stood on the stoop watching after the departing wagon, he moved closer to her so only she would hear him complete his thought. "Penny, their parents may still consider them boys, but they are men. And I'll send Vic back to you a great deal stronger. He'll be the better for it."

Though she was but seventeen, Penny Carson had a maturity beyond her years. "If anyone can help us get back my brother and Vic's father, Mr. Ryerson, it's you. God, somehow, answered my prayers."

Ryerson was moved by the statement. "I appreciate your

faith, Penny. It helps. And I'll do everything possible to measure up to it."

She started to come closer as though prompted to make some tangible gesture, but held back. "You'll be in my prayers, Mr. Ryerson," she said.

"And you in mine," Ryerson lied, but warmed that it was a meaningful lie. Somehow he'd never learned to speak with God, something in which others seemed to find great consolation.

Penny turned and darted into the house. Ryerson, musing over their conversation, made his way toward the stable and his thoughtful smoke. Clute was away helping Sam Carson and the neighboring ranchers sharpen their tactics. He hunkered down in the barn's shade, not far from where the five of them had gathered previously, and dug for his tobacco sack.

Time, he thought, enjoying the sensory pleasures of his cigarette and only half witnessing the glorious Western morning, was not his ally. The machinery was in motion to alert Doan that a mass attack was brewing. How soon the iron would be hot enough for him to strike he could only guess. He assumed Doan would be smart enough to keep his prisoners alive to assure amnesty when Ryerson and Doan confronted each other in a bargaining session, or as human shields to ensure his escape.

Everything was dicey, more so than anything he'd ever done. Doan, anticipating an attack, might have forward scouts on the prairie to sound the alarm of the approach of any riders from town, whether four or forty. He and Clute, Rick, and Vic would have to sneak in as quietly as Indians with their gear for the proposed sham attack to cover the stealthy rescue of Doan's prisoners.

Could he depend on his assumption that all of Doan's men would abandon the ranch site when Vic and Rick set off their hullabaloo? Could he and Clute scale the cliff face to get on the roof; could he get the heavy shutter open to release Jim and George? Would the prisoners be in a condition to stand the rigors of the chancy rescue he had in mind?

Ryerson rolled another smoke and again studied the sun-blessed landscape from his cool, shaded vantage point. A balmy breeze poked around the corner of the stable to grace him with its pleasance, carrying his smoke softly away. Abruptly his mind recalled the afternoon of Kenny Rollins's killing of the unknown rider on the road to Berdan.

The times, paradoxically, had their similarities; such stark ugliness in the face of so much natural beauty in sky and land. So much of life, he thought, was filled with such ironies; beauty and the beast forever at odds.

He sighed. A man did what he had to do and got on with it. Now it was time to face the challenge of rescuing Doan's prisoners and getting to the seat of the evil besetting Berdan's ranchers. For a moment, he considered how easy it would be if all this were behind him. Or had never taken place. But ugly demon that it was, it had to be faced. He also considered briefly figuring a way to bargain with Doan; the prisoners for Doan's freedom, no strings attached. As quickly, he dismissed it. That's the easy way out, the coward's and the shirker's way. He seldom thought of righteousness, at least in the biblical sense, but he fought on its side and risked his life for it. There could be no backing off, no easy way out. His rescue plan was as bold and daring as it was risky. Perhaps, as Sam Carson had insisted, it was sheer idiocy. But it was the only way a man of his ilk could approach it. Thy will be done, he mused, realizing he'd meditated prayerfully. Maybe it's not such a bad way, he thought.

When it was over and done with, he promised himself a leisurely ride back to Fort Walker. Days and nights to again appreciate solitude and land and sky and being alone with his thoughts. There'd be time and opportunity to knit up after all this and to throw off the stifling cloak of such burdensome responsibility.

It would be done, and his time for his own style of personal rewards and reknitting would come. Ryerson heaved himself up from his perch and began to take stock of what they'd need, how they'd transport it, and how—finally —he'd pull it all off.

And now it was time. Sam Carson's irregulars, who were made to believe their efforts would result in real action, had made no pretense of secrecy as they spent an afternoon in target practice and another day of mock attacks on their entrenched comrades-in-arms. They held early-evening meetings on two occasions, ostensibly to discuss strategies of attack.

Around town, there were few secrets as to what was going on. Though no one spoke in specifics, it was common knowledge that the rustler camp was due for a cleaning out, mainly stemming from the death of Luther Moseley and George Douglas's loss of his land claim.

Knowledge of the whereabouts of Douglas and Jim Carson was carefully guarded by Ryerson and Sam Carson. Carson's army was only told what Ryerson wanted them to know.

Word was also leaked that the lawman behind the organization of ranchers was not Kenny Rollins but Judge Winfield's top lawman, Marshal Boot Hill Cole Ryerson. Ryerson had no idea how such word would affect Doan and whatever confederates the rustler chief had in Berdan. It was a cinch that the ranchers involved in the armed organization were mightily impressed.

Ryerson was almost certain that by now word of the ranchers' armed assembly had leaked to Doan, who, he hoped, would be duped into thinking that an attack by the settlers was imminent. Specifically warned against it, no one expressed any idea of the timing of their planned attack. Ryerson, through Carson, let the settlers know the attack would be mounted in about a week. Doan's spy, he thought, could be in their very midst. He hoped his own four-man guerrilla squad might pull off its sneak invasion before

Doan thought to place outriders on the prairie and in the thicket.

Ryerson decisively roused up and stretched muscles cramped from crouching so long. He squinted thoughtfully out over the sun-spread prairie. The iron had to be hot enough now. He'd move against Doan the following night.

· 13 ·

Knowing that much of the time for the next few days they'd travel without horses, Ryerson and Clute selected runty mustangs barely broken to saddle from Sam Carson's herd. Vic and Rick would lead these spare horses back, but in the event they had to make a run for it, loss of these particular mounts would not be serious. Ryerson wouldn't risk losing Rusty nor Clute his faithful paint.

With their gear for the action properly stowed, the four rode out after supper as dusk gave way to full dark. The ride to the thicket, to Ryerson's relief, was uneventful and the four spoke little.

Ryerson realized happily that his fears over encountering Doan men on his trail had been unfounded.

Also to their leader's enormous pleasure, Ryerson's squad found the thicket littered with dead leaves, sticks, and good-size limbs. He guessed the area at twenty to twenty-five acres. A fire any place would quickly have the entire expanse ablaze.

They'd drilled large cavities in odd leftovers of thick barn timber, and filled each with about a half pound of black powder; a wood plug was forced in to contain and compress the powder and provide a proper explosive canister. Ryerson also designed each with a small flash hole.

All was quiet around them as their preparations at the thicket got under way. Clute slipped away to near the entrance to Doan's canyon, alert to the approach of any riders from the vicinity of the ranch.

In the dark of the thicket, Ryerson again coached Vic and Rick on procedures. Rick had his father's watch and Clute owned one he'd taken off the body of a Federal officer during one of his military skirmishes.

"It's ten-fifteen now," Ryerson said softly as the pair leaned close to him in the eerie and dark stillness. "It's quite a hike up that canyon and I'll have to deal with Doan's sentry as quietly as I can."

The two young men nodded, attentive to Ryerson's words.

"We ought to be in position by twelve-thirty. No, let's not trifle with fate. Make it one A.M. Got that?"

Rick squinted at the watch face in the dark. "Got it, Cole," he said.

"Make a thin trail of powder around through the woods. Here and there drop off about half of our firecrackers in line with the powder trail. Keep the flash holes exposed so the traveling spark can get to them. Leave the others here and there, but in sure places that the flames will get to when the thicket burns."

"Yeah," Vic said. "That's the way we planned it."

"At one o'clock, start a hell of a ruckus with your Winchesters and your handguns. Keep it up for ten minutes or so. Then set the woods on fire and, as you hightail it, touch off the powder trail."

Both young men grinned like schoolboys conspiring to tip over outhouses on Halloween. They were aware of the risk but they surely were not blind to the thrill of adventure that went along with it.

"The gunfire will alert them. You'll be on your way when the first of our torpedoes goes off. By the time the fire reaches the others, I expect you'll be way out of any danger zone. Whatever you do, don't hang around to watch."

Ryerson tried to see their faces in the pitch darkness to make sure his message was getting through to them. He had also committed himself to Sam Carson to make certain these two made it home in one piece.

"And stay away from those things after the fuse trail is lit," he added. "There'll be a lot of dangerous scrap flying around when those thunder tubes of ours start to blow up."

"We'll see enough fireworks from out on the prairie," Rick said, grinning.

"It won't take you till one o'clock to set things up, so while you're waiting, keep yourselves hidden and the horses quiet. We don't know who might be coming in or out. I doubt anybody would be, but there's always an outside chance. Rick, your dad'll skin me alive if you fellas run into trouble. And Vic, there's a certain young lady back there's holdin' me accountable for your well-bein', and I'm not naming names."

Vic's face beamed in the faint light. "You can depend on us, Cole."

"There's another thing we haven't talked about. Clute and I might just stub our toes. Run into trouble, so to speak. If you hear any commotion, gunfire or anything of that sort, from up the direction Clute and I are going, set everything off and beat it. We're figuring we'll sneak in unobserved, but if they catch us, it'll come down to a fight and you'll sure hear some shooting."

"You'll make it, Cole," Rick assured him.

"Let me tell you I by God better. A lot's ridin' on it." He hesitated. "You fellas all set? Clear on everything?"

They both mumbled an assent.

"Clute and I better get to hoofin' it. Time's a-wastin'." He picked up the two huge coils of rope they'd freighted in and slung them over his shoulders. "See you in a few days." He reached out and shook their hands and stepped away into the darkness.

"Cole?" one of them called after him.

He stopped. "Yeah?"

"Good luck."

"Same to you. Now keep quiet."

Near the canyon's mouth he found Clute waiting along the trail and got rid of half his burden of rope by looping it over his companion's shoulder.

"No sense me doin' all the work," he said softly in the dark.

"Dunno why not," Clute responded.

"Talk like that'll get you this ball of twine I got around my neck, too," Ryerson said, pleased that he'd found an old skirmisher to tie up with who so willingly shared the risks with him. "I'm still in charge, y'know."

"And you forget, too, that your side lost, mister. The victor always gets to lord it over the loser."

"Then we're even. We both carry rope. All right, from here on out, we better remain quiet, Clute. Or at least only what needs to be said. Check your watch. The boys are going to turn the wolf loose exactly at one A.M."

"Time's a-wastin'. How'll we take out Doan's guard?"

"Let me know when you think we're getting to the guard post and I'll try to sneak up on him. Hope I don't have to kill him."

"That's the riskiest part," Clute said. "He sits there on a perch he has to climb to. Got to go up a ledge to get up there. I don't think it'll work, Cole."

"It's got to be done," Ryerson said emphatically. "I'll figure something."

They trudged silently for about a quarter hour and approached Doan's canyon before Clute again spoke, this time in even more hushed tones.

"Seems to me we just did this the other day on horses comin' the other way."

"And you had a better trick for getting past the guard."

Ryerson could see Clute's grin through the dark; Clute waved his arm loosely in a "let's go" sign and they resumed the slow, foot-slogging march up the canyon. They struggled silently through the loose gravel and rock of the canyon bed for more than a half hour before Ryerson began to recognize the terrain nearing the canyon bend where Doan's sentry was posted.

Clute reached out and silently grasped Ryerson's arm. He pulled him toward the rock wall, shielded from the sentry by the trail's bend, and moved close to get his mouth close to Ryerson's ear. "Wait," Clute hissed.

"What?"

"I been thinkin'. This is foolish. You ain't going to sneak up on him."

"So? Somehow we got to get by without spreading the alarm to Doan."

"Let's try to sneak past instead. Pull off your boots. Won't make sound. Stay close to the rocks on his side. If he's awake, he'll be listening for a horse coming, anyway. Won't be expecting anyone on foot."

"It's risky."

"What ain't about all this business, Cole?"

"Okay." Ryerson sat on a boulder to pull off his boots. Clute wasn't finished. He moved closer.

"I'll go first. You wait a minute or two then you come. No sense both of us gettin' nailed."

"I get your point." Ryerson chuckled silently at his choice of words.

"I hope you weren't makin' a joke, mister. If he gets me, you hightail it back and figure something else." Clute sat down to tug at his boots. They were still close enough to hear each other's whisper.

"How about this? If he hears me," Clute said, "I'll change my voice, make him think it's somebody comin' down from up above. I'll call him down off his perch and you can lodgepole him from behind."

"You're taking a hell of a chance, Clute."

"We been through all that before. Let's get movin'."

In moments, they neared the canyon's bend, hugging the

rock face on their right, the sentry's side. Ryerson stopped, shielded by the tall shoulder of granite. The full moon of a few nights before was gone; the pitch-black night worked in their favor.

Ahead of him, Clute disappeared into the inky stillness leaving Ryerson alone with his fast-thumping heart. He counted to sixty slowly, waited a bit longer, and eased past the obstacle blocking him from the sentry's view. He moved cautiously and silently, inching through the night nearly brushing the jagged canyon wall.

He took his breath in short, noiseless gulps, hoping against a wheeze. His stockinged feet felt every pebble and rock. He ignored any pain from a sharp projection. Clute had made it past without incident. Ryerson gathered that he must be directly beneath the guard's lofty perch.

Abruptly, causing him to freeze in place in panic, a match flared out of the dark scant feet above him. Alert to any movement, Ryerson stayed in a tense crouch, rigid as a statue. As he watched, a cigarette tip took on a glow in the night and the match flame disappeared.

The oblivious guard had just rolled and fired a smoke.

Ryerson waited a bit longer, watching the ruby glow brighten and dim as the man puffed on his smoke.

Confident their movements were undetected, he commanded his muscles to relax and continued to inch along the rock wall. An outcropping behind the guard soon shielded the cigarette's glow from Ryerson's vision and he proceeded, only somewhat less cautiously.

In another twenty-five yards, he found Clute struggling into his boots. He leaned down to congratulate him, but the old-timer got the jump on him.

"Where the hell you been?" Clute asked softly. "Took you long enough."

"God! When I was right below him, he lit a cigarette. When he struck that match, I thought my hash had been settled for good."

"I hope you went up and asked him to share his makin's."

Sensing great elation with the success of their ploy, Ryerson belted Clute a good one on the shoulder for his bum joke and sat down to cram his feet into his boots. "Let's go," he whispered, getting up. Clute started away.

"Hey, Clute," he called guardedly. "What time is it?"

Clute held his watch close to his face. "Pushin' midnight."

"We got to be hid on the rimrock over Doan's place in an hour," Ryerson said.

"We'll be there," Clute assured him. "There's a big cottonwood this side of the house. Doan sleeps on the other side and the bunkhouse is a long ways off, if you remember. We'll toss a rope and snub it on a big limb. You climb a ways and I think you can edge out and get footing on the rock ledge. That'll take you to near the roof."

"You *think* we can?"

"Hell, Cole, I never done it. I'm new at this, too."

"It better work."

"We got to be up there in an hour. Quit your jawin'."

As they continued their sneak up the canyon in the dark, all the possible hitches raced again through Ryerson's mind. What if the guard's relief came riding down and caught them? What if they couldn't get on the roof? What if Doan left a few men at the ranch and he was discovered dangling in front of the shuttered attic window? What if he couldn't open it?

He was roused out of his skeptical speculations by the faint odor of cattle, horses, and woodsmoke drifting down to them and growing stronger. The canyon bed leveled off now on the approach to Doan's ranch yard.

Abruptly it seemed, the canyon walls slipped away and the flat box valley was spread before him, its cubes and giant boxes of buildings bulking darkly and ominously in the night. The toughest part of the dangerous gamble was at hand.

He couldn't see a light. It must be half-past midnight. They'd have to move fast and surely from here.

Clute motioned Ryerson toward the giant cottonwood, a lump of dark in the night next to the house. As Ryerson started past him, Clute grabbed him again by the forearm and gripped it tightly, pulling him close.

"I got bad news," he said sheepishly. "My watch stopped!"

"Oh, shit!" Ryerson gasped. "What's it say?"

"Twelve thirty-eight."

"When'd you notice it?"

"Just now."

"Let's get up that damned tree. We may be too late!"

In the pitch dark, it took three throws of the coiled rope to finally loop the trailing end over a large branch. His fingers trembling in urgency, Ryerson fastened a loop and tugged the loose rope down and secured his loop against the thick limb about fifteen feet overhead. He tested it with his weight. It held.

He'd tied knots at intervals of about a foot to help them in getting up and down the ropes. Grabbing one, he whispered, "Here goes." He began his shinny up the side of the tree.

The climb took precious minutes but at last he found himself on the big limb, straddling it for balance. He whipped the rope to signal Clute to begin his ascent.

Clute seemed to take forever and Ryerson's breathing was tensed as he anticipated the sounding of the alarm from the thicket miles away.

The climbing Clute came into view beneath him and he watched his form inching up the tree in the dark. Clute was nearly to the limb when Ryerson heard it.

The muffled rattle of rifle shots drifted to him in the dark stillness. One, then another were followed by a veritable volley as Rick and Vic emptied their Winchesters into the night.

He slid back to make room for Clute on the limb when a massive explosion, enormous but also muted by the distance, belched thunder through the night. He smiled. The boys had touched off the powder trail. That meant the thicket had also been fired. Everything had worked so far. Closer to him, he heard the alarmed shouts of waking rustlers and scuffling in the house almost directly below him.

"We might as well figure how to get on the rimrock," Clute said softly. "They'll be so damned busy for the next few minutes that nobody'll care about what's up in this tree."

"Look," Ryerson said, "off there. Down the canyon."

"The boys done it," Clute said, looking in that direction.

A rosy glow lit the horizon, a narrow band of orange at first that grew in width and intensity. At only about a several-second interval, the roar of two more of Rick and Vic's torpedo canisters tore at the night air as Clute and Ryerson hugged their limb.

"Well, let's not sit here enjoying the fireworks," Ryerson whispered. "The commotion's started. Let's see how we get on the roof."

Below them, Doan's ranch house door slammed and a figure sprinted across the yard toward the bunkhouse. It was Doan himself, fully dressed, guns strapped on and waving a Winchester.

At that moment, men began pouring out of the bunkhouse.

"We're attacked!" Doan's frenzied scream rose up to the two figures hugging their tree limb. "We're attacked! Grab your guns and mount up!"

Crouching uncomfortably among the leaves, Ryerson sensed great relief wash over him. Secretly he had feared that a man as shrewd and cunning as Jubal Doan would see straight through the mock attack and catch the invaders red-handed.

But then he reasoned, Jubal Doan was surely crazy as he heard him racing around the ranch yard babbling commands and screaming curses, totally disorganized. Ryerson

151

figured he ought to have realized the man's mental condition just knowing about his ridiculous lifestyle.

Crazy men did crazy things and just now Jubal Doan was running true to form.

It was all going so much according to plan that Ryerson began to think that he might as well have pulled it off in broad daylight.

Also true to form, no rustler wanted to be left out of the fracas. As Ryerson and Clute coiled their climbing rope and moved higher into the tree to find a limb leading to the rock ledge, the scene below them was little short of a comic melee.

While the explosive roar of distant thunder tubes resounded through the night, and with Doan screeching commands at a soprano pitch, his crew skittered about like disorganized ants. They ran back and forth for forgotten guns or ammunition or hats or boots. The night filled with the shouts and curses of men battling for bridles and saddle blankets in the dense blackness while horses milling in the corral picked up the panic to become an unruly and skittish swarm of bucking heads and plunging hooves.

One by one, men got their fighting gear together, found and saddled satisfactory mounts, and charged down the canyon. Somewhere in the bunch of horsemen that piled piecemeal and pell-mell across the ranch yard was Jubal Doan himself, screaming orders at the top of his lungs.

Ryerson grinned into the night. Doan had built a perfect setup for defense but obviously had never established strategies with the very men who would be responsible for that defense.

Ryerson and Clute worked fast. A cottonwood limb growing close to the ledge over Doan's roof was precariously slim. In the dark, ignoring possible apprehension from the chaos below him, Ryerson scooted along on his crotch and hoisted himself to the ledge. He raised up on the rock lip as Clute followed him, edging out on the same tenative limb, burdened as was Ryerson with his great loops of rope slung over his shoulder.

Knifing through the night from miles away, the torpedo tubes continued their concerto of concussion, adding more panic to the scrambling scene in Doan's ranch yard. The thicket's conflagration thrust ruby fingers into the night to dance along and over the distant horizon.

When Clute was scant inches from the security of the ledge, the brittle limb suddenly dipped beneath him to break off close to the trunk with an abrupt and sharp splintering crack unheard in the commotion still going on in the yard.

"Owww shat!" Clute screamed as he dropped away from Ryerson's sight down into the jumble of cottonwood branches below. Miraculously, the broken limb wedged against the cliff face, partly supported by the mesh of lower branches.

Clute hung there, three feet below the ledge, gripping his precarious perch for dear life, too petrified to move a muscle.

"Easy, now," Ryerson called, certain no one would hear him. The ledge offered barely enough room for him to crouch. He thrust down a hand, feeling Clute's fingers brush his. Their fingers hooked in a grasp and they struggled until their palms clenched.

"Careful," Ryerson said, closer now to Clute. "Pull me off here and we're both in the soup!" Clute's other hand grasped Ryerson's forearm and with the support, he eased erect, testing the branch's staying power. It held.

Their breaths coming in short sobs, the two worked against gravity and a limb threatening to give way any second. Slowly Ryerson pulled as Clute came fully erect. Clute found a narrow foothold of granite below the ledge and trusted his weight to it, stepping off the limb with one leg dangling.

"Easy, now," Ryerson cautioned with a grunt, struggling erect with both of Clute's fists painfully gripping his arm. Straining and trembling with his burden and fighting to keep from falling, Ryerson stood up. Clute cooperated by swinging his dangling leg up to the ledge, finding solid footing and boosting himself off his narrow rock step.

At last he dropped his grip on Ryerson's arm and stood up on the ledge.

"I'll tell you one thing, son," Clute grunted almost breathlessly. "That's about as close to hell as I ever hope to get."

Below them in the night, the confusion had wound down to a few fumbling cowboys still searching for saddles and shouting angrily at skittish horses to calm down. Now and again one of them got himself organized and thundered down the canyon toward the scene of anticipated action.

"You're okay now," Ryerson whispered. "Let's go. When Doan gets down below and finds he's been bulldozed, he'll have them back up here like a herd of damned riled hornets to see if they still have their prisoners."

"You don't care a damn that I come near to bustin' my ass," Clute said in a mock simper.

"Well now, Clute," Ryerson said consolingly, "if we get out of all this in one piece, I promise to kiss it and make it well. Now, dammit, let's quit all this lollygaggin'!"

The ridge of Doan's roof was but a few feet away and Ryerson made for it along the narrow ledge, still struggling for balance against the huge rope coil on his shoulder. Over the middle of the house, he sized up the drop at fewer than four feet. All seemed quiet in the ranch yard. In their preoccupation, they hadn't heard the last cowboy ride out.

"I think we can get down without ropes," he said over his shoulder to Clute. "Hit it square and you won't roll off. Here goes." He slipped over the rock ledge, landing evenly at the roof's ridge line. He caught his balance, arms extended like a high-wire walker.

Clute dropped behind him, hitting to one side. Ryerson grabbed at him before Clute could slide down the roof's steep pitch. Together they inched along the ridge, awkwardly straddling its line.

Ryerson heard movement through the shingles and the muffled questions of those below. His only concern was that Douglas and Carson would be in condition for the demands the next few hours would bring.

The next question was if any of Doan's men remained to guard the place; he couldn't be certain till he looked past the end of the roof.

Another problem was solved when he poked out his head. Nothing moved in the yard below him and he noted with satisfaction that the ridgepole projected past the roof about two feet, a perfect snubbing post for his escape rope. Ryerson leaned down and smacked the flat of his hand against the siding. "George Douglas!" he hissed loudly.

"Who's there?" came a muffled voice in the attic.

"No matter. Sam Carson sent me. Does the shutter latch from inside?"

"Yeah."

"Thank God. Enough opening to climb out?"

"Sure."

"Now listen close. I'm only saying this once. I know you've been there a while and may be feeling puny. I'll drop a rope past while you open up. It's got knots to climb down. Jim goes first. I'll be right under him. If you have problems, Jim, just drop your feet on my shoulders and we'll ease down together."

"Okay," came another muffled voice. It had to be Jim Carson. The shutter latch whined its release and the hinges flexed noisily open on rusty pins.

A head poked out and he recognized George Douglas's ring of graying hair.

"There's a man with me, George. He'll get down the rope ahead of you. If you have trouble, slide down till your feet hit his shoulders and both of you ease to the ground."

"I'll make it on my own," Douglas insisted.

"I've seen you in action before. I figured you would. Now move!" He built his loop and snubbed it to the roof projection. He swung out and started down. As he passed the opening, two bearded, haggard faces peered out of the attic's darkness at him. He paused there, hanging tight to a knot.

"Jim, when you hit the ground, head for the horse corral and saddle up four mounts. George, we'll need as much of this rope as we can salvage. Try to loosen it from the ground."

He started down again, but another thought stopped him. "Clute," he called up at the dark figure peering over the roof at him. "We need at least two axes, hatchets, and knives. You know where Doan keeps 'em?"

"Yeah," Clute responded.

"If you know where you can lay your hands on 'em, these boys here could use sixguns and belts, and a couple of Winchesters may come in handy."

"They're all in the house probably locked up," Clute said. "Cole?"

"Yeah? What now?"

"What are you gonna do?"

Ryerson grunted with mock impatience. "How about I sit on the porch and roll a smoke? Get movin'!"

Ryerson scooted down and watched as Jim Carson swung out and gripped the rope and dropped toward him hand-over-hand. "I'm all right," Jim called. "Go on down."

In turn, Clute lowered himself off the roof, sliding past the open window. Ryerson heard him say, "Evenin', Mr. Douglas," as he went by. Douglas reached out for the rope and stepped out into space.

"Need help?" Clute called up.

"No," Douglas responded, moving down the rope at a speed that forced Clute to drop faster toward the ground.

Ryerson landed first, Jim Carson right behind. Ryerson reached out to grip him by the shoulders. "You all right, Jim?"

"I'm okay. Who are you?"

"No time for introductions. We got to move. For now, it's just Ryerson. My pard up there is Clute. Used to be here with Doan, but he's trusty. Tell you everything later. You got a job. Can you do it?"

"Boot Hill Cole?"

"Yeah."

"Heard of you. I'm a little light-headed and stiff in the joints but I'll make it."

"Then head out . . . Jim?"

"Yeah?"

"A lot of people want to see you home safe in one piece. Your dad and mother . . . and a pretty young lady named Melissa."

Carson bowed his head in unashamed emotion. "Not any more than I want to see them."

"One more thing, Jim, to think about. And be proud. You heard the shooting and explosions that sent Doan's men hightailing?"

"Sure did."

"You can thank a couple of brave young bucks you know. Rick Carson and Vic Douglas. I figured to give them a chance to take part in the action when we headed in to save you. It wasn't too risky for them and they got the job done right. It sure cleared Doan and his men out of here so Clute and I could get to you fellas."

"No fooling? Where are they?"

"Just now probably halfway back to your dad's place. Now, boy, get a wiggle on!" Jim disappeared into the dark in the direction of the corral.

Clute hit the ground with George Douglas right behind him.

"Okay," Ryerson said. "You know what to do. Clute's going to lead us to the river west of here, George. Get moving."

Clute headed for the barn for tools while George began expertly whipsawing the dangling rope to try to loosen its loop's hold on the ridgepole. Ryerson watched the canyon for the return of any of Doan's men.

As he passed the darkened veranda, movement in the dark near Doan's front door flashed a signal of alarm. That fast, Ryerson involuntarily tensed, crouched, and pivoted, drawing and cocking his Navy as he did.

"Make no moves!" he hissed hoarsely into the dark. "You're covered. Drop your weapon and step out!"

The voice that came to him out of the night was female. "Mr. Rollins? Is that you? I don't have a gun."

His mind raced. Of course. Ruby Montez.

"Go back in the house, Miss Montez," he called. "You're not a part of all this. Don't give me any trouble. Just go back in. Jubal will be back soon."

"Clute's with you. I know all about you. About the other night. And Homer. You're a lawman."

"Just go back inside, Ruby."

"You're taking those two men from upstairs, ain't you?"

"Ruby, I don't have time . . ."

"Take me with you, Mr. Rollins. I need to escape, too."

"You? Escape? But aren't you . . . Doan's girl?"

"No . . . not Doan's girl!" She spoke emotionally, her words rapid-fire. "I'm just . . . Ruby Montez. I'm an orphan, Mr. Rollins. I had to do some sinful things to stay alive. He promised me money and a good life to come work for him. Now he's kept me here and made me work and . . . you know."

"He wouldn't let you leave?"

"He's been awful. When you came here before, I thought

maybe I could trust you. But I couldn't get to where I could tell you anything privately." She came closer to emphasize her appeal. "The only way I knew to try to get someone, one of the men, to talk to me was maybe to flirt. Then I could tell them. Ask them for help. But Jubal would've killed anybody he caught with me. I need to get away from here, Mr. Rollins. Away from Jubal."

Ryerson's insides churned. All this was too unexpected, too impossible. What she suggested was insane. "I can't take you, Ruby."

"This is the first chance I've had in three years, Mr. Rollins. I've been bad. I admit that. I want to be better and I know I can be. But I need a chance. Need to get away from here. Please, Mr. Rollins."

Ryerson squinted and shook his head in dismay. "We're going out the river way. No one's ever done it. It's rough water, rapids, rocks, fast water, maybe even waterfalls. None of us may make it out the other end. Ruby, I can't . . . just can't."

"It's a chance I'm willing to take. I'll work. I'll cook for you. I'll hunt. I'm a good shot. I'll hold up my end. You'll see."

"Ruby, I'd like to, but it's . . . it's all wrong." Ryerson felt himself weakening. Ruby was attractive and she was strong, physically and spiritually, in spite of her sordid life. Here, he thought, was a woman of the West. A craving stirred in him, but there wasn't time to analyze his feelings.

The bearded, haggard, and emaciated form of Jim Carson materialized out of the dark leading four saddled horses.

Near them, George Douglas marched up proudly, the huge coil of knotted rope slung over his shoulder. Ryerson recalled the awful night Doan's sentry dragged Douglas in. And the near-calamity that followed his stepping in on Douglas's behalf.

"We drew that noose damned tight up there with our weight," Douglas said, intruding on Ryerson's thoughts. "Took a lot of work but, by damn, I got 'er!"

160

Ryerson studied his released prisoners and pondered. Clute showed up grinning, hefting a large axe in each hand with hatchets and utility knives stuck in his belt.

Ryerson sighed deeply. "Gents. Those of you who don't know, this is Miss Ruby Montez."

Clute said, "Mornin', Ruby."

"Sometimes she brought us our meals," Jim said. "Never knew your name, Miss Montez, but you always seemed gentle and sympathetic." He touched a finger to his forehead out of respect for her womanhood.

"Well, I don't know," Ryerson said, bewildered. "We've got to get moving. Aw, hell! Ruby, do you know where the key is to Doan's gun rack and the ammunition drawer?"

"Sure do!"

"We need some Winchesters and sixgun rigs and cartridges for George and Jim here."

Ruby seemed energized by Ryerson's sudden encouragement. In asking her about the guns, Ryerson felt that somehow he'd taken her on his crew. He still knew it was idiotic but what he guessed was his code left him with no outs.

Deep inside, something told him he'd come around to feeling as good about taking her along as he did right now with Jim and George free and standing there eagerly at his elbow. He'd released two from Doan's evil snare and maybe the third was also meant to be freed.

"Jim?"

"Yeah?"

"Any horses left in the corral?"

"Quite a few."

"Well, tie up those there and go back and catch and saddle another while we're inside getting some guns." Ryerson paused and studied the faces around him.

"Gents. Miss Montez will be joining us. One more escapee."

This time no one questioned him, not even Clute, and he was thankful.

With his final commitment, he rolled his eyes at the sky still wondering if he was doing the right thing. He stopped as another reality dawned on him.

The rosy tint of the thicket fire had left the sky.

Without doubt, Jubal Doan was on his way home; or soon would be.

"Okay, you all got your orders. Clute, you and George stow the ropes and your tools on the horses. Ruby, you and I'll get the guns. We ride in two minutes!"

· 15 ·

True to Clute's estimate, Ryerson guessed it had been eight miles to the river, a trip that took most of what was left of the night. Behind them down the narrow canyon-like pass, back toward Doan's, dawn seeped in as a blue-gray band along the horizon.

The cleft in the land ended abruptly and hazardously at the rim and drop-off of the Black River gorge fifty feet below. Ryerson wouldn't have cared to ride in at night. In the gray pallor of approaching day, the river below them picked up speed as it funneled through the narrow, cliff-like sides of the gorge. The roar of its turbulence rose up to him, a surging, pounding torrent, frightening in its violence.

The five riders paused near the edge only momentarily. Ryerson heaved out of the saddle.

"What now, captain?" Clute asked.

"The next step. Where's that ledge you told me about?"

"Right over there."

Ryerson spoke up to the group. "Unsaddle. Throw the saddles and bridles in the river. We've got no choice but to send the horses home. I don't want to help Doan any more than I have to. Roll your saddle blanket and tie it over your

163

shoulder like a horseshoe. We may need them before this is over."

Everyone stepped down and got busy. In the early light, he saw that Ruby Montez had found a sixgun rig and snugged it around the waist of her long dress. Ryerson grinned at her in the pale light, her eyes reflecting a glow that even Ryerson felt. Most of her coppery hair was hidden under one of Doan's black hats; maybe his only one. He'd seen Doan race across the yard bareheaded. Ryerson beamed. Ruby looked rugged enough to stand the test; hell, he thought, remembering Dan Sturgis fondly, redheads—good ones—can be depended on.

"Ruby and Jim each take a Winchester," he ordered as he flipped up his stirrup and began loosening the cinches. "Divide the hatchets and knives and stick them in your belts. Clute and George take the axes. I'll try to manage the ropes. Get busy!"

None of them dallied. They had no illusions about their fate if Doan caught up with them. In moments they were rigged for the trail. Clute led them to his ledge, a three-foot wide projection from the cliff face. "This is it, folks," Ryerson announced. "Not much, but it's the next leg of our escape route."

"This is like a wagon road to what's coming," Clute advised. "It narrows plenty down a ways. But like Cole says, it's all we got."

"We're hauling a lot of gear," Douglas said. "Can we make it?"

Clute's eyes narrowed. "You got two alternatives, George. Go back and face Doan or jump in that river down there. Take your pick."

"Let's move," Ryerson urged. "I don't favor Doan catching us on that ledge like sitting ducks. Clute tells me there's a nice woods down there, near the waterline. Landlocked. Easy to defend from anyone coming down the ledge. We'll build a raft and take on the gorge."

"What?" Douglas was incredulous. "That's suicide! I've heard of that gorge. There's no way out over land?"

"Nope," Ryerson said decisively. "Clute's scouted this country plenty. The river's our only way."

Douglas whistled his astonishment under his breath.

Ryerson spoke up. "George, you're no greenhorn. You got a couple fingers off and a nose that don't run plumb center. I take it you've been over a few rough trails in your time."

"For a fact," Douglas said.

"Anybody ever tell you life was fair or that it was going to be easy?"

"Not at any of the places I've been."

"Then how'd you expect getting jerked out from under Jubal Doan's nose was going to be a Sunday School picnic?"

"I didn't."

"That's what I been tryin' to tell you. It ain't."

"You're the boss," Douglas said. "I'm just happy as all get-out to be away from that damned prison of his. I'll take my chances out here after all."

Ryerson looked around at the rest of them. "Clute, you go first and warn us of the hazards. Jim you're next, then George. Ruby, you go ahead of me. How far is it to our landing, Clute?"

"As the crow flies about an eighth of a mile, but you're going to think it's a thousand."

"Doan could show up any minute. Now, folks, I'm honor-bound to a lot of people in Berdan if not to Judge Winfield in Fort Walker to get you all out of here safe and sound. So no slip-ups. Everybody gets through. Is that clear?"

He saw grins on their faces. Jim Carson, he figured, was the weakest because of his long captivity. But the eyes he looked at, though showing the strain, also glinted with the challenge. Ryerson took hope from that.

"Cole," Clute called back. "There's something I forgot to tell you."

"Here it comes!" Ryerson said, prickling with apprehension. "What now?"

"Remember me sayin' I figured to come back here and camp some time?"

"Yeah. So what?"

"I got a nice little cache buried down there. Some jerky and beans. Got some coffee and a good-size jug of old Bravemaker. All safe and secure in little tins you can cook with."

Ryerson roared with relief. "Ruby!" he enthused. "Your first chore in camp is to fix breakfast!"

"Gladly," she chirped and headed after George Douglas along the ledge.

"Those that want can sample Clute's liquid courage," Ryerson added.

As Clute had warned, the width of the ledge narrowed after about the first hundred yards of optimistic width. They were quickly forced, hampered additionally by their equipment, to face the cliff and edge along sidewise, taking precarious handholds where they could find them.

Wind, squeezing down the narrow gorge, pummeled and pulled at them with frequent buffeting gusts. They hung there like flies on a wall, nothing above or below but straight up and straight down.

Fifty feet down the sheer cliff, like a hungry, yawning, and bellowing demon, roared the Black River. White water churned up as it gathered speed in its rush through the opposing cliffs. Its thunder filled the ears of the small band clinging tenaciously to the canyon wall.

Ryerson made the mistake of glancing down and his breath caught in his throat. A misstep spelled instant death on the rocks or in the rapids.

He drew close to Ruby Montez. "Don't look down. Keep your eyes on your foothold and where you put your hands. Pass the word."

Ruby turned to call the warning to George Douglas, shouting over the turbulent din.

Ryerson looked back the way they had come. They'd made miserable progress. He could clearly see the shelf where they'd left the horses and guessed they could be picked off easily if Doan showed up before they got down farther and hidden from view.

Like something dark and evil growing abruptly out of the ground up there, a trio of horsemen emerged at the chasm's edge, and were quickly joined by more.

"They're here!" he screeched, raising his voice over the river's roar. He couldn't tell if the others heard him.

Something smacked like a sledgehammer into the heavy rope coils and blanket roll on his shoulder; the coughing bark of a distant .44-40 Winchester was nearly drowned out by the thundering roar beneath him. Instantly he felt a violent sting in his shoulder and a sudden ache ricocheted through his back and chest. He almost fell as he flinched with the impact.

Grimacing against it, Ryerson dug his fingers into his handhold and pressed his cheek against the rock wall in agony, feeling tears of pain starting out of his eyes. "I'm hit!" he screamed. "Keep moving!" Another bullet sang past him, and through his fluid-like vision he saw the puff of muzzle blast from above.

He turned his head to check their progress. The others inched faster along the ledge. Clute seemed nearly to a point where it dipped past a granite projection. If they could all make that point, they'd be out of gun range.

He knew he was the prime target as he generally shielded the others from the outlaws' gunsights bearing down on them. Ruby had moved away from him as he reacted to the wound. Aside from the first bone-jarring shock of the hit, the pain—miraculously—subsided. The agony was still there, but not as intense as he expected. Another bullet chipped off a large chunk of granite and sprayed him with gravel. He flexed the injured shoulder. Nothing like fractured bone grated around the wound and everything seemed functional.

Painfully, commanding his brain and his muscles to control themselves, Ryerson continued to edge along the granite lip. He swiveled his head again to check the progress of the others. Clute had disappeared around the outcropping, George Douglas was close to inching past. Jim Carson, his strength possibly flagging, had allowed a considerable gap between his position and Douglas.

Ruby Montez was now several feet ahead of Ryerson and closer to Jim.

Another bullet howled past Ryerson's head, too close for comfort.

The barrage continued as those exposed to the gunfire tried to speed up their agonizingly slow traverse of the ledge. All the bullets so far had missed except for the first that hit Ryerson. Sheer will power pushed him on. Jim Carson paused for a brief moment at the projecting tip to look past it and then slipped around it to safety from the gunfire at least, with Ruby close behind.

Ryerson darted a glance back up the ledge as three of Doan's men, all that could fit in the confined area to shoot, furiously jacked cartridges into their rifles' breeches and lobbed rounds his way.

"You were lucky on that first one!" Ryerson screamed at them, not caring if they heard. He reached past the stone projection feeling for a handhold. Something warm and soft moved over his hand; he craned his neck around as Ruby reached out for him, her hand guiding his, their eyes meeting. She squeezed his groping hand. "You okay, Cole?"

"Not in much of a position to check," he grunted. "But you don't know how nice it seems that you're concerned." He meant it to be a bit facetious, but it came out sounding sincere.

Another bullet spat granite slivers around him as he crept past the sharp edge of cliff, Ruby's comforting hand still over his. The slug twanged away to oblivion with a high-pitched shriek.

"They won't get us now, Ruby. I'll just have to keep going.

The sooner we get down below, the sooner I can check how bad off I am."

"I can't do much, but I'll help guide you," she said; she clung to his hand, helping him find holds. Again, despite the anxieties of the moment, Ryerson sensed strange stirrings inside him. "If you feel faint," Ruby said, "tell me and I'll try to hold you. At least we'll go down together." She grinned at him and he found it a lovely grin.

In the distance, down near the waterline, he saw a fringe of trees emerging. That had to be Clute's destination.

It was still a hell of a ways.

· 16 ·

The ledge widened on its approach to the forested flats. They were able to throw down their gear, except for the rifles, and leap to lower ground. Clute carefully took the rifles before Jim and Ruby made the short drop. Ryerson heaved down the heavy ropes and painfully eased off the rock shelf. Ruby came to look after his injuries.

"Let Clute do it, Ruby," Ryerson said, hoping his expression registered proper appreciation. "You and Jim take the rifles and watch that ledge. I know full well Doan isn't going to risk coming down here after us, but we'll take no chances. And you did tell me you were a crack shot." He winked at her. Ruby grinned and said nothing. She swung up the Winchester muzzle to touch her forehead in a sort of acknowledging salute. Ryerson felt his insides churn; Sturgis at Helena. Or was he reading more into things than were meant to be?

"Where'd he get you?" Clute asked, disturbing Ryerson's thoughts.

"Right shoulder. Feels like under the shoulder blade. I can't reach it." He shoved his left hand under his right armpit, pointing to the wound. "And we'll take my shirt off careful. It's the only one I've got just now." He worked at skinning out of his trail coat, letting it drop off his dangling right arm, and unbuttoned his shirt and tried to wiggle out of it the same way.

"Just let it drop off your shoulder a little, Cole," Clute said, getting behind him. George Douglas came by to look at the wound. Clute carefully pulled up Ryerson's shirt and peeled it away from his wound.

Clute let out a quick laugh. "Look there, George," he said, and Douglas leaned over to study the wound.

"I'm damned," Douglas said.

"Well, how the hell does it look?" Ryerson demanded.

"Well, Cole, I ain't no doctor but I'd be willing to wager that you got a while longer to live."

"Looks like a big gray wart back here, Cole," Douglas said.

"Well, what the hell's that all about."

"Looks like the ropes and that blanket roll and your heavy coat took most of the damage," Clute observed. "Hell, you ain't hurt at all."

"It's layin' there right under the skin, Cole," Douglas said with a snicker. "Hardly even any blood. I could squeeze 'er right out of there like a blackhead."

Ryerson could sense they were relieved that the wound was minor.

"Well, if you two sawbones are through with your medical consultation, get on with it!" he growled.

"I think we ought to cut the skin and get it out. That'd make it bleed and wash out any poison. What do you think, doctor?" Clute asked George.

"I'm inclined to agree. No tellin' where that ca'tridge might've been," Douglas said. "Doan's man might've dropped it in the cowshit when he was trying to load his carbine."

"Will you get it over with!" Ryerson's voice was loud with mock impatience.

Clute whipped out his knife, lanced the protrusion and caught the bloodied bullet. The work only caused the area to smart a little. "Here she is, Cole," he said, handing the gory slug to Ryerson. "Your souvenir of this trip."

The soft-nosed bullet had mushroomed slightly in passing through the rope and blanket. Ryerson could still see clearly the striations of the rifle's lands and grooves as he hefted it in his palm.

"She's bleedin' a little, Cole," Douglas said. "That's good."

"I'll rustle up that coffin varnish I've got stashed," Clute told Douglas. "A drop or two on there'll help knock down any infection. Then we can find something to pack in there and tie down for a bandage and he'll be good as new."

"Don't go splashing too much of that hootch around," Ryerson said. "We've got a raft to build and I've a hunch that stuff's going to come in handy before we're through."

Clute went to unearth his cache of food, tins, and his whiskey jug. Douglas dragged up the ropes from where Ryerson had dropped them. Ryerson perched on a rock with his right shoulder still bare, patiently waiting for Clute's administering of the antiseptic and crude bandaging.

"I'll take a look at these ropes and see how badly they're damaged," Douglas said. "If you're so dead set on building a raft, you're going to need every inch of them."

"If they're broke, just throw a square knot into it and it'll be okay," Ryerson said. Clute trudged back with a big cream-colored crockery jug.

"You don't know much about rope, Ryerson," Douglas said, with a kind of uppity tone that brought an edge of irritation to the wounded marshal.

"Now, Cole," Clute said, "I'm just going to dab a little of this on here. Might sting some." The whiskey's bite against the wound was only momentary.

"That's a lot better, Clute," he said. "Now tie 'er up and let's set about building our raft. I don't suppose we have enough food here for too much frittering time."

"Cole," Douglas interrupted. He paused as he carefully played the coil of rope with the possible damage through his fingers. He found two places nearly cut through by the bullet. "While I'm at it, I'll show you how to splice a hemp rope by weaving it. Saves a bulky knot, looks and handles better, and saves you several inches of rope."

"Heard a man could do that," Clute said. "Never seen it done. I'm told sailors know a lot of that stuff. Was you a sailor, George?"

"Only on a prairie schooner. I worked at a ropewalk up in Missouri before the war."

"A what?" Ryerson said. "A ropewalk? I thought that's what happened to the guest of honor at a necktie party."

"A ropewalk is what you call a rope factory. I worked on one spreading hemp when I was a kid in Missouri."

"Do tell!" Clute said. "So you know all about rope?"

"Well, I'm not much of a hand to brag, but I learned a thing or two. I could also show you how to weave the end so it won't fray."

"You from Missouri, George? I'm from Kansas."

"There was a time," Douglas said, "we'd be at one another's throats, Clute."

"Glad them days are past," Clute responded.

"If you're from Kansas, you may've heard of the man I worked for. Made his fortune in rope before the war. Then raised particular hell for the Yankees in Kansas and Missouri. Man by the name of Shelby. Ever heard of him? Jo Shelby? They made him a general in the Confederate cavalry."

Clute belted out a laugh. "We heard of him sure enough. Cole and me both."

"I rode with him, George," Ryerson said. "Four years. I rode with Shelby against Clute here, I guess, at Newtonia. Maybe some other skirmishes we haven't had time to talk about."

Clute had torn a strip from the hem of Ruby Montez's long dress. He folded a bandage pad and used the rest to tie it in place against Ryerson's shoulder.

"You rode with Kansas, Clute?" Douglas asked.

"Company A, Ninth Kansas Volunteer Calvary." Clute said it proudly.

"You mean cavalry," Douglas said.

"That's what I said. Calvary."

Douglas let it pass. His eyes roved the tall pines in the wide and long river-bottom flats around them.

"I see there's sure enough no way to climb out of here. It'll have to be a raft. You fellas know anything about rafting? Down a mean and miserable stretch of water like that?" He waved at the roaring rapids charging past them a few yards away.

"I figure you cut down trees, cut a bunch of logs and lash 'em together," Ryerson said.

"I suppose that's the basic idea," Douglas said. "But unless we build it right, it'll take you about to the first big rock, maybe a hundred yards." He paused meaningfully. "Then you'll swim the rest of the way if your log pileup doesn't bash your brains in."

"Sounds like you know something about rafting we don't, George."

"I've seen a few, saw how they were lashed. When I was working in the rope business with Mr. Shelby."

Ryerson was suddenly glad George Douglas was with them. The man knew his ropes and he knew a great deal about rafts. All that knowledge would help get them through if it was possible at all. George spoke up again.

"Where'd you expect to build it?"

"Oh, I don't know," Ryerson said. "Out there on the flats somewhere, I suppose."

"You're a pretty good lawman, Boot Hill Cole," Douglas said. "But you're not much of a mechanic." Something about Douglas's manner was a little irritating to Ryerson in spite of his value to the raft project.

"What are you getting at, George?"

"Say you lash together several tons of logs some distance from the riverbank. Then, how do you propose to get it in

174

the water? To tell that young lady over there to nudge it over the edge for you?"

Ryerson looked at him. "Well, now that you're here, George, I suspect you'll tell us about an easier way."

"You got to build it on a slope or on skids near the water, blocked off or roped off from rolling away. Then when you're ready to go, you knock out the blocks or cut the rope and it slides into the water."

"I suppose we could do that," Clute said.

"You'd better have a sweep, too."

"A sweep? What's that?" Ryerson asked.

"You might call it a rudder. All the rafts I ever saw had one."

"Huh!" Ryerson grunted. "Hadn't thought about that."

"Well, you got to think about these things. A sweep might steer you away from getting busted to flinders on the rocks. I'm not saying it will. But it'll be better'n starting down there with no means of navigation."

"You know how to rig one, George?" Clute asked.

"Oh, I've some ideas in mind. I think we could fashion something tolerable to fill the bill. Seen a few. Got a fair idea how she ought to work. Once you've got an idea of the mechanics of what it's supposed to do for you, why, you go ahead and build it to suit your purpose."

Ryerson had to hand it to Douglas for having a head on his shoulders in spite of a kind of irritating way he had of showing it.

"We'd best get busy," Ryerson said, rousing up and adjusting his shirt and buttoning it. His right arm and shoulder were stiff, but in working the shirt buttons, they limbered up. "We'll spell one another with the axes," he added. "Whoever isn't working with an axe can go to lopping off limbs with a hatchet."

George Douglas got up from his crouch near Ryerson's rock and reached for a rope. "I got to get busy weaving these frayed sections. We won't need big trees. Medium-size is fine, I think, and easier to handle on the ground. Want to get them as close to the same general dimension—girth—as we can. And enough for four people to ride and maneuvering room for the one handling the sweep."

Deep in the gorge, a benevolent twilight came early but spent a long time with its balmy, waning light. Ruby cleaned up around the cook fire after fixing a grand—to them— meal of jerked beef, beans, and coffee. Ryerson ambled to where she worked and perched on a convenient rock. Jim had celebrated his first night of freedom by getting to bed early. George and Clute were off discussing trees and rafts. Ryerson was accustomed now to the river's roar a few rods from their camp and imagined the others were, too. As he smoked by the fire, Ruby joined him, drying her hands on her long skirt, and sat near him. "How's your shoulder, Cole?"

Ryerson raised his arm and flexed it. "Muscles a little tight, some soreness, but that's to be expected. I was lucky." He studied her face, now a great deal different from the powdered, rouged Jezebel he'd met at Doan's. Freedom had also softened the lines of her face, and relaxed her body. Her red hair, no longer confined by Doan's purloined hat, flowed like copper filaments down her shoulders. To Ryerson, her hair gleamed—unlike the dull, lifeless strands he remembered from the day in Doan's lodge room. Freedom, he thought, puts the gleam back in the hair as well as in the eyes. He felt good—real good—about having brought her.

"I'm lucky too, Cole. Lucky you came along when you did and helped me get away from Jubal. I think I'm a lot smarter now than when I had to go to work for him. I don't apologize for my life, if that's the way it sounds. I did what I had to do to survive."

"A lot of us find ourselves in that kind of pickle, Ruby."

"I guess you don't know how I lived. I never told any man about me, not even Jubal. They wouldn't care. But you're different, Cole. I know I could tell you and you'd understand. You understand about people . . . about me."

For no particular reason, Ryerson took her hand. "If being someone who's done his own share of suffering means anything, I guess I would understand. At least, I could always try." His grin at her was self-conscious. He figured he wasn't good at giving advice, so when someone began talking about their problems or just wanting to get something off their chest, he listened and only heard their feelings. Such folks seemed to work things through without much of his help. They were grateful to him, though he never knew exactly why.

"Cole, it's easy to think that my feelings for you are plain gratitude for one of the best things any man ever did for me." Ryerson studied her, his eyes questioning. "But, dammit, it's more than that, and I know it. This morning, when you got shot, it was like I got shot too!" She put her other hand over his and gripped it. "If you'd've fallen, I'd've jumped right behind you!" Ruby bit her lip and her eyes, searching his, were moist.

"I've no right to say such things to any man, especially you, who was so kind to me. And I've no right to the feelings I have for you, the kind of person I am, the kind of life I've lived."

Ryerson decided not to get into how Ruby felt about him; still he couldn't account for his pleasant sensations in being near her. "Anybody can learn from the rough roads of the past, Ruby, and pick out a new trail for their lives."

"Cole, I'm such a nobody I don't even know my real name, if I ever had one. I was an orphan, or maybe a foundling. I don't know where she got me—I've got some ideas—but the only mother I knew was a woman named Rosa Montez and that's where I got my name. She, ah, well, she ran a house . . . not far from the Texas cattle trail. I was always kind of tall for my age, so when I got big enough that the cowboys started sniffing around me, Rosa put me to work."

"How'd you come to meet Jubal?"

"He came through on a cattle drive. He gave Rosa some money and they said I was indentured, or some such. Plain truth was she sold me to him. There was no way I could get away, so I decided to get used to it. And that's about what you saw when you showed up at Doan's."

"My stepfather bound me to a gunsmith in St. Louis. I jumped my bond and went to Texas," Ryerson said.

"We're more like two peas in a pod than I thought, Cole," she said. "I guess if we get out of the river, you'll go after Jubal."

"He's murdered, kidnapped, rustled, conspired to defraud, and held you against your will, and that's slavery. That's been abolished for black or white folks. He's got a lot to answer for."

"You be careful around him, Cole Ryerson. He's evil and he's vicious. Cole?" She gripped his hand firmly in both of hers.

"What, Ruby?"

"Am I wrong in my feelings for you? Because of who I've been? You don't know how I've longed to live a decent life; to be good and to be the wife of a good and decent man. Is that wrong?"

Ryerson pulled her to him. "None of it's wrong, Ruby."

Tree-cutting and raft-building took three days. Clute's jerky lasted two days and there were enough beans for the balance of their time. They passed the whiskey jug before their noon meals as a midday tonic and in the evening, made jokes about after-supper brandies.

While Ryerson observed an easy-going companionship developing among his escapees, raft-building was foremost in their thoughts.

Douglas suggested they build it longer than it was wide. "Seems reasonable," he said. "Should keep the head-end pointed downriver and the stern and sweep in the proper position." Ryerson and Clute agreed that their chief engineer made sense.

Douglas also designed and built what Ryerson considered a quite proper and sturdy sweep—a long pole affixed to a post on the raft and with a good-size length of hand-hewn plank securely pegged to the pole's end. The sweep's post on the raft could swivel more than 180 degrees in a hole Douglas laboriously carved out of the middle log of the raft. He explained to Ryerson that back and forth movement of the sweep, he hoped, would move the raft in the direction of the sweep's thrust, improving its navigation and perhaps saving its riders from catastrophe.

Douglas's sweep pole or handle was also pegged to the upright to easily hoist his rudder out of the water to avoid damage on rocks or shoals.

George supervised the secure lashing together of the logs. Loops of ropes were fashioned as handholds to save the raft's travelers from tumbling overboard. They hewed a slide out of the granite gravel of the river's bank and built the raft perched on its edge; a long log wedged between two nearby trees at the bank's edge served to keep the raft in place.

On launch day, Douglas's "keeper" log would be cut through, allowing the raft to slide down and be water-borne. They had quickly and affectionately dubbed it "the lodgepole."

Ryerson purposely kept Jim Carson on guard at the ledge. The young man, though basically strong and responding well to freedom, was still weak from his weeks of inactivity as Doan's prisoner.

Ruby attended to much of the cooking and camp chores, occasionally stepping in to lop branches off the giant logs with a hatchet.

Relaxing over the first night's fire, with one big tree felled during the day and rolled into position against the lodgepole, Ryerson lit a smoke and gulped a swig from the whiskey jug and looked at young Carson and George Douglas, their faces a-gleam in the firelight across from him.

"Well, we got a start on 'er," he said. "Only time will tell how she works. Now . . ." Ryerson purposely paused. "Jim —and I suppose you, too, George—I've got to ask this. Especially of you Jim, but I know you fellas had your heads together up there in Doan's prison."

The two looked at him quizzically.

"The reason, Jim, that Doan came to capture you and put you up there in the first place? Namely, I got a hunch you know who Doan's in cahoots with in Berdan."

George Douglas looked at Jim, giving him the opportunity to respond.

"I do. The thought that brought me through all that was that some day I'd get away from Doan and see this man get what's coming to him. But Mr. Douglas has an almost bigger stake in this than I do. So we both were living only to get out of there and deal with him together. We talked it all out."

"Before you go any farther, might I ask who that man is?"

"Maybe you don't know him, Cole," George said. "Nor any of the others here." He looked at Jim, who spoke up.

"My father's business associate. Martin Rathburn."

"We'll get him, boys," Ryerson said soberly. "Your suffering will be avenged. Justice is on our side and for once, justice will out."

"First order of business, though," Clute chimed in, "is getting the raft finished and taking on that river."

"And keep an eye peeled for old Doan trying to send some of his boys down that ledge," Ryerson said.

"Pshaw!" Douglas chided. "Look at it up there, Cole. What is it? Fifty, seventy-five yards of exposed ledge not eight inches at its widest spot. We can pick 'em off like squirrels on a bare limb if they try coming down here."

"And I'm telling you, there's no other way in here," Clute added. "Even if he got up to the rimrock, we're still safe. You can't see up there from down here, so he can't see us from up there to try any potshots."

"We'll still post a daylight guard," Ryerson said.

"Granted." Clute watched Ryerson as he spoke. "Doan doesn't know about this place. He knows if we try to make it out along the river we're drowned meat. I'm bettin' he's got the top end of the ledge sealed off. He'll have a sharpshooter or two at the end of the rapids in case we make it out."

"Then we'll be the ones like sittin' ducks," Ryerson said glumly.

· 17 ·

Ruby had taken a turn guarding the ledge with a Winchester. Ryerson walked up to the cook-fire ring where embers of the noon fire were blanketed under powdery gray ash. Before he went back to work, Clute crouched at the fire ring, chatting with Jim Carson. A lumpy and soggy stub of cigarette dangled at the side of Clute's mouth.

"It'd take a lot of work to hack it off," Ryerson heard Clute say, the cigarette bobbing as he talked. His jowls were salt-and-peppery with several days' stubble.

Ryerson slid down near them and rolled himself a smoke as Clute continued. "We got soap for lather and I suppose I could whet and hone a proper edge on my knife. I've had to shave with it a time or two and it works tol'able well."

Jim Carson touseled his abundant growth of beard. "I just don't want to go home looking like this."

"What's all that about?" Ryerson asked.

"Jim here wants a shave before we shove off in the mornin'," Clute responded.

Jim watched Ryerson as he knelt by the fire and pulled out a glowing stick to fire his smoke.

"I'll feel better going out of here if I can shave," Carson

told them. "I look peaked enough as it is, but getting off these whiskers would make a great improvement."

Ryerson fingered his own abrasive growth of several days' neglect. "You don't look too good yourself, Clute," he said. "We could all do with a little cleaning up that way. We can land down below looking like men and not just a bunch of seedy saddle tramps."

"Shaving ain't going to be easy," Clute said.

"Clute," Ryerson reminded, "you've told me that about this whole fracas. Now, dig out your soap and get to stropping your knife. I'll heat up a mess of water. George could stand to scrape his chin, too."

When they went back to work an hour later, the four men were clean-shaven and feeling cleaner in their souls as well; their smooth faces gleamed as bright as their spirits.

Ryerson excused himself on the pretense of checking on Ruby. She was leaned against a tree trunk, eyes on the narrow ledge that inched up the cliff face, the Winchester across her lap. Her stiff-brimmed black hat was shoved back to reveal her coppery hairline.

Ryerson felt an old familiar stirring; he was attracted to her, and she to him. She accepted him for who and what he was. He quickly made up his mind. His feelings for her were about as close to what he figured was love as he'd ever get.

"Well, Mr. Ryerson," she said, observing his clean jowls. "Aren't you the handsome one under all those whiskers now that they're gone!"

"Hoped you'd notice," Ryerson said. "I reckon I did it for you."

"We go tomorrow, Cole?"

"Looks that way, Ruby."

"We'll make it. I know that. I've got faith in you, Cole. Because you say it'll work, it'll work. Then what'll happen to us, Cole? You and me? Our talk the other night. When you held me."

"Ruby, I'll have a lot to nail down. Doan and this man

Rathburn who's in cahoots with Doan. Maybe you could stay with Jim's family."

"The question is, Mr. Ryerson, do you want me to wait for you?"

"Guess I'm saying so. Ruby, I'll tell you straight out, I'm not much of a hand with the women. Drawing room manners and all such as that. I'm truthful and steady. I don't give my word without a lot of thought. When I give my word, I never back off from it."

Ruby's pretty dark eyes again searched his. "Meaning?"

Ryerson grabbed her abruptly and held her shoulders. "Meaning yes, wait for me! Go back to Fort Walker with me. I'll find you decent quarters there for a lady. We'll begin seeing each other like proper folks do. Ruby, from here on out, the past is forgotten!"

"Thank you, dear Cole."

Everything was ready at daybreak. They lashed the Winchesters on the raft, but left the axes and hatchets in camp. In the pre-dawn light, they filled up on their only food supply, warmed-over beans, knowing full well they'd not eat until they were out of danger. A small ceremony—with a slug apiece—went along with reburying Clute's jug.

Ruby, Jim, and Ryerson lay on the raft clutching rope handholds. Clute was given the honor of cutting through the lodgepole. Douglas stood, his sweep pole in his grip, holding it high until they were in the water.

"All right, folks," Ryerson announced from his prone position. "Hang on and be ready for the ride of your life!"

Scant feet below him the Black River roared, angry and swollen with a vicious, unpredictable vitality.

"Won't be much of a chance to talk until we hit calm water," Ryerson added. "Just plant this idea in your head and don't turn loose of it. We are going to get through! Clute! Do your duty!"

"To the five of us!" Jim Carson shouted jubilantly.

"Yahoo!" Clute yelled and stepped toward the lodgepole

with his axe poised. The others chimed in with a bracing cheer.

Clute's axe, specially re-sharpened for the occasion, rang against the lodgepole, first right and then left of his notch. The axe bites barked in the early-morning air. White chips spun skyward. With a great cracking sound, the restraining log succumbed and the raft roared down their slide to plummet into the ferocious water.

Clute hurled the axe away and dropped to grab his rope support.

At once and with a jarring shudder of the lashed logs, the aggressive current swept them away downstream, spinning the raft one full turn, putting Douglas and the sweep he'd lashed himself to at the wrong end. The roar around them was deafening. At this point, no rocks loomed in sight, only pitching and tossing waves of surging, turbulent current slamming at the raft from what seemed every direction.

Douglas dipped the sweep into the churning water carefully and the raft quickly veered sideways to the massive current as it was tumbled and tossed, dipping and rising with the fury of the raging torrent.

Hanging onto his stout pole with both arms, Douglas allowed it to dip again into the forceful current, this time to right itself with the sweep at the rear.

They had slipped to midstream and with no visible rocks ahead, Douglas lifted the sweep by pushing down on his pole; he clung to it for his balance on the deck of the dipping, rocking, and slippery raft. The cliff walls spun past them at dizzying speeds.

"She's working like a whiz-bang!" Ryerson heard George shout jubilantly over the river's thundering tumult. Water flew from his curly-tight hair and showered off his arms and clothing as the raft bounced and bucked in the powerful current. Everyone was drenched.

Almost like an afterthought, Douglas's voice rose again over the din. "Jee-zuss! Hang on!"

Ryerson raised his head to see the river end at a pitching,

tossing horizon about two hundred yards ahead. He saw nothing beyond but sky and canyon walls. A waterfall! The sting of cold spray dashing from the front of the raft lashed his face.

Ryerson took a tighter hold on his rope loop with both hands. The others gripped theirs and watched with fear-widened eyes as the unknown brink rushed at them, trying to make themselves smaller against the logs. Ryerson felt his breath torn from his lungs.

Then they were in it. The raft pitched out like a cannon shot, its head-end momentarily airborne. Almost impulsively it was sucked down a chute of tremendous force and pressure, more an angling slide than a sheer drop-off. Geysers of water slammed skyward around them as their log vessel plowed down with a jolting slam. Ryerson felt the logs twist and buckle under him, but Douglas's lashings held.

A giant wave plunged over the raft and slammed the grizzled helmsman square on. Ryerson was sure that when his vision cleared Douglas would have been swept overboard. But there he stood at his post, stoutly working his sweep. The man had uncommon pluck.

The raft pitched and bucked down the steep incline of violent water, but miraculously held its head-first course. Once, as it began to pitch sidewise in its pell-mell plunge down the rapids, he felt Douglas dip the sweep in and almost abruptly the raft responded, thrusting itself squarely into the force of the dynamic current.

In the midst of the churning chaos, a ridiculous thought spun through Ryerson's mind. Longer than it was wide; Douglas had proved his engineering genius. Its short side, Douglas had predicted, would naturally go with the current and the rear sweep would keep the front end properly aligned with the flow's violence.

At the end of the rampant chute and the savage beating the raft had taken, the head-end again plowed into the turbulent, swirling water, immersing the front half. That fast, it bounced upright and swiveled; Douglas dipped the sweep, guiding the raft as it corrected in line with the current.

Towering over the inert Ryerson, Douglas shook his head to rid his eyes of the streaming water. Ryerson dared to raise his head again to see the raging river all but blocked by giant boulders, tumbled down the gorge at flood tide just past the bottom of the giant flume of wild water.

Ryerson watched Douglas fight the sweep pole with both arms, struggling to steer the raft past the onrushing house-size rocks.

"Cole!" Douglas screamed. "Help!"

Dropping one hand from his restraining rope, Ryerson reached out and caught hold of the slippery sweep support post. The current had hardly lessened its speed past the end of the chute and the raft pitched like a bucking bronc. He dropped his hold rope with the other hand and rolled to grip the post with both hands. With great effort, he pulled himself erect with the sweep pole between him and George.

"Push to me!" Douglas screamed over the roar, straining with all his might against the pole. As Douglas pulled, Ryerson pushed and the raft lurched past a giant rock with scant inches to spare.

"There's another!" George bellowed. "Now pull to you," and he strained to push the shaft to Ryerson, who felt the sweep pole shudder and tremble under the force as their jury-rigged rudder tore through the raging water. Ryerson feared the vicious current would snap the long pole. The raft obediently veered from its collision course with the rock and swung past it.

Ryerson was not lashed to the post as Douglas was. His only support was the water-slick pole he clutched. One mistake, one slip and he'd be hurled into the charging current and swept away to his death.

"Now back to me!" Douglas ordered loudly and they evened the sweep with the current. The raft again corrected its plunge down the river, bobbing and bucking ferociously, but holding true course.

A sudden scream from Ruby rose over the river's roar. In a horrified glance, Ryerson saw that she'd lost her grip on the slippery rope hold. She called out his name once.

"Cole!"

Startled by the sudden crisis, Ryerson watched her frantically claw and scratch at the logs and scramble to catch herself as she slid in the direction of the raft's slope. Dropping his grip on the sweep, he quickly crouched, one arm around the post to reach out to catch her. The raft lurched, and she rolled away to bump against a terrified Jim Carson. When it tilted again, Ruby spun past Ryerson. His arm lashed out to catch hers slipping past as she dropped over the edge of the logs into the raging torrent. Her eyes beseeched him as the water's force tugged and tore at her full skirt, sucking her away from him. His hand, unable to maintain a hold on her slick arm, caught her wrist; Ryerson dug in his fingers and gripped it with all the force he could summon. Vainly, he tried to pull her away from the river's fiendish clutches. "Hang on, Ruby!" his voice shrieked.

A violent wave slammed the raft, drenching them again, tossing the raft like a bobbing cork. Ryerson's hold on the sweep post began to slip. Douglas screamed at him for help. Clute struggled to raise up to aid George, but was hurled back to the logs. Ruby screamed Ryerson's name over and over. In desperation, he stretched to reach out with a foot to hook his boot toe into a nearby handhold to free both hands to drag her back. It was too far and too dangerous.

Douglas shouted another warning a moment before the raft glanced off a huge rock with shuddering impact to carom into the ferocious current. Ryerson was slammed by a monstrous wave and Ruby's wrist slipped from his grasp. One arm still circling the sweep post, Ryerson hooked the other around it and slumped to the logs gasping with exertion and dread. His eyes searched for her in the raging water, but there was no one; she had been swept under and was gone.

With great effort, Clute made it to George's side to take over Ryerson's place at the sweep. He was able to crouch and guide Ryerson's hand to a rope hold; numbed by the suddenness of the catastrophe, Ryerson gripped it and the vacant one beside it, for several moments incapable of anything more than holding on.

Abruptly, his self-control came back. He and Jim and Clute and George still had to make it to safety; he had to set aside dealing his loss of Ruby until later. And he would; at the right time and the right place. This was neither. He'd learned that bitter lesson at Helena, and for that matter, in a dozen other battles and skirmishes when good men—first-class soldiers—under his command made the casualty lists. The man leading the column ignores personal tragedy, however devastating, in favor of winning the day, in favor of those still in the saddle.

He forced himself to clear his head for the problem at hand by taking stock. He had no notion how far they'd come or how long they'd been in the stream. In some respects it seemed like seconds, in others, an eternity. The turbulence still roared around him, tossing the raft like a wood chip.

Clute and George worked together manning the sweep, getting smarter about small corrections and adjustments to avoid rocks or plunging waves looming ahead. Long anxious moments were consumed in their weaving course past the silent granite obstacles. Ryerson lost track of time and place as his helmsmen battled with the sweep to keep the raft straight in the furious, raging current. His mind remained vacant.

"Easy now," he heard Douglas call to Clute. "Just a bit to me!" and they eased the sweep slowly as the raft plunged past a submerged rock or avoided a giant white-capped wave flinging itself skyward.

Jim and Cole were sodden piles of rags at their feet,

sometimes rolling with the pitching raft as they clutched their rope loops and flopped back as the raft leveled itself. When the raft began to slide sideways to the powerful current, the helmsmen pulled or pushed the sweep arm to correct it with the river's flow of monstrous force.

Ryerson hugged the logs, hoping the unbearable ordeal would end soon; his gut knotted with guilt. "If I'd only hung on. Should have grabbed her sooner . . . made sure she was lashed down better."

Then they plunged out like a rock flung from a scoop shovel. The cliffs veered apart to soften into hills with sparse vegetation, spreading and gentling the water's force. Flat land appeared at either side of them. The malevolent river's course widened and while the current remained strong, the waves and turbulence diminished.

Ryerson dared to look around him at the water for some sign of Ruby's body; everything he saw that might be it turned out to be something else. Despite his growing desolation, a kind of sublime relief, tuned to the lessening of the raging waters, overwhelmed him; he sensed a jubilance in the others as well, despite the dark cloud that clung to them.

The stream's force was still a power to be reckoned with, but control was easier, with only surface eddies and whorls to remind them of the violence they had challenged and bested.

The chasm gentled to the eye as it receded in the distance. The river widened and lay smooth as a mirror with the flat, rolling miles of lonesome prairie stretching away on both sides. The peaceful vista was broken only by cottonwoods taking advantage of easy water at the side of the whispering river gliding scant feet from their roots.

Again Ryerson battled to stay in control despite his devastating calamity. He couldn't afford to let his mind wander; had to stay alert. Jubal Doan and thirty or so rustler cronies would shoot him on sight. He had no notion what kind of tricks the slimy Martin Rathburn might have up his sleeve.

He looked out at the river, letting his mind be with her in a moment as serene as the water around him. "Sorry, Ruby," he thought. "It was awfully good while it lasted." And he found himself again thinking prayerfully. "Take good care of her, Lord. She's a good woman." Suddenly he felt looted, deprived and empty; an aching, hollow void inside him. He knew again the bitter desolation that followed the death of Dan Sturgis.

The raft rode gently on the glass-smooth reflective surface. Fighting back bitter thoughts about Ruby, he battled again to bring calm to his mind, as he laid aside the evils of the gorge and the havoc they had wreaked. The future with all its promises, its threats, and its challenges lay ahead. Fading into the oblivion of memory were the precarious rescue of Jim and George, the flight from Doan's, his minor wound. The perilous plunge down the Black River gorge and the brutal forces that lay behind him could also be relegated to memory but for the bitterly vivid picture of Ruby slipping from his grasp.

Ryerson glanced at George Douglas and Clute Mills, their eyes still fixed downstream, manning the sweep to keep the raft correct in the bland flow. Clute could have stepped aside so far as need was concerned, but, Ryerson thought, Clute stood rooted as if, by God, he had earned the spot and figured to stick with it.

Jim Carson and Ryerson crouched silently in their soggy clothing; Ryerson knew that Jim's mind was full of relief at having made it out of the perilous clutches of the rustler chieftan. George and Clute were left with the now-pleasant task of guiding the soft-flowing raft in its midstream course; it was easy now, almost enjoyable for the grizzled rancher and the aging ex-Union "calvaryman." Ryerson felt Clute's eyes on him. Clute was the first to speak since they hit calm water. "What a hell of a thing to have happen, Cole."

George also spoke up. "Cole. I'm damned sorry about Ruby. But we made it. Your guts and mule-headed stubbornness brought us out."

Ryerson looked wistfully out into the distant prairies. "We all should've made it. It's not the grand feeling it should be, without her. We made it, and I guess just now that's all that matters. For me right now, nothing else seems to." Almost absentmindedly, Ryerson hunted through his clothing in hopes his smoke makin's had stayed dry. "Naw, George, my willfulness only got Ruby dead. Besides . . . without you, none of us would've made the rapids past midstream."

Clute was jubilant despite the calamity. "Chalk it up to guts," he said. "A little bit of savvy and one hell of a lot of luck."

"For us, maybe," Ryerson said dryly.

"What'll we do, Cole?" Jim asked. "Keep floating or get off and walk?"

"Float. Eventually we'll see somebody or wind up at a ranch. Or maybe we'll drift clear to Berdan."

Ryerson had found his smoke makin's intact, rolled one and hunted a dry place to scratch his match. From somewhere Clute produced a dry match and snapped its head into flame with his thick thumbnail and reached over to fire Ryerson's smoke. In turn, Ryerson offered Clute his makin's sack.

"What do you think happened to Ruby?" Jim asked, his voice now halting and hoarse with emotion.

Ryerson looked at him, feeling an abrupt burning spurt of impatience. "Why, dammit, she drowned!" His snapped-out words were loud and bitter. Instantly, he was sorry he'd vented his feelings and frustrations. "Sorry, Jim. Didn't mean that the way it sounded. She's dead and her body's in the river some place. We'll probably never know."

"You're not to blame yourself, Cole," George said. "You did everything that was humanly possible."

"I saw it all," Clute said. "I don't know how you held onto her as long as you did."

"Let's leave it be, fellas. It's over and done with. We're lucky any of us made it."

The others nodded in agreement. "Now, we got to get on to the next problem," Ryerson continued. "Better unlimber the Winchesters. They're wet, but they'll work. Doan may figure we'll try to come out of the gorge. We ought to stay close to the west side, George, in case we have visitors on the east side, Doan's side."

"Good thinking," Douglas said, dipping the sweep and pulling it to his right. The raft quartered in favor of the west half of the river, but still out from the bank.

"Wait a minute!" Jim Carson called, apprehension quivering in his normally level voice. "Down there! At the bend!"

All eyes swung in that direction. In the distance, Ryerson saw what appeared to be a camp on the west bank. Several wagons loomed into sight through the trees; a dozen or more horses were secured to a picket line and a pillar of gray smoke issued from a campfire. People moved around in the vicinity of the camp.

"Doan's slicker'n I figured!" Ryerson growled. "He's crossed over and set up an ambush. George! Get us to the east side! Fast!"

Douglas dipped the sweep, and obediently but agonizingly slowly the raft angled toward the east bank. Ryerson pulled out his Navy and checked his percussion caps and the plug of grease over each bullet sealing it watertight.

"Jim!" he called softly. "Hand me a Winchester and paint for war. Clute, get down here. George, you get down too; the raft'll stay mostly midstream by itself."

"We're moving awful slow," Douglas moaned. "Doan's got us boxed. Fish in a barrel. We may have to swim for it."

A voice drifted to them over the serene water. "Hallooooo! The raft!"

A pair of figures materialized around some trees along the west bank opposite them and moved down toward the lush, reedy grass at the water's edge.

"Don't shoot!" the voice called again. "Jim! Cole!"

Jim Carson's voice rose, quaking with emotion. "It's my brother Rick! And Vic Douglas! George! There's Vic!"

Douglas stood up again to reef on the sweep pole and send the raft quartering for the river's west bank.

· 18 ·

"Let's not lose the raft!" George called as they neared the shore. To Ryerson it sounded like George might want to drag it home and keep it in the barn to brag on in years to come. Rick and Vic moved close to the water's edge to help. George tossed his support rope, still snubbed to the sweep post, toward land. "Here, Vic," he called, "grab this, son." Vic caught the short length of rope and stood by, hauling and holding the raft close to the bank.

Ryerson watched the Carson and Douglas families race happily along the bank toward them from their downstream campsite. Ryerson knew that he would be quickly engulfed in a jubilance he'd be unable to share, but would have to. None of his raft mates knew his true feelings for Ruby. Their feeling of loss was heartfelt and sincere, but all that was overwhelmed by their relief at their deliverance.

In a corner of his mind, Ryerson was not so sure it wouldn't be better to have drowned in the river with Ruby; it seemed that whenever he began to love and care about someone, something came to snatch that person away from him.

Ryerson shook himself as he raised up to follow the others off the raft. Again he told himself to reorder his thinking.

Preoccupation with Ruby's tragedy could lower his guard; could get him dead.

"Wait a minute," Clute yelled jubilantly. He bent down in mock ceremony to kiss the sodden shaggy bark. "Thanks, raft," he called loudly as people began to cluster on the bank. "You brought us out to freedom." Clute grabbed up his Winchester and stepped off.

"For our deliverance," Jim Carson said, leaning down to caress the logs before scooping up the other rifle. Ryerson looked at George Douglas, their eyes acknowledging the leveling influence of Ruby on an otherwise joyous occasion. To Ryerson, it was time for him, as well as the others, to lighten things up.

"Well, cap'n," he said loudly, "the master, I'm told, is supposed to be the last to leave the vessel. In your honor, I step off first. My idea, but your creation, George." And then more softly. "We got out."

"Damned if we didn't," George agreed, his eyes on those swarming the bank, his face crinkling pleasantly at Melissa and his wife, Hanna.

Sam, Nora, and Penny Carson engulfed Jim with hugs, their eyes glistening with tears of joyous relief. The scene was the same with the Douglases. Ryerson strolled over to Rick Carson and Vic Douglas as they finished securing the raft's tether to a cottonwood.

"See you boys got home in one piece," he said. "You did yourselves proud. Your timing was perfect. Tell you about it later."

"Just followed our plan, Cole. Like you asked us to," Rick said.

Vic piped up. "Heard Clute and my dad talking about a lady on the raft with you, but she fell off. What happened?"

"It was bad, fellas. I don't really want to talk about it. Maybe later. I will tell you that Doan had a young woman there against her will—didn't want to be there. She persuaded me to take her along. I wish now I hadn't. She fell off in the wild water and we lost her. Just let it go at that."

"That's awful, Cole," Vic said. "But the rest of you made it and I suppose we ought to be thankful for that."

Their conversation was interrupted by George Douglas's voice booming with authority near them. "Jim Carson! Come on over here!"

Jim broke away from his jubilant family and obediently stepped to where George stood with Melissa and her mother. "Young man," George called loudly enough for all to hear as his former fellow prisoner approached, "we've been through a lot together these last few weeks and days. I've learned a lot more about you. You're a good man, Jim Carson, a decent and strong man. Now! Whether or not it's appropriate for me to say this, I'll say it anyway. I'll be proud to have you come formally calling on my daughter Melissa!"

"Go to him, child," Hanna Douglas urged and Melissa stepped away to meet Jim, arms outstretched. Ryerson saw great tears welling up in Jim's eyes as his arms came up to embrace Melissa. "Jim, Jim, Jim," she murmured, a sob of relieved emotion in her voice.

Jim was speechless as he hugged Melissa, his eyes clamped shut. When he opened them, still in Melissa's arms, he looked straight at Ryerson, his lips forming silent words: "Thanks, Cole."

Ryerson turned away, his heart sinking, his eyes moist; he only hoped the others would view his actions as his being moved by the joy shared by Jim and Melissa. Instead he saw Ruby in his mind's eye, on guard at the foot of the ledge and her words: "Do you want me to wait for you?" He swallowed hard and turned back to the others, his face composed.

Sam Carson stepped forward and stuck out his hand to George Douglas, gripping his forearm to emphasize his emotion. "You made it, George," he said. "All's well that ends well."

"Not quite," Ryerson said loudly. "Meat ain't meat till it's in the pan. All this isn't settled yet."

Sam's eyes swung on him. "I know, Cole. But you've been through a hell of an ordeal, taking all the responsibility to see that this wonderful moment could come to pass. You all need time to recover, to rest. You can at least take time to do that. Let's all go down to our camp. We've got plenty of good, hot food and tents and blankets for all you folks to rest up. There'll be time to hear about the young woman, too."

George Douglas looked at the raft and its mooring to a convenient sapling. "She looks secure," he said, viewing his log lash-up, standing and looking prouder than the master of a Mississippi sternwheeler. He strode to Vic standing nearby. "Son, Cole tells me you and Rick had yourselves quite an adventure. I'm proud of you." George's joy and his pride were stamped all over his face. He swung up his arms and caught his son in a fatherly hug. Vic's eyes swung around until they found Penny, standing nearby with her mother; he grinned broadly.

With Ryerson again telling himself to keep his mind off Ruby and on matters at hand and with the Douglases and the Carsons bubbling over with euphoria, they headed for the camp a short distance downstream. The women bustled around and soon spread a bounteous meal for the escapees; everyone showed great concern for their comfort.

By the time they had eaten, the sun, low in the west, threw long shadows across the prairie. The distance filled with a powdery bluish haze. His mind easing, Ryerson settled on a perfect word: the gloaming. With plans for everyone to stay in camp and return home in the morning, Ryerson built a smoke and sat away from the others, alone with his cigarette and his thoughts.

His exhaustion began to take over with the responsibility off his shoulders. He closed his eyes and leaned back, focusing his mind to purge it of recent trials and tragedies.

Clute had drifted away somewhere to sleep. George Douglas and Jim Carson were in deep conversation with Sam Carson—giving him the details of the sinister plots of his business partner, Martin Rathburn.

Ryerson further forced himself to relax and catch a few winks. Too late in the day to start for Berdan to arrest Martin Rathburn; first thing in the morning, he thought, his consciousness giving way to sleep.

As twilight fell over Berdan some miles distant, a coal-black horse with a white blaze on its forehead came up from the south, carrying a small man in dark clothing with a black hat and black leather vest.

Berdan's Broad Street was dark, aside from patches of light from the windows and doorways of two or three buildings.

Jack Reno wore matching ivory-gripped sixguns low in a tie-down rig on a specially built cartridge belt.

Keeping his horse at an easy walk, Reno rode boldly up to the hitch rail in front of the Berdan Bar. He got down and looped the reins over the crossbar. Through the dark, he could see the sign at Martin Rathburn's office and a rectangle of light from a window playing on the rutted street, assuring him that Rathburn was there at work.

A horse left any other place in town at this time of night, Reno calculated, might arouse suspicion. Other horses were tied nearby, their owners obviously in the saloon. His gunslinger's cunning glinting in his hard, black eyes, Reno looked up and down the deserted street and, seeing no activity, turned to loosen his horse's cinch before starting cautiously across to report to Rathburn.

Reno's usually keen eyes missed the slight and age-bent figure of Dad Burns lurking in the alley next to the saloon. Dad was on the verge of stepping out of the darkness with his usual greeting to a stranger and fawning attempts to mooch a drink. A recognition of the man's bearing and behavior stopped Dad as he watched the stranger fiddle with his saddle in the dim light from the saloon window.

"Jack," Dad whispered under his breath. "Jack Reno!" Astonished and fearful, Burns ducked out of sight again and disappeared down the alley.

Again, Reno cautiously glanced up and down the street before walking with an assured stride across to Rathburn's office. He rapped on a door panel and stepped back into the shadows to await Rathburn. When the door opened, Reno waved Rathburn aside and ducked in.

"I tried to keep from being spotted, Mart," he said gruffly to the portly financier. "Got anything to drink around this place?"

Rathburn released the drape-like curtains to cover his front window and went to the rear window to assure himself it was closed, and pulled a rolled shade down over it as well.

"I'd about given up on you," Rathburn growled impatiently. "Things here have turned very touchy."

When Reno spoke, his teeth were bared in a tight-lipped snarl. "Got here as quick as I could. It's a long ride from El Paso."

Rathburn got a fresh glass for Reno and filled it, as well as refilling his own gleaming thick tumbler beside the paperwork on his desk. They each took hefty sips. "So what is it you need, Mart?"

"At this point, I'm not exactly sure anymore. It's all gotten stickier than I had expected. The major problem is there's a lawman hereabouts, a Federal marshal from Judge Winfield's jurisdiction. The settlers are ganging up for an assault on a rustler's hideout some miles south of town. I expected them to move to the attack before this."

"How do I figure into that? Or you?"

"Let's say I've had some dealings with the rustlers and I won't be in a very favorable light if it comes out. A lot of the heat would be off me if a stranger was to come to town and just happened to egg this marshal into a gunfight and come out on top."

"Who's this enforcer?"

"Ever heard of Cole Ryerson?"

A sardonic grin flitted at the corners of Reno's mouth. He grunted.

"Heard of him? Who hasn't? Boot Hill Cole. Never saw

him. He's supposed to have killed eight or ten men as a lawman. But I never heard that any of them were any kind of specialists with a sixgun. I don't see a particular problem in calling him out once I find him. That'll be something. Sending Boot Hill Cole to Boot Hill!"

"Came to town masquerading as a prospective land buyer named Kenny Rollins. Even wangled his way into the rustlers' stronghold but got found out. Escaped by the skin of his teeth. He's been staying with my business associate, Sam Carson. Probably helping get this army of ranchers drilled for an attack on the rustlers' camp. I haven't seen Carson for three or four days, either. Among other things, Sam Carson's son was killed by the rustlers, so Sam's going out there to try to even the score."

"This Ryerson been to town lately?"

"Not that I know of. I'm sure I'd've heard."

"Won't do for me to go hunting him. I'll stick around town a day or so to see if he comes in. I won't dally too long. I'll get him here. Make it look like a clean calling out, one gunfighter up against another. Tracking him out there is too much like a hired gun at work. There might be embarrassing questions."

"Get it done. That's all I ask. What's the tariff on your work these days, Jack?"

Reno grunted a sinister half chuckle and looked Rathburn in the eye. "For you, Mart, even considering the reputation of the man I'm going up against, make it a thousand."

"Get it done soon and clean and there's another five hundred in it."

"Mighty generous."

"I'm desperate. I stand to lose a lot the longer this Ryerson sees daylight."

"You got the money here?"

"Do it and go into camp five or so miles south of town. I'll bring it out as soon as the coast is clear."

"Huh-uh. Cash on the barrelhead."

"You drive a hard bargain."

"And you're falling on hard times, Rathburn. You need me more than the other way around."

"Eight hundred now. That's better than half."

"Do I have a choice?" Reno's tone was sarcastic.

Rathburn's lip curled in easy cynicism. "Yeah. Ride on out of here. There's an old rummy that hangs around the saloon. I could get him to drygulch Ryerson with a shotgun for two bottles of cheap whiskey. Then I could become a hero by shooting the old bastard for killing Boot Hill Cole."

"You got the eight hundred? I need some sleep."

Again, Rathburn leered evilly at Jack Reno. "I knew you'd see it my way, Jack." He slid out a desk drawer to produce a banded stack of crisp bills. He rapped the bundle loudly against the edge of his desk before tossing it across to Reno. "Eight hundred. Count it. See you in your camp when the job's done."

"Foldin' money?" Reno queried suspiciously. "You sure it's good? I hoped for silver. I'm not sure there's a bank that would guarantee it."

Rathburn's grin had all the outward signs of gloating. "It's as good as my word, Jack."

"That bein' the case, take it back and get me silver."

"You don't trust my word, Jack?"

"Jack Reno doesn't trust any man's word. Yours about the least, Rathburn."

"And I thought we were friends, Jack."

"Silver or no deal."

"Jack, you have any idea how much fifteen hundred silver dollars weigh? You'd need at least two pack horses. And Sam Carson might sic some of his men on you."

"Let me work that out. How about it?"

"You wouldn't get far, Jack. You deal with the banker Emmett Muldoon in El Paso, don't you? Emmett deals with a lot of us who sometimes operate, you might say, outside the law. He'll guarantee my paper money."

Reno slid the bills inside his shirt. "Don't make me come back to claim it, Rathburn. You might regret it."

"Jack, is that any way to talk to an old friend?" Rathburn heaved his bulk out of the chair to show Jack Reno to the door.

For a long time after Reno slipped out, Rathburn sat in the murky gloom of one lamp pondering the next few days. Getting Ryerson out of the way was the linchpin in his plans. If Sam Carson's army attacked Jubal Doan, they'd be sure to be repulsed. A few ranchers would die and he'd have to foreclose their land claims and improvements. Doan would know that Judge Winfield would mount a militia-size posse to drive him out; with that prospect looming, Doan would surely be persuaded to leave the territory.

Rathburn sighed; things might not look so bleak after all. There'd be profits to be made with sales to new buyers and business might return to better than normal.

A tentative tapping at his office door alerted him. Jack Reno back? he wondered. He cautiously opened the door a crack. The dim bar of light from his office lamp lit the expectant but whiskery features of old Dad Burns.

"Mr. Rathburn?"

"It's Dad, isn't it?"

"Yessir. I never come here before. Never spoke to you."

"What can I do for you?"

"I think we ought to talk."

"I can't imagine what we'd possibly have to talk about, Dad. But come in."

"Maybe it might be about Jack Reno."

"Come in. Quickly!" Rathburn closed the door behind Dad after looking up and down the dark, deserted street to assure himself no one had seen the confrontation with Dad. He found the old man surveying his office.

"You got a lot to drink in here, Mr. Rathburn. Don't suppose you could spare a man a little dab?"

"Have a chair, Dad," Rathburn said. "Sure. Sure. Let me pour you one."

For a moment, Rathburn's hand paused at the brandy bottle with its special red-diamond symbol. Better, he thought, to hear the old man out. He filled a glass from a bottle of his cheapest whiskey and set it in front of the eager derelict who sat across the desk licking his lips in anticipation.

He retrieved his own empty glass from his desk and refilled it with a fine vintage brandy. He handed Dad's glass to him and watched the whiskey disappear almost as fast as he could bat an eye. He poured Dad another.

"Now, Dad. Who is this person you wanted to talk with me about?"

"Jack Reno. The gunslinger from Texas. I know him from the old days. I know you talked with him. A few minutes ago." Dad took a long sip of his second drink.

"It happens a man did stop by this evening to talk about registering for a land claim. But he didn't tell me he was Jack Reno or anything about the nature of his work."

"Well, Jack was here talking to you and don't try to con me. I watched him come and leave. He took his horse down to the livery and then went over and put up for the night at the Berdan House. He's a dangerous man, Mr. Rathburn. If you don't know it, he's trouble in big doses."

"I'll sure take that into account in my dealings, Dad, and I thank you."

"Don't suppose you could spare another?" Dad asked, tossing off the dregs in his glass.

Rathburn took Dad's glass back to the liquor cabinet and again looked at the bottle with its glaring red-diamond warning emblem. Again he chose his bottle of cheap whiskey.

He handed the full glass back to Dad.

"I could tell you a lot, Mr. Rathburn. Like I seen Jubal Doan in here with you one night, a long time ago. Just after they killed Mr. Moseley."

"Strictly business, Dad," Rathburn assured him. "People around here have the wrong impression of Mr. Doan. And there's no evidence linking him to Moseley's death."

"But they come to see you at night, sneaking into town

like Jack Reno done. And lately some of Doan's men have been back to see you. They came in the night, too, so's not to be seen."

"Have another, Dad?" Rathburn's mind raced with the old drunk's revelations. Dad handed him his empty glass. The whiskey had turned the old man bold.

"And I seen the time they hauled young Jim Carson out of here all beat up. I've kept quiet about it. But Kenny Rollins or whatever his name is has gone out to get Jim away from Doan. Gonna sneak in and fetch the boy right out from under Doan's nose."

"Young Carson's dead," Rathburn protested. "Had an accident out on the prairie most likely. How do you know all this?"

"I watch what goes on around here. I listen to the talk in the s'loon. People don't care what they say around me because I'm a no-account. Once in a while I put things together. Like what's going on over here with you."

Rathburn stared at the old geezer in astonishment, unable to speak.

"There's some have heard," Dad said, "that Rollins is bringing young Carson down the Black River gorge on a raft. Sam Carson and a bunch of people are camped out there right now, waitin' for 'em."

Rathburn almost gasped aloud. "Goddamn Doan," he whistled under his breath. That explained the delay in Sam's attack at Doan's. The rancher army was only a smokescreen for Ryerson's rescue attempt. And Doan probably hadn't disposed of young Carson in time.

Rathburn calmed, turning coolly calculating. This was no time for panic, he told himself. To treat Dad to the poisoned brandy now would be foolish. There'd be no easy way to get rid of the body. But if the old man met with an unfortunate accident when Rathburn was away, he couldn't be blamed.

Dad's voice intruded on his thoughts. "I could forget about knowing Jack Reno and the other stuff I've seen and heard."

Rathburn looked at him. The old sot wasn't as lamebrained as he appeared. Still Rathburn knew that his golden goose in Berdan was cooked—and burned.

"You're pretty clever, old-timer. What's loss of memory cost these days?"

"What's it worth to you?"

"A thousand dollars. Take it or leave it. I need friends and I'm willing to make it worth your while, Dad."

Dad's eyes lit up. "You got it here? Tonight?"

"I'll have it here first thing in the morning. You come by. If I'm not here, you come in anyway and wait. Help yourself to a drink if you're of a mind."

"Good enough by me. Any more of that whiskey left, partner? Just to seal our deal?"

Rathburn grimaced at Dad's familiarity and sudden self-assurance. "Sure, partner," he said. Rathburn again avoided the red-diamond bottle; it would serve its purpose in the morning.

Dad slugged down the hefty portion Rathburn had poured and got up to leave. "See you in the mornin'," he mumbled, sidling toward the door, a bit unsteady on his feet.

As soon as the door closed, Rathburn mentally inventoried his supply of ready cash, glad that he hadn't offered more to Jack Reno. He quickly cleaned his safe of currency, stuffing it in a leather valise.

He pondered any incriminating documents, particularly those that showed his clear title to claims that were defaulted. They quickly disappeared up the flue of his office stove.

He looked the place over as he prepared to leave. He was out about three thousand dollars plus the eight hundred he'd advanced to Jack Reno. Let Reno go ahead and do Cole Ryerson in, he thought. He didn't worry about Reno chasing him down for the remainder; he'd head east where he had major investments, change his name. Besides, gunslingers had short life expectancies anyway.

His final act was to leave Dad's glass on his desk. He put two bottles beside it—one of pure hooch, nearly empty, and the red-diamond flask. At his back window, he drained the poisoned bottle of all but a good-size swig. Dad could be counted on to drain them both in the morning and destroy the evidence along with himself. People would assume Dad had learned about Rathburn's liquor supply, had broken in and drunk himself to death.

Martin Rathburn gloated; men were easier to dispose of than wolves.

His final bit of business in Berdan would be to stop at the saloon for an alleged nightcap and just happen to tell the bartender that he'd be gone on a business trip for several days.

· 19 ·

In the chilly moments of pre-dawn, Ryerson warmed himself over a small fire while the camp slept, boiled a pot of coffee and gnawed cold beef and baking-powder biscuits, leftovers from the grand feast spread by the joyous Carson and Douglas families.

He recalled another dawn—when he'd ridden to the river with Ruby and the others—as a blue-gray streak oozed along the eastern skyline. Off in that direction, the hills were cloaked in a purple haze, jagged and standing in each other's way between him and the vast distance to the east.

The river's gorge and its malevolence and death, conquered now, had been left behind and flat, chaparral-choked miles of granite-gravel stretched toward Berdan and the next challenge in his troubled quest to restore peace in the Ramirez Plateau country.

The morning mists rose and above the knobs to the east the sun appeared, a globe of red whose shine was spread out and heatless. Ryerson eyed it in the quiet, but disquieting moments of dawn, sipping the dregs of his coffee. After the stark tragedy and monumental relief of yesterday, the day coming up had him on edge. With a sigh, he heaved up and strode to where Rusty waited, saddled and alert.

As he rode for Berdan, the land flattened. Back there, beyond the camp, where trees thinned, he could still see the dark arches of hills that flanked the river—the frowning scarps where he'd lost Ruby. As he rode that way, the land was broken only by low ridges dotted with scrub oaks and an occasional massive sycamore, a scabby trunk standing naked and white away from the rest.

Dawn painted a bleak picture of leaden clouds hovering over the hills ahead. As if on a whim, the wind boiled down from the sky in one angry, chilling sweep. Dust was roiled in little gusts and dancing funnel-like clouds ahead of him. Tumbleweeds in great bouncing balls chased each other across the vast and open flatlands.

As Ryerson rode into the storm, the wind, like an impetuous woman who changed her mind by the minute, quickly grew wilder and more daring, pushing massive slate-colored clouds over the peaks ahead. Turning rougher and sharper, the wind slashed through the chaparral, keening like a grieving squaw, drumming and shoving at him and drowning out any other prairie sounds.

As though he were riding from twilight into deep night, a shadow fell across the land. In the distance lightning flickered and thunder growled. A splash of rain, like an omen of something fierce, slapped Ryerson's hand holding the reins.

"Hell," he muttered. "I only just got dried out from the soaking I took yesterday!" He hauled Rusty to a halt and got down and unlimbered his "fish," his bright yellow rubberized slicker that cloaked him from chin to boot heels and covered much of Rusty's flanks as well.

As he shrugged into the giant raincoat, the dark clouds filled the sky as far as his eye could see. Out ahead, over where Berdan probably lay, a bolt of golden light forked down from the sky with a sizzling hiss, and thunder rattled again in an ominous, throaty rumble.

At least partly protected now from cold, wind, and wet, Ryerson remounted and pushed on toward Berdan, probably drenched by the same onrushing torrent. He saw a sky growing close and gray with distant tattered streaks of rain. If there was a sun this day, it was hidden in clouds like dirty fleece that hung in sheets over the flatlands.

When it finally hit, Ryerson was pleased that a promised force was less than he had anticipated. A sluggish and gray rain poured forth as the wind abated; near him the river-bank trees sagged heavily with sodden leaves and branches. In a few hours, he thought, that gorge would be even more treacherous to tackle. They hadn't started a day too soon. He pulled down his hat to further isolate himself from the rain, bent his head and let Rusty set his own pace.

With it, the rain brought a chill that found its way through his protective gear, making him long for a snug shanty, a roaring fire to toast himself against, hot coffee, and a companionable swig or two of good whiskey.

The steady rain continued as Rusty's gentle gait ate the miles and Ryerson lived alone in his thoughts and his yearnings.

Abruptly, Berdan lay ahead of him in the valley. It was out there two or three miles, with wet, slate-gray boxes of buildings grouped along Broad Street, and a random scatter-ing of smaller houses, barns, and sheds imposing themselves on the rolling prairie country in all directions out from the town.

The rain had settled into a steady downpour that rattled tin roofs and gushed in downspouts and turned Broad Street into a morass of mud. Ryerson rode straight for the sanctu-ary of the livery stable and through its high and massive door into the dry barn, its insides smelling of sweet hay, horseflesh, and pungent manure. But it was dry, something he'd promised Rusty halfway through the rainy ride to town. He tossed the liveryman six bits to unsaddle and rub Rusty down and give him a healthy helping of oats and grain, promising to be back within the hour.

The drenching rain had stopped by the time he stepped out of the stable. He went back to leave his slicker with his gear on Rusty's saddle. Outside, Ryerson walked slowly along the gray, wet street. The rain was over but the sodden walks along Broad Street remained deserted. He crossed the wide street, his boots sucking in the mud, and tried the door of Martin Rathburn's office.

The door yielded as he turned the knob, ready to go for his Navy if need demanded, but he froze, his ears catching a strange sound. He allowed the door to swing open a crack, hoping not to alert anyone inside, and the sound grew more distinct. A gasping, gargling noise mingled with a spasmodic tap-tap-tapping against the floor and brushing sounds not unlike someone writhing in agony.

He drew his gun and opened the door a bit more, almost enough to admit himself. "Rathburn?" he called guardedly. When no response came, Ryerson eased in. Someone or something moved on the floor behind Rathburn's desk. Holding his gun at a business level, ready to fire, he stepped toward the desk. A purple-faced Dad Burns groveled and choked on the floor, eyes bugged, his body convulsed with shakes, arms and legs twitching, his quaking boot-heels drumming fitfully on the wood planks.

A whiskey glass was on the floor beside Dad and two empty bottles lay on their sides on Rathburn's desk.

Quickly Ryerson crouched beside Dad and as he did the old man's convulsions suddenly quieted as though on command. "Dad!" Ryerson called and got no reaction. He put his hand against Dad's warm chest and found no heartbeat. He raised one of the old man's eyelids to see an eye already glazing in death.

He looked around. Rathburn's office was a mess of papers littering the desk and tabletop and piled haphazardly by the open door of the stove. In the firebox, Ryerson could see cold fragments of unburned paper. Rathburn's safe door stood open; it appeared virtually empty.

Clearly, Rathburn was one jump ahead of him and had bolted; Dad, he thought, must have seen Rathburn ride out and seized the opportunity to walk in and loot Rathburn's supply of booze.

At last the old man had drunk himself to death over the sudden windfall.

He checked Dad's body again, certain now that he had breathed his last. For some unaccountable reason, Ryerson picked up the empty glass beside the body and sniffed it. The smell of alcohol was strong, almost overpowering another odor, faint but familiar to Ryerson's keen nose. But what the hell is it? he asked himself. He sniffed again. He'd smelled it before in cattle camps and where wolfers congregated. Hard to believe, he thought. Strychnine! Wolf-killer. He smelled the neck of one of the whiskey bottles, but the distinctive smell was missing.

His whiff of the other bottle, bearing a red diamond on its label, was unmistakable; one and the same odor. Why, he puzzled, would Rathburn poison some of his booze with strychnine? Did he have something against the harmless old mooch?

Or, Ryerson thought, what—perhaps—did Dad have on Rathburn?

He remembered the silver-capped wolf fang Rathburn wore as a watch fob. Wondering at the connection, he rose cautiously. In the rain's wake, the room was damp, dark, musty smelling, and depressing. Dad's bizarre death gnawed at him; another senseless loss. He knelt briefly by the body, pondering this insanity in all its ugliness—Ruby and now this innocent old bum. A dark mood built in him, and with it, anger. He knew his furies and hoped no one would cross him; in such a temper, he could come out of his shell with the rage of a maddened bull.

Forcing himself to come back on center, he reasoned that Rathburn had escaped after setting a death trap for Dad Burns. Ryerson would have to learn which way Rathburn went and ride him down, with murder now added to his bill of particulars.

In the street, the only activity on this drizzly day was at the saloon. He mushed across the quagmire and swung through the batwing doors to alert the bartender about Dad and to ask about Rathburn.

A pair of men Ryerson didn't recognize stood at the bar drinking and talking. The only other customer was a small man in dark clothing with a black hat and black leather vest engrossed in a game of solitaire at one of the back tables.

"Hey, barkeep," Ryerson called. The ruddy-cheeked and slightly overweight man started his way. "A glass of your best stuff."

The bartender grabbed a glass and a bottle on his way along the bar, set the glass in front of Ryerson and poured a stiff one.

"It's turned chilly with that rain," the man said. "This ought to bring back the glow."

"Much obliged. You know Dad Burns, don't you?" Ryerson inquired.

"Like the itchin' piles, he's hard to forget. Mr. Rollins, ain't ya?"

Ryerson heard chair legs squeal abruptly on the floor behind him, but when he turned around, the solitaire player was nervously adjusting himself in his chair and resuming his game. Ryerson paid it no mind.

"The name's Ryerson. I just wanted somebody to know that when I went over to pay a call on Rathburn just now, I found Dad Burns dying on his office floor. Been at Rathburn's liquor cupboard." He decided not to mention his suspicions about the poison.

"Dad?" the barkeep gasped.

"Somebody better go over and get him taken care of. That ain't the only reason I'm here." Ryerson lifted the glass and had his first drink since burying Clute's jug alongside the Black River gorge more than twenty-four hours before; already it seemed like an eternity had passed.

"Did Martin Rathburn tell you he was leavin' town?"

"Did as a matter of fact. Last evenin'. Late. Said he'd be on a business trip for a few days. He does that every now and again."

"Rathburn won't be gone long," came the voice of the solitaire player. Ryerson turned to regard him.

"You happen to know that, sir?" Ryerson inquired. The small man was lean and hard with piercing, dark eyes, a tight, angular hint of danger in his features. The man's eyes boring into Ryerson's were mean looking and searching, as though he might know more than he'd be willing to reveal.

"I've had business dealings with him. Just yesterday. I know for a fact he'll be around tomorrow or next day for sure."

"I'm glad to know that, and I thank you," Ryerson called. He was persuaded that Rathburn was gone for good. He turned back to the bartender. "You see which way he went?"

"Not for sure. His house is out east of town. He didn't come back through town this mornin' that I know of, so I suspect he's headed east somewhere. Maybe he's got business over in Fort Walker."

"But you don't know for certain."

"Nosir. I'd tell you if I did. You're a marshal I'm told, and I don't need to go obstructin' justice."

"Maybe I'll go out and check at his house."

"Care for another?"

"No, thank you. I'll be back." Ryerson tossed more than enough coins on the bar, spun on his heel, and started for the door, hearing a chair squeak against the floor again. He turned his head slightly to see out of the corner of his eye as the short, darkly dressed man folded his cards and got up. Something he couldn't come to grips with had suddenly turned the air tense.

Outside, Ryerson had started across the muddy Broad Street on an angle toward the livery stable when he heard the saloon's batwing doors creak behind him.

"Ryerson!"

Ryerson spun back to see the small, dark man in a

menacing stance in the mud of the street as he was. Ryerson's arm tensed; the man posed as though he was spoiling for a gunfight.

"Should I know you?" he called.

The man straightened himself, standing taller, with a killer glint in his dark, squinted eyes. His voice was harsh and cold-toned. "Not yet, but maybe you will." A quick shadow of cruelty darkened his face as he adjusted himself more in the posture of a man ready to go for his guns. Every stiff line of his form was sharp with tension and hostility.

Ryerson felt himself stiffening as well; he had all the signs down pat. It wasn't the first time some brash gunslinger had tried to call his hand. And he had little use for a jasper who carried two guns anyway. He'd always figured that a man needing two guns was like a bullfrog—mostly mouth.

"You must know me," Ryerson growled. "Otherwise you wouldn't be calling me out. What is it, boy? You heard Boot Hill Cole's in town and you want to take a crack at some kind of title?"

"I don't need no title. You've heard of me, Ryerson. Reno. Jack Reno."

"Well, well. The El Paso Kid, eh? Yeah, your name's around here and there, Reno. Who bought your gun this time, punk? Rathburn, maybe?"

Reno's hard-set eyes gathered in Ryerson and his stance of unflinching challenge. A hard cynicism touched the corners of his mouth as he smiled and spoke. "For me to know and for you to find out."

For effect, Ryerson returned his scowling glare. Out of the corner of his eye, he saw the bartender and his two customers crowded together, staring over the saloon's doors at the adversaries scant feet apart.

Jack Reno was also aware of movement behind him, but dared not look.

Seized with sudden inspiration, Ryerson allowed his glance to turn fully to the saloon door.

"Don't do it, Clute!" he commanded. "Let me take him! He's mine!"

Reno drew and spun around, ready to drill an antagonist behind him. The trio at the saloon door had already retreated in fear.

In the seconds it took Reno to turn, realize he'd been bluffed, and spin back to confront Ryerson, he found himself staring down the muzzle of a gleaming, blue-steel Colt Navy scant feet away. His own single-action Colt was only halfway up to a business posture.

"Take your pick, Reno!" Ryerson growled. "Sleeve that piece and ride on out of here and there'll be no hard feelings. 'Course I can't guarantee your reputation if you do. Otherwise get on with it. It's your first move."

"You're a slimy backshooter, Ryerson." Reno's words grated like gravel. "Pulling a cheap stunt like that!" Ryerson sensed he'd chipped away at the brazen gunfighter's brittle nerve.

"You're the one that wants to kill me, boy. I got no bone to pick with you. I'm offering you your life, which is a helluva lot more than you're willing to do for me. 'Course, you can stand there all day with that peashooter and try to talk me to death!"

Far from being threatened or frightened by Reno, Ryerson was angry. He'd had enough obstacles tossed in his path on this wretched assignment without some hothead pipsqueak trying to haze him into gunplay. Seemed like every time he turned around he was sticking his neck out in this ridiculous country. Or somebody was sticking it out for him.

Still Ryerson stayed cool, in control of himself. He knew the muzzle of his Navy was pointed on a direct line with Jack Reno's breastbone.

"Shit, Reno!" he screamed, "or get off the goddam pot!"

Reno reacted as though he'd already been shot. His features stiffened and fire darted from his eyes as the Colt swung up and his thumb automatically eared back the hammer. Ryerson kept his unwavering stare on the man's crazed eyes.

Reno's Colt barked a split second before the Navy; Ryerson felt a bullet cuff his shirtsleeve at the elbow at the same moment the Navy bucked in his hand. The guns' rapid-fire staccato blasts died abruptly in the soggy air.

Jack Reno doubled in the middle with the shock of the Navy's .36 ball backed by twenty-five grains of black powder at close range. He landed clumsily on his butt in the oozy muck, his eyes wide in surprise, and—still in motion— slammed back to half bury his head and shoulders in the sticky mud of Broad Street. From the hit Reno had taken, Ryerson was convinced that the loudmouth gunslinger was dead meat.

Trembling now that it was over, Ryerson studied his dead assailant a moment before angrily poking the Navy back into its holster. He quickly regained his equilibrium.

"Hey you in there," he yelled at the saloon, and three ashen faces materialized over the doors. "Now you folks have got two funerals to go to. I'm riding on out to find our Mr. Rathburn!"

He pivoted angrily and sloshed through the mud toward the livery stable. "Hell!" he sputtered, "tore another hole in the only good shirt I got left!"

· 20 ·

Clute saw an opportunity and grabbed it—a chance to get away for some hunting. Watching the camp come to life, he figured he'd spent too many days on a high wire of anxiety and adventure. This was sure to be an easier day with the Carson and Douglas families breaking camp—a fine time to ride out and enjoy his newfound freedom as an exoutlaw.

The rain squall that woke them at daybreak was over. When the sullen clouds departed, the sun emerged bright and warm. An hour later the land was dry, but smelled fresh and clean-washed; a fine day to get out and move around, Clute thought.

He wondered at Cole's unexplained disappearance, but knew the lawman needed to apprehend Rathburn on his own. Feeling only a little peeved at not being asked along, Clute also understood that Cole needed time to deal with the loss of Ruby; Clute had nothing to go on, but felt that something had been building between Cole and Ruby. Cole was uncommonly devastated by the young woman's tragic death.

So, he thought, there was no rush with the hunting. He squatted across the morning fire from Sam Carson and sipped his coffee. "Guess Cole's gone to town to pay Mart Rathburn a visit," Sam observed.

"Seems so. Sorry about your partner, Sam."

"Needn't be," Sam responded with a faraway look. "Berdan will get on without him. I still can't see how I allowed myself to be taken in by him. I always prided myself on being a good judge of character. Sure missed that one by a mile."

"Confidence men are in the business of fooling people, Sam. Cole knows how to handle him."

"I hope so. Hope Rathburn doesn't offer him a drink. Jim tells me one of those bottles in his office is laced with poison to take care of anybody who gets unruly. Can you imagine that? God, how I misjudged."

"What little I know of him, I wouldn't put it past the likes of that man," Clute said. "But maybe you don't know Cole Ryerson, Sam." Clute set down his coffee to roll a smoke. "He don't often drink this early in the day. Besides he'd see through that kind of stunt like fresh-scrubbed glass."

"I wish he'd waited and talked to me before charging out like that."

"Cole Ryerson rides his own trails, Sam. We talked it over a little. He's on his way to arrest Rathburn and lock him up some place in town. Then we'll go out and get Doan's sentry to take a message to him to surrender. If he doesn't, Cole will post your home guard out there, seal off the canyon and starve Doan out."

Sam Carson brightened. "I knew we hadn't organized and prepared ourselves for nothing."

"Cole just didn't want to put them in danger needlessly. Keeping that canyon bottled up wouldn't offer much threat. Say, Sam, while you folks are breaking camp this morning, I been figuring to get in a little hunting. Maybe I can find some fresh game to give you a little variety from beef all the time."

"I'd look forward to that, Clute. Jim used to do that, but he was gone a long time. Thank the Lord he's back safe with us."

"Thank the Lord and Cole Ryerson. I'll ride on over to your place a little later in the day."

"Good hunting."

Clute roused up and set off to locate one of the Doan Winchesters. He saddled and mounted his paint, brought out by the Carson family.

About a mile downstream of the camp, he spied two mule deer in the distance and eased the horse that way, keeping the Winchester at the ready. As he rode cautiously and silently toward the spot where he'd seen the deer walk up a bank and out of his sight, the riverbank trees thinned. Movement across the river and through the trees attracted him. A body of horsemen appeared in the distance. Clute urged the paint into a screen of trees to watch them from about a half mile away.

Doan, with his entire rustler band, rode with grim intent downriver toward Berdan. Clute could see it in the stiffness of the men on horseback. By all appearances, they were definitely not out on a lark.

His breath caught in his throat. Forgetting the deer, Clute urged the paint around and, hoping he wouldn't be seen by Doan's force, rode with all haste back to camp.

The families were packed, ready to move, the women in the wagons with Nora Carson and Hanna Douglas at the reins of the respective wagons. George and Vic Douglas and Sam Carson, along with Jim and Rick, were in the saddle as Clute galloped up. He was breathless.

"Doan's on the prod!" he shouted. "Saw them downriver. Headed for Berdan, most likely."

"What the hell for?" George Douglas called. He eased his horse toward Clute, who had ridden close to the Carson men. Vic rode beside his father.

"We stole his prisoners and took away Ruby—the lady that was drowned yesterday. But Doan don't know it. On top of that, his days in this country are all done. He had a perfect setup till you folks moved in and sicked the law on him. If I know Doan, he's probably mad enough to sack and burn your town, maybe wipe out a few ranchers and round up what stock he can before pullin' freight out of the territory. He probably doesn't know about your home guard."

The faces around him were anxious. "As Cole would say, it looks like it's time to paint for war," he added.

Carson took command. "No time to lose. Clute, you'd best ride to town to find Cole and warn him. George, you and I will alert the ranchers west of town. Rick, you and Vic head east to the ranches that way. Have the men assemble at the river ford south of town. Doan's men will come in from the north." Sam paused, seeing Jim watching him anxiously from horseback.

"Jimmy, I know how much you'd want to ride with us, but I'm going to ask you to escort your mother and Mrs. Douglas and Melissa to our place. It's the best I can do, son, considering all you've been through. I just don't think you're up to it yet."

Jim Carson's eyes held a disappointed look. He nodded grimly. "All right, Dad."

"Tell the men to have the women and children gather at our place," Sam called. "If Doan's out for blood, it'll be safer for them that way. Vic and Rick, go there when you're through and help Jim look after things."

Sam looked at the group of men around him. "All right! Let's not let Doan harm our town or our ranches!"

Two hours later, having alerted ranchers east of the river, Vic Douglas and Rick Carson led their jaded horses up a rise on the way back to the Carson ranch; home was still several miles away. As they rested on the ridge, their eyes swept the sprawling prairie below them, clumped with blue-green piñon and juniper against straw-colored grass and dotted here and there with sage and mesquite. Several miles away over the vast flats, a dark, beetle-like speck poked ahead of a flurry of tawny dust along an east-west wagon road that lay twisted and sometimes straight like a carelessly tossed ribbon across the rolling landscape.

From a distance so great the two had to nearly squint to make out the form, they perceived the moving object to be a small one-horse buggy with its single, overweight passenger.

"Who you suppose that is?" Rick asked.

"If I didn't know better, I'd say it's Mr. Rathburn," Vic replied.

"Sure looks like his rig."

"Can't be. Cole went to arrest him in town this morning."

"We don't know that for sure, Vic."

"Think we ought to ride down and see for ourselves?"

"What if it is Mr. Rathburn? What do we do then?"

"I don't know. Maybe we'll get in trouble. Maybe Cole and Mr. Rathburn already had a talk and maybe Cole turned him loose," Rick said. "But I don't think Cole would let him off that easy. From what Jim was saying last evening, Mr. Rathburn's in as deep as that rustler Doan. I know Cole wouldn't just turn him loose like that. Not Cole."

"What'll we tell him if that is Mr. Rathburn?" Vic asked.

"We'll just tell him he's needed back in town. If he puts up a fuss, we may have to take him in under guard."

"I think we'd be doing the right thing, Rick."

"If we get in trouble, we'll be in it together. I think Cole would back us either way."

"We did talk it over and we both agreed on the decision. We tried to use our best judgment."

"So we'll take whatever comes like men, right, Vic?"

"Let's get down there before he gets away!"

The two young men spurred their horses off the knoll and rode at a gallop across the prairie's flat sprawl.

Still tense and aware of strange emotions over the abrupt and violent confrontation with Jack Reno, Ryerson hastened to the livery stable. He saddled Rusty, reloaded the

Navy's empty chambers and checked the cartridges in his Winchester in its under-stirrup boot.

Riding out of the wide stable door, he headed south on Broad Street toward the river ford at the edge of town and the road leading east to Rathburn's place. He cocked an eye at the lately emerged sun, guessing the time was pushing noon.

He glanced down the street toward the saloon, noting with grim satisfaction that Jack Reno's body had already been dragged away.

From behind him to the north where Broad Street merged with prairie roads, came a flurry of movement and sound. Then, blaring in the quiet of Berdan's main street, shattering the silence, shots roared, bringing Ryerson abruptly alert to a new threat.

"What the hell?" he muttered. "Doan? For God's sake! Doan!"

A bullet whizzed past his ear; on the walk in front of the saloon a man half whirled and then crumpled, flopping over into a curiously small and flat huddle of clothing, downed by a bullet intended for Ryerson. He recognized him as one of the two customers he'd seen in the bar less than a half hour before. "Hell!" he muttered. "First Reno, now this!"

Horses pounded toward him from north of town despite the sound-deadening mud. A man shouted, high and shrill, a kind of victory screech over first blood in Berdan; Doan had his men whipped into a frenzy of violence.

Ryerson distinctly heard Doan's unmistakable hard, brittle voice barking commands. "There's Rollins! Get him! Get him!" The attack had begun; Doan was making his move to wipe out Ryerson and, along with him, Sam Carson's town.

The sound of horses from behind him came with a swelling rush. Shod hooves pounded like a stampede in the drying mud and saddle leather squealed in the split second Ryerson twisted around to see Doan's attack force. The men riding down on him were hard-bitten, armed, and menacing, keeping close to the cover of bunches of sage and mesquite. Some of the charging horsemen dipped out of sight, the brush that came to the edge of town hiding them, and the long, folded bank of an arroyo giving them cover.

Ryerson reefed against Rusty's reins and swung away from the charging band, seeking the security of an alley between the buildings. When he reached it, he turned Rusty back toward Broad Street and poked out his head.

Two horses of Doan's vanguard, their riders bent low, came into view. Rusty was motionless and in that moment, Ryerson caught sight of one of the riders over the barrel of his Navy and pulled the trigger.

One of the speeding horsemen reeled in the saddle under the bullet's impact. Ryerson saw him sway and his hat fall. Then the riders were gone, passed beyond his vision. Doan's other riders disappeared around and behind buildings in the town, preparing to fight on foot, or kill anyone who showed himself.

Ryerson was sure the town was all but deserted, save for a handful of merchants whose lives now were threatened. Sam Carson, Clute, and George Douglas, he remembered suddenly, were still at the river camp. Members of Carson's settler army were spread over the countryside, engaged in their ranch chores, too far out even to hear gunfire. He was virtually alone against Doan's mob.

His life, along with the lives of the few people in town, was surely measured in minutes. In a split second, Ryerson vowed to find a spot to defend himself and make Doan pay dearly for his scalp.

The south end of town was still open and he determined to ride for it. Possibly by riding out he could decoy Doan away from harming the town or its merchants. He sleeved the Navy and yanked out his Winchester. Broad Street again seemed deserted, Doan's men infiltrating the town and probably moving up behind Broad Street's buildings. He'd be flanked or surrounded at any moment.

Broad Street now was his most promising means of escape and he charged out boldly, turning Rusty south toward the ford.

Across from Ryerson's charge out of the alley, a man on foot appeared between the buildings across the street, his rifle at his shoulder. As Ryerson watched, another outlaw joined him. Again lead sang past Ryerson as he reined Rusty short and changed course. Rifle slugs thudded into a building near him as the horse's quick maneuver saved his life.

At the brief distance that separated him from his attackers, Ryerson—the reins looped over the saddle horn— whipped the Winchester to his shoulder and fired. He missed, but the bullet's trajectory was enough to send the pair scuttling for safety back down the alley.

Ryerson again pulled the horse around and pounded south. The two he'd faced, bolder now that Ryerson's back was to them, reappeared to fire at him as he spurred Rusty out of town.

Galloping toward sanctuary, however fragile, Ryerson carried the Winchester in his right hand like a pistol, his strong thumb ready to latch back the hammer. As he rode, he pivoted and lined his sights and fired back at the pair, ducking when another bullet whined overhead.

Ryerson's blunt spur rowels touched Rusty's flanks and the horse, hooves grinding in the hardening mud, leaped expertly and struck full stride down Broad Street.

Behind Ryerson, more outlaws emerged into the street amid shouts and cries and exploding rifles. Beyond the plank buildings, glancing right and left for enemies as he rode, Ryerson saw others, still on horseback, charging him from behind and from the side, appearing out of alleyways.

Once more he spun in the saddle and fired into the horde bearing down on him.

In the headlong flight to safety outside of town, a bullet creased Rusty's neck and, flinching from the sudden pain, the horse broke stride. Ryerson, off-balance as he leaned back to cover his retreat, lost his grip in the stirrups and plummeted from the saddle in an abrupt twisting, dizzying spill.

The ground rushed up to meet him and Ryerson was brutally slammed down, landing on his shoulder and rolling. He lay a long moment collecting his wits, groggy, trying to check the hard rasp of his breath and his pounding heart. His eyes fuzzily registered Rusty's dash toward the Black River ford.

Near Ryerson was a huge boulder perched on the lip of a low, dry arroyo. He grabbed his dropped Winchester and, crouching low, sprinted to drop behind the boulder for cover. Poking out the rifle's barrel, Ryerson sought a target in the men moving through the town toward him, some advancing on foot from one bit of cover to the next, others still on horseback, charging his way with a determined vengeance.

Ryerson shrank himself small beside the sheltering rock, covered as well by the lip of the dry wash. His carbine cracking and spitting death, he kept his determined killers at bay. Bullets ricocheted as they hit Ryerson's hasty breastworks and on shrill whines quartered away into the air.

From the south, behind him, Ryerson heard pounding hooves along the road from the river ford. Surprised at an attacker coming from that direction, he spun back to meet that adversary.

He drew a bead and nearly fired before he recognized Clute Mills's pinto bearing down on him at a high gallop. As the paint neared the road crossing of Ryerson's shielding draw, Clute slowed the horse and vaulted from the saddle, Winchester upraised. Catching himself in his jump, his momentum propelled him at the dead run down the wash bed.

Ryerson watched him in wonderment at how spry the old campaigner was.

Bullets from Doan's riflemen howled even more intensely as Clute, reaching Ryerson's position, fought his churning legs to slow him down. Clute flung himself at the protective bank beside Ryerson, rolled into position, and aggressively poked out his rifle, ready for business. Their eyes met and Ryerson grinned.

"Looks like you got your hands full again, marshal," Clute muttered.

"Thanks for joining me," Ryerson grunted. "You just doubled my odds of getting out of this alive."

· 21 ·

Doan's besiegers infiltrated the edge of town, concentrating their fire, doggedly determined to wipe out the two men Doan despised most, Ryerson, the interloper, and Clute Mills, the traitor. They fired from the splendid cover of buildings at the edge of town, some of them sniping from upstairs windows, and from the cover of chaparral and the irregular terrain.

A hundred yards separated Ryerson and Clute from their closest adversaries. The pair effectively kept them at that distance, the air resounding with the crack of Winchesters on both sides.

Clute poured lead into the town opposite the dubious protection of the boulder and wash bank. Angry rifle slugs thudded into the dirt around them as both squinted along carbine sights, watchful for enemy movement.

Keeping his eyes fixed intently on the town's outskirts, Ryerson called to Clute over the rattle of gunfire. "How in hell did you get here?"

"Out by the river camp. Saw Doan riding for town. Couple of hours ago. Figured a fight was brewing." Clute paused to direct a round at a clump of chaparral where they'd seen several puffs of muzzle smoke.

The brush shook and a crouching gunman spun sidewise to slump immobile beside it, dropping his rifle as he fell.

"You got him!" Ryerson yelled.

"Looked like Curly," came Clute's grim response. "Rode with him a lot of years."

"He'd've done it to you," Ryerson called. "Does Sam know? About Doan?"

Despite his apparent killing of Curly, Clute's old eyes were bright with the zest of battle as he darted a glance at Ryerson. "Sam and George are out rounding up their army. If we can hold out, they'll be here before long."

Ryerson popped additional rounds at likely targets before him. "I'm sure as hell happy about that. This isn't a situation we can hang onto forever."

"Just hope they get here in time."

Almost as Clute said it, from behind them, beyond the cover of a long and low gravel bank near the river ford, bullets twanged over their heads to howl in the direction of the town buildings.

"Yahoo!" Ryerson screeched. "Sounds like some of them are here already."

"Ask and it shall be given," Clute shouted back over the rising roar of gunfire.

"Seek and ye shall find," Ryerson hollered. The rifle fire over their heads directed at Doan's force increased in tempo.

"Doan'll have to pull out! He's outgunned now!" Ryerson yelled jubilantly. "Watch for clear targets when they jump and run."

Lead from the massing force behind them spewed recklessly, but beat back the entrenched rustlers. From the south, Ryerson heard shouts and firing with renewed energy as more ranchers raced in to join the fray. At the edge of town and from the buildings, he could see figures moving, giving up their cover, pulling back.

He picked targets among the disappearing rustlers and let fly with his Winchester. The outlaws were on the run, not waiting to see the strength of their new enemy. Shots from the town had all but ceased in the mad scramble of Doan's men to retreat or pull back to more secure cover.

Confident now, Ryerson and Clute rose from behind the wash bank to seek targets among the fleeing rustlers. Ryerson sped two shots into a spot where gray puffs of gunsmoke announced an enemy. The first round flushed the terrorized rifleman crouched under the tentative cover of a bush; the second shot sent him sprawling.

Behind them, the long, low hummock of gravel came alive with a swarm of ranchers, their dark forms looming against the sky like nothing more than a massed infantry charge, yowling like banshees and pouring lead into the town. Ahead of them by fifty yards, Ryerson and Clute led the charge along the approach to Broad Street, Winchesters up and ready. Involuntarily the old rebel yell rose in Ryerson's throat and Clute—the old Yankee campaigner—picked up the call. "Eeee-yowwww!" Ryerson heard the thuds of their sprinting feet hammering on the sun-dried mud.

His eye sensed movement in an upstairs window at the edge of town; a gloom-shrouded figure poked a gun muzzle into the sunlight. Still at a dead run, Ryerson whipped up the Winchester and fired. He saw the rifleman's muzzle flash ahead of a puff of gray smoke.

Beside him, Clute's rifle spun from his grip. His arms dropped and his torso sagged, his legs still propelling him forward; Clute ran a few steps before one leg buckled and he pitched, headfirst, into the dust.

From the window, a body slumped precariously out of the open sash while a carbine spun to the ground below. The dead or dying outlaw hung there a brief moment before jerking with a death convulsion to tumble out, plummet like a rock, and bounce once as the body landed.

Ryerson wheeled in midstride to race back to Clute, nearly overrun by the horde of howling ranchers converging on the road into Berdan, bloody vengeance darting in their eyes, Winchesters bristling in their grips. In the crowd,

Ryerson spied Sam Carson and George Douglas side by side sprinting among the mob of attackers.

The charging, shouting men swirling around him, Ryerson gently turned Clute over. "Sam! George!" he shouted after them. "Doan! I want Doan alive!" He had no idea if they'd heard him.

Clute's eyelids flickered. "Got me, Cole. I'm done," he grunted against the extreme pain. "Finally caught the one to finish the job at Newtonia."

"No, dammit! No!" Ryerson's words were shrill with insistence. "You're not leaving me now. Not after I lost Ruby! And just when we're winding this up. You're going to pull through, Clute. Get that through your head here and now!" He peeled back Clute's shirt and faded red union suit top to find a small bullet hole just under the rib cage on Clute's right side. He ran his hand around to Clute's back to feel a similar exit hole. It was probably not a mortal wound but again, he thought, Clute was an old man.

"You'll be all right, pardner," he whispered into Clute's ear as he crouched beside him. "I'll get somebody to look after you."

Clute's eyes were closed. "You go, Cole. Go ahead. Don't bother with me. Get Doan."

A swift, hot fire of fury ran through Ryerson. Clute had risked a lot to take sides against his old boss and his old saddle mates. Gritting his teeth against unkind fate, he leaped to his feet, his mind whirling with the urgency of getting aid to Clute and getting on with making sure he took Doan into custody.

His ears pricked at a new sound, a rattle of buggy wheels up the road from the ford behind him. As he spun to hunt the source of the sound, Martin Rathburn's horse and buggy emerged over the rise and started down the gradual slope toward where Ryerson stood watching and wondering beside Clute's inert form. The ranchers had gained the town and he could still hear the staccato of gunfire from that direction.

Ryerson's heart leaped at the sight approaching him.

Pried uncomfortably on the buggy seat with the corpulent, glowering Rathburn, Vic Douglas controlled the reins, his horse tied and trotting along behind. Beside the buggy, guarding Rathburn, Rick Carson rode his horse jubilantly, his left hand clutching his reins, his right holding the Winchester's butt on his hip, muzzle angled arrogantly skyward like a stubby cavalry guidon without regimental pennant.

"Rick!" Ryerson bellowed. "Good for you boys! Keep an eye on Rathburn but for God's sake, get to town and get some help for Clute. He's been bad shot. I got to get moving!"

"We'll look after things, Cole," Vic shouted. "Don't worry."

Ryerson again bent over Clute. "The boys are here, Clute," he said, reassuringly. "They'll look after you. You're going to be okay."

Clute weakly waved him away without a word. With Rick keeping his guard over Rathburn, Vic appeared beside Ryerson and Clute.

"Handle him gently," Ryerson commanded. "Get him to town and to bed. If there's a doctor in your town, this man gets first priority. Do you understand me, Mr. Douglas?"

Vic's youthful face, serious with the gravity of the situation, nonetheless softened into a small grin. "Depend on us, Cole."

"You brought in Rathburn. I know I can depend on you boys." He rousted himself up, eyes sweeping the area around him for a sign of Rusty. His horse was nowhere in sight.

It suddenly occurred to him, rankling him, that the disappearance of a faithful horse was like losing a right hand; nay, a right arm.

"Ryerson!" a voice over him boomed. Ryerson looked up at the buggy seat and into the fat, florid face of Martin Rathburn. "I demand to know the meaning of this!"

Rathburn's cheeks and jowls were ruddier than he remembered, the eyes slitted and sparking. Ryerson regarded the face for a long moment, collecting his patience.

"Mister, right now I'm in the midst of protecting your town, as if you give a damn. The meaning of what?"

"These children masquerading as your deputized agents. Manhandling and kidnapping me on the prairie like a . . . a craven outlaw! Dragging me back here against my will."

"They just saved me the trouble, Rathburn. I'd've come after you myself for I'm certain Judge Winfield in Fort Walker will have some questions he'd like to ask you."

"This is intolerable!" Rathburn sputtered. "I have well-placed friends in Santa Fe and others of considerable influence in Washington. Both you and your Judge Winfield are public servants. They'll have your heads for this!"

Ryerson's cup of patience drained. "All right. Let's quit the damned bickering. You're charged with criminal negligence in the death of one John Doe, also known as Dad Burns. And I'm charging you with conspiracy to defraud."

"You'll never make it stick!"

"Can it and put a lid on it, Rathburn. These boys will see that you are comfortable as well as secure. You'll have to excuse me as I've got to look into the whereabouts of our Mr. Jubal Doan. You'll be needing him to go before Judge Winfield to testify in your behalf, I'm sure."

Ryerson spun on his heel and angrily started off at a brisk pace toward town. His day of violence wasn't over.

Despite the bright shine of sunny daylight, a pall of silence and destruction lay over the place; the gunfire had ceased, the rustlers scattered to the four winds or pinned down in town.

Here and there in the gravelly, brushy outskirts, the bodies of dead or wounded rustlers rested in the dirt, undisturbed and abandoned. Through Berdan's buildings and alleys the ranchers probed and poked, hoping to comb out any rustlers still entrenched.

Doan, Ryerson thought angrily, had made good his escape. There was no way he could track him in the sea of fleeing hoofprints in all directions.

Aside from an occasional armed rancher emerging on the street as they swept the town for stragglers, all seemed quiet and deserted. The horses of Carson's army had been left south of town in favor of the charge on foot.

He imagined—and hoped—that when he had time, he'd find Rusty among them. A lone horse, a stubby, poorly kept buckskin, stood meekly at the hitchrail in front of the saloon.

He had no idea whether the horse belonged to rancher or rustler. A Winchester hung in the saddle boot and Ryerson assumed he'd find cartridges in the saddlebags to replenish his dwindling supply; renewed shooting could erupt at any moment.

As he neared the horse, shots rang out to the north of him, close to the livery stable. From that direction, he heard alarmed shouts.

Three riders burst out of an alley, wheeled, and pounded out to the north end of Broad Street. One of them was unmistakable, clothed in black, hatless, his thick red hair like a flame on top of his head.

Doan!

From out of buildings and alleys, small knots of ranchers appeared to root themselves on wide-spread legs and empty their carbines at the riders thundering away from them.

Afire with urgency, beside the only saddled horse in town, Ryerson quickly checked to find a box of cartridges in the saddlebags before leaping to the horse's back.

With the shooting trailing off, Ryerson swung the horse out, looking at the distant riders galloping at top speed, the sounds of their retreat diminishing even as he started after them. The buckskin responded obediently under him, but it wasn't Rusty, and that made a lot of difference. As Ryerson pounded past the knots of astonished ranchers, he saw Sam Carson among them and he shouted at Sam.

"Your boys have Rathburn outside of town! Get him locked up! Look after Clute. He's bad hurt!"

Sam Carson's face was a mask of astonishment, but his eyes registered understanding.

Ahead of him, on horses far superior to the buckskin, Doan and his two henchmen were shrouded in a cloud of dust. Ryerson reined the horse to a sudden stop and as quickly as it quit prancing, took careful aim with the Winchester at one of the riders beside Doan.

He felt the .44's explosion buck against his shoulder. As he watched, the man reeled in the saddle to drop sideways against Doan's horse and slam into the middle of the road. Ryerson touched spurs to the buckskin's flanks and was again racing after the fleeing rustlers.

The rider still with Doan peeled away from him on the road to race across the prairie, knowing he, himself, was in no danger of immediate pursuit. Ryerson saw Doan's head pivot angrily as he was abandoned by the last of his gang; he heard Doan yell something at the escaping rustler, probably profane, but Ryerson couldn't hear it.

The buckskin's top speed was considerably less than that of Rusty, a fact that maddened and frustrated Ryerson as he watched Doan easily outdistance him to disappear over a series of low ridges into the virtually trackless prairie.

Ryerson rode hard, as hard as the buckskin's stamina would allow, his eyes cold and grim and his mouth twisted into a bitter, hard line. Ryerson swore to keep on, as long as it took, riding Doan down. Somewhere, the outlaw had to make a stand. He slowed the horse's pace.

As if to mock the violently stormy and cold morning of Ryerson's ride to Berdan, the sun wheeled across the sky and seemed to hang suspended through the long, hot afternoon; Ryerson felt a film of sweat form on his forehead. He frequently whipped off his hat to swipe with his hand at his moist brow and hairline.

The country he rode through was open; flats and low

ridges, arroyos and benchlands. With late afternoon, the sun dipped behind a starkly barren western horizon, the ridges and draws casting long shadows, the brush along wash banks softening to dim clumps. Ryerson halted the horse and got down to walk, giving the buckskin a rest.

Ryerson strode along, bitterness filling him, his anger seething. Without the specter of Jubal Doan out there someplace with murder in his heart and perhaps even setting a trap, the desolate silence out here could incline Ryerson toward giving vent to his grief, coming to grips with his anger over the tragedy of Ruby's loss. His head almost ached with the frustration of it all; days too full of threat and tragedy for a man to comfortably tolerate. Keeping alert to danger, his mind worked back over the rescue, the perilous ride down the gorge and Ruby's disaster, the death of Dad Burns, and the escape of Martin Rathburn. His mind also relived the gunfight and death of Jack Reno, Doan's attack on Berdan, his and Clute's fight for life, and Clute's grave wound. Trudging along, he prayed for Ruby's soul and for old Clute's survival.

Now he found himself alone again with no allies, stalking strange country for a man who would kill him from ambush if possible, a deadly, desperate enemy whose own survival depended on Cole Ryerson's death.

But Jubal Doan had been abandoned by the men he relied on. How the outlaw leader would fare on his own might be a totally new story. Ryerson mounted again and rode on.

Dusk lay gray and heavy all around, thick and concealing. The horse, tired as it was, swung its head from side to side as it picked its path. Darkness fell and Ryerson knew only that the horse was laboring up a long, gradual climb.

Then the cut between the ridges began to slope downward. A valley opened out of the darkness ahead and Ryerson let the horse pick its way, sure the animal would keep to the beaten trail. Overhead the stars came out, their light pallid against a moonless sky. Horse and rider came down the slope, a course that took them across the ruts of a wagon road. For perhaps two hours he followed the road through the night, a poor target for a dry gulcher but still keenly alert. At last thoroughly confused, he stopped. He had no idea which direction Doan had gone, and it was too dark to check for fresh hoofprints in the dusty road. There was no use in going farther, no point in wearing himself and the horse out and wasting the pitiful reserves of man and horse.

He got down again and walked the road, leading the horse, allowing it a much-deserved rest without a man on its back. Ryerson sensed that he, too, was exhausted with the rigors of the past few days. But he would not sleep; rest, maybe, he thought, would help.

When light came he would go on. The night was cool, but not cold. Ryerson found a bank with sand at its base and, stretching out on the ground, he rested. His muscles relaxed, but his mind remained active, seething and bitter. He blamed Doan for a lot—the imprisonment of Jim Carson and George Douglas, the brutal repression of Ruby Montez, and possibly the death of Clute Mills. He blinked his eyes and then shut them in bitter memory; he, himself—he, alone—was responsible for the greatest calamity. If he had used better sense, Ruby would at least be alive, if only as Doan's prisoner. But she'd be alive!

It was a full-star-shining night. Out of it, a distant coyote yipped a mournful dirge through the darkness. The wind— in silent accompaniment—felt cool but moved virtually soundless over the land.

Clutching the buckskin's reins, Ryerson catnapped, a thankfully dreamless sleep. When his eyes opened, the emerging dawn gave him a better look at the valley. Low hills stretched to either side. The faint pink in the east changed to salmon color and then to gold. Beneath the gold, marked strongly against the hills, the bulk of buildings showed through the gray murkiness that clung close to the land, maybe a half mile away.

The place seemed deserted; probably its owner was in

town with Carson's army, the women and children taking refuge at the Carson ranch.

Ryerson left the road and, circling cautiously, approached the buildings. A windmill's eerie squeal sliced monotonously at the silence and water splashed from a pipe into an earthen tank next to a stable, lending a sense of desolation and depression to Ryerson's already jangling nerves. An ominous tension clung to the air; a foreboding. It would be a perfect place for Jubal Doan to make a stand from the cover of the house and outbuildings as Ryerson approached, exposed and vulnerable.

· 22 ·

Ryerson realized he had found Doan when a bullet whined past his head and he heard the muzzle report caroming from the ranch house. He whirled the buckskin into a deep, covering draw and lifted the saddle gun in his right hand. Looking out from his meager cover, he saw a puff of powder smoke from the deserted house about a hundred yards away.

Again, through a vacant window, a gun muzzle burst flame in the gray dawn and a bullet sang over him as he rolled off the horse, hit the ground and came up, Winchester at the ready. A heavy clump of mesquite, growing down into the draw, afforded him the sheltering vantage point he sought. He poked the rifle around it, taking his sight picture on the exposed window frame from a prone position.

Without a specific target, Ryerson laid two rounds through the window, shattering the glass of the overlapping top panes. As he waited breathlessly for some response from Doan, he saw the rustler chief burst from the house and dash into a small and windowless stable. It was the opportunity Ryerson needed.

Quickly he leaped to his feet and sprinted to the ranch house, circling it from opposite the stable; if Doan hadn't

239

seen him run—and he doubted he had—Ryerson could achieve a strategic position behind Doan; if he was looking for Ryerson, he'd be watching the wrong way.

Long moments passed as morning came up stronger. Ryerson waited, his heart pounding and his skin prickling, behind a corner of the house. By poking out his head, he had a clear view of the quiet stable. He picked up a good-size rock alongside the house foundation, hefted it, and waited a moment for any movement in the stable.

He quickly stepped out from the cover of the house and hurled the rock to resound with a sharp crack against the side of the stable. From inside, Doan poured three rounds through the closed stable door. Ryerson heard the rifle's muffled reports and saw the holes appear in the planking door and splinter the dry, gray wood.

Grinning, Ryerson waited for more reaction from Doan; there was none. He hefted another rock and heaved it to thud loudly in the dirt on the opposite side of the barn, the side from which Doan anticipated Ryerson's approach.

He pitched another and waited. Long moments passed. The stable door eased open enough for the muzzle of Doan's saddle gun to poke out; the man behind it was obviously looking for a glimpse of his adversary. The door swung wide and Doan's carrot-topped head inched out, swiveling, looking anxiously for Ryerson. Doan looked both ways along the side of the barn, at the house and at the sprawling prairie around him.

Ryerson nearly giggled in delight; he had the outlaw chief spooked.

Doan inched out and along to the corner of the stable from which the sounds of the rocks had come, his back to Ryerson cautiously easing out enough of his head for one eye to see around the corner of the house.

Ryerson held his fire; he wanted Doan alive if possible.

Doan reached the corner of the stable, brought the rifle up, hammer back, and strode around it boldly, thinking he'd catch Ryerson off guard. Doan disappeared around that corner of the barn. Ryerson stepped away from the house into the sun-flooded ranch yard and waited, keeping an eye on both corners of the barn for Doan's reappearance. The rustler chief took a long time making his circuit of the stable.

Doan's gun muzzle emerged first and then the red-haired and hatless outlaw stepped out, unaware of Ryerson standing motionless midway between the house and stable. "Hello, Jubal!" he shouted. "Toss down the gun!"

Doan, recoiling in surprise, glared out of an anger-pinched face and sparking eyes as he whipped up his Winchester from the hip to take aim at Ryerson. Despite his fury, Doan held his fire, aware that Ryerson also had a trigger finger tensed on a Winchester aimed dead center.

"Ryerson! You slime! You sneak!" he screamed. "On top of everything, you took my woman! What have you done with her?"

"Put down the gun, Jubal. Don't make me kill you. Ruby's dead. Drowned in the river."

Doan shrieked an animal-sounding howl. "I'll kill ya! I'll kill ya with my bare hands!" Doan's bullet slammed past Ryerson to bury itself with a solid thunking sound into the clapboard siding of the house behind him. The anger and the frustration built up over several harrowing days boiled out of him in a fiery surge. "Not this way!" he bellowed. "You're askin' for it! You're makin' me do it!"

With forced deliberation, Ryerson swung the Winchester to his shoulder in a blurring motion and his eye aligned with the sights. Again the big-bore lever-action bucked against his shoulder; Doan's body recoiled with the impact. The intensity of his insane fury kept him on his feet to clumsily lever another round into his Winchester's breech. A circle of blood stained Doan's white shirt front where his black cloth coat was swept back.

"Damn you, go down!" Ryerson screeched out of his own

rage as he laid another round into Doan's midsection. Despite the bullets' shock, the dogged outlaw kept his balance. With hardly the strength to lever a fresh round into the chamber, Doan began a staggering, lopsided lope across the yard toward Ryerson for a closer shot, screaming out of a deranged compulsion to kill or be killed by the man who had deprived him of his life's pursuits and its pleasures. Still enraged himself, Ryerson cranked in another cartridge and again brought up the gun.

Ryerson's third shot stiffened Doan in midstride with a round square in the center of the chest. He spun around to slam down on his back, his jaw slacked, blood spilling from his mouth as his glazing eyes stared at the sky. An angry Ryerson strode to the body to confirm his kill. He stood over Doan to nudge him contemptuously with his gun muzzle; Jubal Doan was good and dead. Ryerson looked at the eyes' fixed and glassy stare.

"You could have had an easier time of it," he muttered bitterly to the corpse.

His shoulders slumping with emotional and physical exhaustion, Ryerson clumped slowly away to peer vacantly into the dusky interior of the stable at Doan's horse. If he hurried, he could be in Berdan before evening. It was all over, but concern for Clute weighed heavily.

He started at a rapid stride out into the prairie where he'd left the buckskin.

Ryerson leaned against the door frame of the Carson's spare room and watched the dozing Clute Mills, propped up with pillows in a big spool bed and under a thick quilt dominated by red and white geometric patterns. Clute had been shaved and scrubbed and someone kept his sparse gray hair regularly slicked down. He wore one of Sam Carson's cotton nightshirts.

Sunlight peeked in around curtains thoughtfully closed so the patient could sleep as much as possible. From Sam

Carson, Ryerson had learned that Clute's wound was serious but hardly fatal. The doctor from town predicted the old-timer would be laid up in bed about two weeks and on the mend for a month more.

As Ryerson stepped lightly across the room, Clute's eyes opened and without moving his head, he watched the marshal skid a chair close to the bed. "Forgive me if I don't get up, Cole," Clute said softly, in obvious pain. "I ache in every joint."

"You ought to know I don't stand on ceremony, Clute," Ryerson said, parking himself on the bedside chair. "I sit on it every chance I get. You feel like talking?"

"About all I got left to do just now. But I'm still among the living and for that I'm grateful. Yeah, talking don't hurt that much and I am glad to see you. Just don't try to make me laugh. That *would* hurt."

"Don't worry. Not much has happened to joke about. I'm grateful and glad on all counts for you, Clute. You made it."

"The ladies, Miz Carson and Miz Douglas and Melissa and Penny—can't do enough for me. Cole, Melissa sat up with me all that first night after they brought me out from town. Jim Carson stayed outside the door, too, in case I took a turn. And Vic comes over every day."

Ryerson chuckled. "Nice of him, but he's here for more than to see you."

"Him and Penny. I know."

Ryerson's voice lowered. "I got Doan, Clute."

Clute carefully twisted his head to look Ryerson in the eye. "Dead or alive?"

"We buried him this morning."

"You had to kill him, I expect. How'd he die?"

"Went down fighting. Died without a whimper. Tough as nails right to the last. Took three solid hits before he'd quit. *Muy hombre.*"

"Say that for Doan. In lots of ways he was stupid, but he knew how to die like a man."

"Buried five more of his cronies. Curly was one of them, Clute."

Clute swung his eyes at the ceiling. "Yup . . . And I came damned close to perishin' by the sword, too."

"All got decent funerals. Cleaned up and buried in good pine boxes and proper forgiving and understanding words said over 'em. Sang from the hymnals, too. A requiem, they called it. Only lost one townsman. Of course old Dad Burns, too. And there was a gunslinger by the name of Jack Reno."

"I heard about that. Heard tell of Jack Reno before. You beat him in a straight-across showdown. You must've put in quite a day that day."

"All past now. All that death. So useless, so stupid. Ah, well, I'm riding for Fort Walker in the morning. Taking Rathburn in to stand trial before Judge Winfield. His money won't buy him out of this one."

Clute mustered a grin. "Now that sure sounds like pleasant duty. Six or seven days on the trail with that old pisspot."

"Could be worse. Looks like I'll have company. Sam and George are letting Rick and Vic ride along and help me out. The boys want to talk to Judge Winfield about being appointed or deputized to serve the cause of law and order here in Berdan."

"Those boys'd be prime candidates. They're stout stuff. One more step in Berdan's progress. It's decent here, Cole."

"You thought any of staying, Clute?"

"Me? Ahh, I don't know."

"You've got lots of good friends, now. Doan's place is up for grabs. It's a good setup. Comfortable for a man who might like to do some light ranching or horse breeding to keep himself occupied."

"Hadn't thought about it. What about you?"

"Back to Fort Walker and the next job, I suppose. If

Winfield appoints a couple of young friends of mine as deputy marshals here, I expect I'll have to come by now and again to check on 'em. Might have to look in on you to make sure you're toeing the line."

Clute paused, reflecting. "That's still somethin' that's chewin' on me, Cole."

"I can't imagine what."

"I've still been an outlaw. I want to stand trial, take my medicine, get my slate cleaned."

"All right!" Ryerson said in mock anger. "We'll attend to that right now. And only because of your weakened condition. By the authority vested in me as an officer in the Federal court of Judge Isaac Winfield, I find you, Clute Mills, guilty on all counts. I pronounce an indeterminate sentence and release you on your own recognizance or whatever the lawyers say. Maybe a better word is probation. Now, does that help calm your dander, Mr. Mills?"

Clute cocked his head, but was unamused. "I suppose if you say so, Marshal Ryerson. I'll try to live with it. Maybe I will talk to Sam about Doan's old place after all. That way I could put something back into this town that's been so good to me."

"Do and I'll be back to see you, Clute. You can depend on it. Consider, if you want, that I'll be checking on my prisoner."

"You'll have to come over for the weddin's too."

"Weddings?"

"Like we was just talking. Whether we know it or not, we set something in motion around here, solving people's problems and bringing them together. There's love in bloom all over the place."

Ryerson grinned and got up, his expression turning thoughtful. "Like the caterpillar and the moth."

"Huh?"

"Out of all that ugliness comes beauty. I got to go, Clute. But I'll be back." He shook Clute's frail hand.

Ryerson headed for the door, but was stopped by Clute's feeble call.

"Cole?"

"Huh?"

"I figure you and I ain't made our last camp. No, sir, not by a damn sight!"

About the Author

R. C. House's previous novel, *Trackdown at Immigrant Lake,* introduced a fresh and fascinating character in the Western field, Cole Ryerson. Mr. House is also the author of *Drumm's War* and *The Sudden Gun* ("House's best book so far . . . terrific. . . ." —*Rocky Mountain News*). *Spindrift Ridge* is forthcoming from Pocket Books. Mr. House is a past president of the Western Writers of America.